# Tin Angel

Tin Angel
Text © 2007 Shannon Cowan

Published by Lobster Press™
1620 Sherbrooke Street West, Suites C & D
Montréal, Québec   H3H 1C9
Tel. (514) 904-1100 • Fax (514) 904-1101 • www.lobsterpress.com

Publisher: Alison Fripp
Editors: Alison Fripp & Meghan Nolan
Editorial Assistant: Alison Kilian & Faye Smailes
Graphic Design & Production: Tammy Desnoyers

We acknowledge the financial support of the Government of Canada through the Book Publishing Industry Development Program (BPIDP) for our publishing activities.

We acknowledge the support of the Canada Council for the Arts for our publishing program.

The Canada Council | Le Conseil des Arts
for the Arts | du Canada

Library and Archives Canada Cataloguing in Publication

Cowan, Shannon, 1973-
    Tin angel / Shannon Cowan.

ISBN 978-1-897073-68-1

    I. Title.

PS8555.O858T55 2007          C813'.6          C2007-901574-3

Printed and bound in Canada.

*For my family*

– Shannon Cowan

Our youths now love luxury, they have bad manners, they have disrespect for authority, disrespect for older people. Children generally are tyrants. They no longer rise when adults enter the room ... They gobble food and tyrannize their teachers.

– Socrates

written by

**Shannon Cowan**

Lobster Press™

# Acknowledgments

Special thanks to everyone who helped me understand the finer points of juvenile law in Canada: Nicholas Bala in the Department of Law at Queen's University, Stephen Biss, Gary Botting, Christine Boyle in the Department of Law at the University of British Columbia, and staff at the BC Courthouse Library Society in Nanaimo and the UBC Law Library. Any errors of interpretation are mine alone. Special thanks to Monica Woelfel for her comments, and also to Keith Maillard and Andreas Schroeder for their never-ending guidance, and to Meghan Nolan at Lobster Press for her super editorial eyes.

# Prologue

I was fourteen years old when they arrested me for the murder of Louis Moss, a man I knew briefly as the man who wrecked my family. I was at his funeral at the time, wearing a black corduroy dress handed down from some girl I had never met, embarrassed by the fact that my toes poked through holes in my leotards. My long hair was drawn back into a ponytail, revealing pink cheeks and a nose chapped from a recent bout of cold air. I had the habit of pinching my nostrils between the sides of a tissue, and as I stood in the hushed interior of the funeral home, steadying myself against swaying bodies and the wail of the pump organ reverberating off the ceiling fans, I imagined my nose to be glowing softly, lighting up the service like a beacon to the North Pole.

Up until that point I had been getting along on

denial and moist air. There had been no visitation, no lineups of mourners shuffling past an open casket to pay respects. For this I was quietly grateful, though the reason for the omission did not strike me until much later, after I was already overcome with more immediate dreads. There could be no visitation because there could be no Louis. There wasn't enough of him left to visit.

By the time the funeral director began eulogizing Louis's qualities, I was already fighting back sickness. I pushed past my sister in her velvet hair band, past my mother with her black tunic and drooping eyelids, away from the wall of bodies concentrating regret with dizzying force. I stepped out into the fresh air and threw up behind a wrought iron gate that led all the way to the vestibule.

I remember rain falling onto the sidewalk, hissing softly like air coming out of a tire, and a row of poinsettias in glazed bowls. I knew these plants would die before the season was out, the same way they always did, and I felt a momentary sadness for their dim reality: it seemed so closely aligned with my own. I wiped my mouth and heard someone cough from the end of the walkway.

"Ronalda?" said a man in a hat, who I knew already as Inspector Lamb. He took a puff from his cigarette and ground it into the concrete with his boot. Apart from the rain and his chuckling, the street was quiet, littered with cars parked illegally at the Handy Dart bus stop. A lone pedestrian struggled along the sidewalk, taking shelter beneath a blue umbrella. "We were going to find you later on today, but now it seems as though you've saved us the trouble."

⁎  ⁎  ⁎

Everything that came after my arrest is well recorded by the local papers. Shelter Bay was a small town, with clean streets and impeccable sanitation. Salmon still ran in nearby rivers, and the smells of cut wood and paper pulp were akin to economic holiness. The price of gasoline may have been on the rise, but people didn't drive very far to get where they were going. As a rule, children did not commit serious crimes. Then I came along and changed all that.

Despite what the papers reported, I hadn't intended to be anywhere near the lodge on the day of Louis's death. I started the morning as any other fourteen-year-old girl – worrying about school and my boyfriend, trying to fit the confounding and jagged pieces of my family back together. Popular opinion placed me in full command of my senses (untrue), harbouring a deep-seated hatred for the man everyone referred to as my benefactor (true). Though the prosecuting lawyer, a rake of a man called Edgar Moyers, failed to convince everyone I was the demon he believed me to be in law, he succeeded in another way. When my acquittal came down, a gasp leaked out of the courtroom. I was let free following the lawyers' press conference, and I stepped out of the courthouse to look into the face of what would become my life: jostling reporters, the shock of camera flashbulbs, questions coming at me like a long and provocative oral exam. *How do you feel after your release, Miss Page? Do you feel that you have received a fair trial? What do you say about continued allegations?* When my face appeared across the national paper, this time beneath the headline *Justice Denied?* I realized the power of popular opinion. I have Mr. Moyers to thank for this honour.

Since that day, I have learned a number of things about justice: if you are a little bit too independent and are known to have opinions of your own, and if you live in a small town, a place like Shelter Bay on the west coast of Canada; if your mother has the watery look induced by too many pills and your sister may or may not be a liar; if you are a girl of fourteen, who doesn't cry when she is interrogated and has a steely look of hatred in her eyes from one too many atrocities – you might as well be guilty, because everyone will treat you that way.

Whether or not I killed Louis Moss has always been the question. Even now, five years since my arrest and subsequent dismissal, the question rears up before me like a recurring late-night dream: blurred edges, lurid and trance-like details emerging and receding from the fog of memory. These details differ from the ones in the courtroom, those tedious dissections of *actus reus* and *mens rea*, which Edgar Moyers was obliged to prove beyond a reasonable doubt. My details are personal, and after all this time, I have not forgotten them, despite the advice of my lawyer.

"Those are incidentals," he assured me at our first meeting. "We will not be needing to speak about them again."

But keeping these details inside has not made the story go away. People have gone on believing in my guilt or innocence. They have gone on organizing appeals, issuing death threats, and soliciting biographies independent of the evidence laid at their feet. Perhaps this is because they have always lacked the right evidence. This is an assumption I am willing to make.

After all this time, I have decided to tell my story, if for no other reason than to make the details known so that they might go away: the details as I saw them, and as I have revisited them, every day for the past five years. The slant of the sun, its glint off the lake. The sweet smell of familiarity. Mountains dusted with a lather of snow. A penumbra of evergreens. My mother's bare feet, slipped for a moment from a pair of sling backs, dancing at the edge of the beach not very far from Louis Moss's. Whether or not I killed him has always been the question. Now you will be able to make your own decision.

# Part I

# Chapter 1

When Louis Moss came into our lives in the summer of 1969, I was too preoccupied to understand what he represented. I was thirteen and content, my long neck perpetually leaning into a book of natural history, my chin dented with the imprint of my thumb from a gesture I considered both scholarly and contemplative. I believed my life to be reaching a sort of perfection. I was a girl in a family of freethinkers, permitted to run wild over a landscape rutted with river valleys and coarse veins of limestone. The place where I lived, known to islanders as Raven's Lodge, sat tucked in the grip of the Coast Mountains, hunkered down on the border of a national park that was at once sparingly visited and internationally renowned. The lodge and its succession of hallways, draughty corridors, and dimly lit dining room, had been in my family for three generations. I had every reason to believe it would stay that way.

That summer was a time of transition. The lodge was suffering from decades of neglect, its roof leaking, its central chimney clogged with a tangle of birds' nests. Crows had pecked holes into the rubber lining around the windows, cheeky with demands after a season of hand-feeding. Shingles were rotting, wiring was short. The front porch slumped into the lake. Before opening for the season, my parents managed to patch up the obvious, soaking holes with tar, and to shore up joists, screening the rot from view with a makeshift succession of shutters. At the same time, they counted on forgiveness, working under the assumption that guests who had visited the lodge as children would permit a certain level of dirt and shabbiness as part of the experience.

These guests, I remember, were city people – soap salesmen, engineers, secretaries and schoolteachers – or dignitaries from nearby Shelter Bay who could afford a holiday close to home. When they were not fishing from the prows of rental boats, they were basking on lawn chairs and beach blankets, or gathering in clusters around fire pits filled with charcoal briquettes. They wore flip-flop sandals and loose-fitting trousers and swimming trunks that exposed flanks of white skin. Most of the time, they joked with my parents, humouring my father into filleting demonstrations, or regaling my mother with nostalgic tales from when she was a girl. They considered themselves to be part of the lodge, as essential as its notched log purlins and river rock foundation. They were right. My mother had inherited Raven's but no money to go along with it. When the numbers of guests started to thin; when they died off or succumbed to the ploys of travel agents advertising holidays in hotter, trendier locales; when their children grew into teenagers who did nothing but sulk, smoke cigarettes, and stare balefully at a lake where nothing exciting ever happened; when they cancelled reservations, held for decades by first names inked into a brown ledger, my parents knew they needed a plan.

The plan to save Raven's included running the lodge as a wilderness education centre. If I had been paying attention, I would have thought more of the choked conversations flowing out of my father's study, my mother's voice always rising in a heat of protest like the fussing of nesting crows. Instead I was content within the boundaries of my world, obsessed with the taxonomy of alpine wildflowers whose own short life spans seemed both angelic and unfair.

Most of that summer, my father worked as a backcountry guide teaching hordes of Boy Scouts to fashion debris huts or start a fire with a piece of flint. My mother continued to serve the guests, fetching pillows, cleaning outhouses, and whisking my sister and me out of everyone's sight. Into this walked Louis Moss one week before Labour Day, driving down the roadway in a blue Lincoln Continental that seemed large and flat enough to

17

ferry across the lake. He had surfaced before – my mother had known him when she was a girl – but it wasn't until that year that he emerged from the blur of sideburns and leather belts to make any lasting impression.

My preoccupations and the fact that I possessed no extrasensory abilities meant that I was unprepared in every way for the disruption that would follow. I could only feel a slight uneasiness with the way he spoke, energized as if by secret information I had no way of knowing. *Ronalda,* he said to me more than once, my name sibilant and reckless on his tongue. I would stand rooted in place, wondering if he was making a statement or asking a question. This was the sort of code I had come to expect from adults and most of the time it had nothing to do with me.

My father and I were just back from a trip, a six-day hike in honour of my thirteenth birthday. We were sticky with sweat and layers of dirt that had accumulated on our faces and necks like the browning of a summer tan. As we shouldered our packs down the side of the mountain, both stuffed with goose-down sleeping bags and extra pairs of wool socks wrapped in sheets of plastic, we saw the gable roof of the lodge rising out of the fir trees. We saw the pillars of smoke from the beach.

"Home," my father said.

I watched the stony path for evidence, for the frequency of grasses my father had characterized as "hitch-hikers," their seeds brought in on generations of tourists' boots. The route we followed had a history, and I knew its past as if it were my own. Not very long ago, men in baggy pants with flyaway haircuts led ladies on horseback from the lodge to the top of the ridge. They picked their way along the bridle path, up steep divisions of rock and over a series of creeks to a succession of alpine meadows. I knew from the fading black-and-white photographs mounted over the registration desk that these women wore high-heeled boots and large, impossible skirts. They were forever padded and frilled, ironed and tucked, everything about them cinched down with laces and buttons and silver brooches, as if threatening to drift away.

Every once in a while, we found artefacts to prove their existence – a rusty horseshoe, a woman's hair comb – worked into the trail beneath layers of scattered fir cones and somehow uncovered by a shifting plate of snow. I kept my eye to the ground as we marched, keen for this bit of proof between specimens of wildflowers. The calls of whiskey jacks faded behind me.

For people who have never lived in the mountains, the idea of sharp changes in temperature and landscape is difficult to understand. Ascending the route from the lodge to the alpine, we usually travelled a distance of six kilometres, gaining one and a half in straight elevation. The farther up we travelled, the thinner the forest became. Eventually there was nothing but sparse clutches of trees huddled against jagged rock, intermittent peaks layered with seams of marble running lengthwise like a

French dessert. Only a select number of plants could find a home in extreme conditions, which included thin air, thin soil, and a ten-month covering of snow. The wildflowers that so fascinated me fell into this category. As soon as the snow retreated, they sprung up, glorious and ephemeral, marking the alpine in brilliant waves of colour. Descending as we now were from the ridge top to the valley bottom, we watched this pattern in reverse. Already the trees were tall and the lupines had gone to seed. A warm current of air rushed up to greet us. My father, trudging along in front of me with the backs of his ankles caked in mud, quoted a verse from Frost: *"The woods around it have it – it is theirs. All animals are smothered in their lairs. I am too absent-spirited to count; The loneliness includes me unawares."*

My father had come from England to the New World, as he liked to call it, seeking to live like a wild man. "But then I tamed him," my mother always said. I knew the truth. They had met shortly after my mother left secretarial school, when my father had come to the lodge on a trip. She had been wowed by his accent. He was dapper and polite, a lot different from the Shelter Bay boys she'd grown up with. His pale and thin body was deceptively strong, and once I came along, I watched him fool and embarrass many guests by shouldering a pack nearly twice his weight. He kept his thinning brown hair tucked under a sportsman's cap and wore long-sleeved shirts and beige trousers, even in the heat of summer. There was a running joke that his high forehead signalled a large brain. I believed this to be true, just as I believed his long pointed nose and scant eyebrows twitching behind the frames of his glasses to be evidence of kindness.

Watching him move as I did now against that familiar backdrop of Raven's Lodge, I felt anxious for the things that comforted me: a hot bath, my mother's spicy shampoo, the shelf of science and history books I was stocking for the coming school year. I knew with certainty that I would live in that valley forever, sealed into my summer long johns, the slits on my woollen undershirt taped shut to protect me from mosquitoes. My father would be there too, a man of forty in a pair of hunter's galoshes with fingers as thin as willow whips, forging ahead as though blazing a trail across the world. Forever and ever we would march down that hillside, sticky and ravenous, thirsty and tired, our lives intertwined like a pair of braided shoelaces. Forever and ever, I said to myself, I will stay thirteen.

When we emerged from the trees at the bottom of the hill, the sun was already slipping behind the mountain. Deep in the valley the sun rose later and set earlier than anywhere else. I had once overheard guests from Shelter Bay name this phenomenon as the reason for my father's white skin. "As white as a beached halibut," they had said over glasses of gin and tonic. But I was used to this sudden departure of light, and looked over my shoulder to catch the last rays illuminating the trees from behind like Christmas ornaments.

"New guests," my father said, motioning ahead.

I looked down the length of trail to the beach where my mother sat nested in a lawn chair. Around her, guests sipped drinks from plastic cups and sent periodic bursts of laughter into the air. We unloaded our packs at the rear porch and circled the lodge to the gathering.

"Might as well make an appearance," my father said. I sensed his mood plummeting.

On the way, I intercepted my sister who was sitting with Taylor Hart on the docks. Taylor was the cook's son, a sulky boy who hid his fierce eyes beneath a lock of stray hair. He never seemed to wear a shirt.

"Marcia," I said.

"I'm busy."

She didn't look busy. She looked bored, leaning back onto her thin wrists in a gesture of practiced composure. I'd seen her do this in front of the mirror, tilting her chin and checking her profile with made-up eyes. I'd asked my mother what it meant. "Leave her be," my mother had said. "She's just sixteen." Now she wore a cardigan thrown over a halter-top. Her shorts were white and impractical, joined at the front like a tennis skirt. She was looking past the group of adults, staring at a woman lying on a beach blanket.

"Who's that?" I asked.

"Some American," said Marcia. "She's divorced."

Prior to that summer, I had good memories of

Marcia. We spent most of our free time exploring the lake in our cedar strip canoe, confident in the pull of the waves, the slant of the wind carrying us this way and that. We stirred the water with our paddles, she at the stern guiding the boat, and me at the bow yelling *left, right, left, left.* We imagined invisible cities, long and cunning histories to make up for a lack of year-round access to other people. We made do with each other.

Now, however, Marcia was interested in other things. Her patience was short; she was niggling and mute. I watched her watching the woman, her long hair fanning out across her shoulders as lustrous and blonde as the princess in a fairy book, and I knew that she was beautiful. I knew that Taylor knew this too, and that was the reason he hunched over Marcia, staring at her as she clacked her gum and stretched her bare legs into a disappearing patch of sun. I saw in their drama something beyond my control, something slipping away from me. There was nothing I could do about it.

"Marcia," I said again.

"*Ssh,*" she hushed. The American turned over on her blanket, wrapping her exposed midsection in a towel. I ran to catch up with my father.

The adults were still gathered around the table, ruddy in the cheeks from too much gin. Three women, some men. The men always seemed to blur together, unified by their tendency toward neutral colours and homogenous haircuts. Their voices were loud and incongruous, rattling up out of their throats like a north wind.

"Look who crawled off a mountaintop," one of them said.

"Louis," my father said.

"Heard you were out being a wild man, putting us all to shame." Louis smiled jokingly.

"All in a day's work."

"Funny you should mention that." He leaned forward and extinguished a cigarette, pressing it into one of the coffee cans my mother distributed around the beach area. The split in his shirt revealed a hairy chest.

"Paul," my mother intercepted. "Louis has some business to discuss. Why don't you go and get cleaned up and we can talk over dinner. There's a chill coming down." She motioned to the other guests who began gathering their things.

"That would imply," my father shrugged, "that I am willing to entertain his idea, which I'm quite certain I'm not."

Louis tutted.

"Paul," my mother said.

"We've gone over this before."

"Louis is our guest. You can hear him out." She emphasized the word "guest," a word synonymous with money.

My father sighed, lingering in the shadows. I stood behind him, weaving the grass. "All right then," he said tiredly. I could see his shoulders falling with the weight of his pack, even though he had already put it down.

∗  ∗  ∗

In the lodge, the smell of roast beef hung in the entryway. After I had taken a bath and scrubbed away the dirt, I went downstairs to the dining hall. Guests congregated around circular tables, looking out at a view of the lake where steep hillsides sloped up to a series of auger-shaped peaks. I made my way across the room.

Back in the days when my grandparents were in charge, my grandfather displayed his collection of stuffed animals in this room. A blue grouse on a stone in the window. A hoary marmot on the mantelpiece. From a tree branch fastened to one of the central pillars, a great horned owl looked eerily askance, its malleable neck twisted one hundred and eighty degrees. These animals had always spooked me. Their feathers were dishevelled; their glass eyes were fossilized and covered in dust. I thought they had seemed like duller, cagier versions of the real things and was pleased with my father when he removed them from sight.

Now the dining hall was spartan. A collection of tables and chairs, a river rock fireplace rising to meet a wooden ceiling. The lodge had a tendency toward darkness at all times of day, and the faint lights twinkling inside orange globes did little to fend off the approaching dusk. I took my seat at the largest table. Marcia was already there.

"Mum and Dad are fighting," she said.

"What?"

"He doesn't like her friends."

"What friends?"

But she shushed me again as the guests began crowding in, filling the other side of the table.

"A toast," my mother said, when we were all quietly seated. "To new beginnings."

"And to second tries," my father added, fitted now in a clean shirt that was an identical match for the one he'd been wearing. His voice sounded strangely girdled.

There was a pause, during which everyone looked into their laps. Eventually Louis said, "To all those things," and everyone took a drink and started eating.

I didn't know who these friends were, or why they were disliked. The guests at our table were the same group from the beach. They chatted with my mother about high school. I realized somewhere in the conversation that the men were business associates of Louis's and at the same time, old friends of my mother's. The women must have been their wives.

"Did you kids know that your mother used to be wild?" said a wide-eyed woman to both Marcia and me. This was the kind of question we knew enough not to answer, misleadingly indulgent, but said for the benefit of other adults. "Caught in a washroom with a mickey of rum. More than once." The woman rolled her eyes.

"Don't tell them that," snapped my mother, but she was laughing.

"Yes," said Louis. "They'll think she was a hell-raiser, which she wasn't," he added sardonically.

"You would know," said my mother. "You were right along with me most of the time."

"In the girls' washroom?" This had come from me. The notion of my mother and this man squeezed in between the napkin dispenser and the garbage can perplexed me. What would they be doing in the girls' washroom? Laughter grew around the table and I felt my cheeks reddening. I disliked making jokes without intending to be funny.

"Of course not, Ronnie," my mother said. "I've just known Louis a long time. His visit is a pleasant surprise." She raised her glass again.

I watched as everyone worked at their meals, knives and forks grating against unbreakable china plates. The conversation went around the table like a ping-pong ball, batted back and forth by Louis, my mother, and a man with a neck rash who laughed wantonly, displaying a moist bolus on the centre of his tongue. I thought again how I did not want to grow up and inhabit a world ruled by gatherings such as these – the rigid smiles gradually loosened by sips of liquor, perplexing relations that demanded lipstick, manners, and cloth napkins flattened around a wine bottle. The women especially seemed painted, simpering creatures with waistlines rising to meet their breasts. Each had hair carefully piled into shellacked mounds or clipped to resemble birds' nests.

Their peasant necklines were tight as collars around their throats. The idea that I would grow up to resemble them seemed preposterous and insulting, but I knew from Marcia that it was a possibility. The men, too, seemed somehow unlikely, concerned now with the state of the lake's trout population, the quality of early morning light and its adequacy for fishing. There was also the situation with the Shelter Bay pulp mill – not enough water to meet the growing demand for paper products – and the American astronaut who hit a golf ball on the moon. Theirs was a world of stumpage fees, gasoline hikes, fishing lures and World Cup soccer, of predictable grumbling and wide-legged pants. I dug into my mashed potatoes, blurred into a mealy heap by the details, as the conversation reached another lull.

"Well," my father said finally. Throughout the exchange he had remained more or less silent, seated beside my mother with a flat smile drawn across his face. "Are we going to get down to business? That's why you've come, isn't it Louis?"

"Paul," my mother said, a piece of meat on the end of her fork. "We're still eating."

"I wasn't aware that business talk interfered with digestion."

"Well it does."

"Never mind, Alice." This was Louis. "Paul is right. Cards on the table." He finished chewing whatever was in his mouth. "You know what I'm going to say Paul, but I think you'll find this offer to be more generous than the last."

"I'm not selling."

"You must be interested in hearing the price."

"Not particularly."

My mother threw down her napkin. "Well," she said. "It appears that Paul and I need to discuss this in private. He seems to have forgotten that I have an opinion, which he has yet to hear."

There was a mulled silence, the sort of gap filled uneasily by the shifting of chairs. One of the wives took a sip of her wine and clanged the glass against her teeth. She followed this with a nervous giggle. Everyone else stared at their plates. I knew my mother's tone of voice. I had adopted it myself when I wanted something badly enough. There would be a private discussion followed by a period of silence and bad feelings. My parents would keep to separate areas of the lodge. Usually my father retired to the shed after an argument where he was attempting to shape a pair of wooden snowshoes around a mould. My mother's reaction would be less predictable. She might clean the pantry or the linen cupboard, meticulously organizing the napkins and towels as if filing them in alphabetical order. Alternatively, she might set out on a walk, striding down the access road in her lace-up boots. Even then she still believed in the power of absence to will my father to listen. She hadn't yet realized he was perfectly happy by himself.

After everyone had finished eating, Louis stayed behind drinking a cup of coffee. I made my usual rounds, clearing away the cups and saucers, removing tablecloths with stains of butter and gravy. Louis took a final sip and handed me his dishes, the weight of his gaze pinning me to the hand-looped rug. "Ronalda," he said. I looked up, expecting to see his two eyes coming at me through a cloud of smoke. Instead I saw him looking elsewhere, across the table at my sister's back as she wandered out the door. He exhaled slowly, flicking the trigger on his lighter so that a flame leaped up from the stainless steel casing. The plume lingered around his head. I thought, for an instant, that he looked like Taylor Hart bent over my sister on the dock.

"That man's handsome," Marcia said later as we helped in the kitchen, drying dishes. "He wants to buy Raven's Lodge."

"What?" I said. I had no idea what she was talking about. I didn't like the sound of it. "Does not."

"Does too." She flipped her hair behind her back with all the grace and elegance I didn't have. "He's rich."

"Dad won't sell. He won't." I felt my face get hot and then cool immediately with the soothing image of my father. "He likes it here."

"Mom doesn't. She wants to move. Louis used to be her boyfriend."

We dried the dishes, the towels thin and moist in our hands. I didn't know how Marcia was coming up with these details, this ridiculousness made up to bother me for no reason at all. She was full of cunning ploys and thorny deceptions, the same way she was full of unearned beauty. I had no way of navigating her deceit. "Not true," I said, but I didn't know. Marcia shrugged and kept on working. What rattled me most of all was her indifference.

*　　*　　*

A few hours later, I was seated in a corner of the parlour playing checkers against myself. My original plan was to intercept my father as he went into the office. Instead he arrived the same time as my mother. Their discussion had already begun. "Are you having an argument?" I said.

"No," said my mother.

"Yes," said my father.

"We're having a talk," said my mother. "And there's nothing wrong with that. I'm trying to convince your father that we can't possibly spend another winter here."

"But I want to spend another winter here," I said.

"See." My father pointed at me.

"Ronnie, this isn't your decision. The lodge is no place for a family in winter. It's dangerous and lonely. We need to take a house in town. The way we used to."

"We can't afford it."

"Of course we can't. Not without guests who pay."

"They pay."

"A fraction of the cost."

"Alice," my father pleaded, "it's the first year of the centre. We don't have a reputation. That's what these first few seasons are for. Establishing ourselves. What do you think I've been doing these past two years? Taking a holiday? I'm drumming up donations. There's plenty of interest."

My mother bit her lower lip. "This used to be my lodge. Don't forget that. I don't like to see it falling apart either, but we can't hold out. I can't hold out. I'm lonely here when you go off. I have no one."

"You have the girls."

My mother looked at me and smiled faintly. Her lipstick was eaten off. All that remained was a bland smudge around her mouth. "You know what I mean." She sat down, bringing a wrist to her forehead. "I'm lonely for you."

My father sat down beside her and I thought he might kiss her. Instead he took her face in his hands. "You told Louis."

"What?"

He released her. "You told Louis we were struggling with money and asked him to make this offer. You've been in contact with him all this time."

My mother stood. Her voice was rough. "How could you say that? You know I haven't spoken to him in years – which I did for you. He was a friend."

"He was more than that."

"I won't listen to this. What happened before you came along has nothing to do with this."

"It has everything to do with this." But he was talking to a blank hallway. When my mother got angry, she disappeared.

"I want to stay," I said quietly, worried they had forgotten me.

"We will stay," my father said.

# Chapter 2

My mother's dissatisfaction with the way things were going was not unusual, although her frustrations were so woven into the patterns of our lives that I scarcely saw them at all. She was a tall woman, soft and loving one moment, harsh and impatient the next. She came from a family where her biggest task had been to marry well. Marry a man and bake occasionally for two older brothers who looked forward to inheriting Raven's Lodge. When the war eliminated that possibility (one brother was killed in action, the other married a Belgian and refused to return), my mother dropped out of secretarial school and began her apprenticeship. Her parents were getting too old to do things by themselves.

The shift was not an easy one. She had grown up expecting a certain amount of leisure time, a house on a boulevard with a two-ended driveway and an electric refrigerator. She had prepared herself for a life of polished kitchen utensils, gravy making, steam press ironing, and afternoon trips to the dry cleaners. A part-time job in a well-lit downtown office was also briefly in the picture. Paper clips. A facility with shorthand. Lemon-oiled wall units. My mother, a polite answering service. All of these things until the right man came around.

For my mother, none of these things implied drudgery because they were far away from hand-washed girdles and slivers driven up under the fingernails while splitting cedar kindling. They did not involve fetching blocks of ice from a lake and then melting them down in a stainless steel pot over the slow-burning heat of a cook stove, nor muddy hikers' boots, the plugs of grass and earth scattered across dining hall carpets that had to be hung and beaten by hand. None of these things, her mother promised, as she seated my own mother on her little girl's bed and wound her hair in rags. None.

So when my mother became the sole inheritor of Raven's Lodge, she was not prepared. She did her best, toughing it out with my father for eight years, watching the snow fall and the mildew grow and the ashes collect in chimney thimbles. She wore headscarves and rubber boots and a plaid lumberjack jacket that made her smell of chainsaw oil. But her heart wasn't there, and when Raven's started crumbling, the Raven's of her childhood – as sunny and ideal as a northland postcard – she couldn't stand around and watch. She wanted to get out.

"An old beau," she called Louis, the day after the altercation with my father. "He can save us, all of us, but most of all you girls."

Marcia and I shrugged, playing a game of Crazy Eights in the dim light of the parlour. I watched as Marcia picked her fingernails, trying to decide what to do with my hand.

"We should be thankful for such an offer," my mother said, her words floating over our heads as if talking to no one in particular – shrill at first, then fading away.

But my father would have none of it. Over the next few days, he avoided Louis and my mother's friends. Periodically I heard his voice rising against my mother's from behind the closed door of the office. Conflict was another thing about the adult world I did not want to embrace. Here my parents were arguing while the last of the summer sun was setting outside the window, turning the lake a steely purple that suggested grape juice or bubble gum. A lone paddler plied the surface of the water, the sun at his back like the blast from a spotlight. On the porch, Marcia played checkers with Louis Moss. Guests moved around the beach, across the lawn, and into the entryway, smoking, laughing, and falling asleep. I knew who won these contests between my parents, who had the bargaining power. For the first time I wondered if this predetermined outcome was fair.

I never considered what Louis Moss would do with

Raven's Lodge if he ever came to own it. It wasn't a thought that entered my head. As far as I could tell, the man in the dark brown pants with the casual shirt and clipped yellow hair would not be buying Raven's. My father had said so, and my father never lied.

"Where's Louis?" Marcia said one day at the beginning of September. "We're supposed to say goodbye. He's leaving today."

"How would I know?" I said. I sat in the window seat of the main lounge, reading a book. I chewed on a strand of hair.

"Never mind," she said. "I'll find him."

I watched her leave the room and wished she would come back, stick by me the way she used to when there was nothing else to do. At least then I would be entertained. Instead she disappeared, leaving a trail of fragrance in the hallway. I looked out the window and down to the lake.

My seat in the lounge was nestled into a shingled extension packed with fabric-covered cushions and a collection of knick-knacks, which included a lumberjack on cross-country skis and a pint-sized, hand-carved canoe. Every day I crept into the comfort of this space and fingered these objects, working my skin against the wood until the surface shone with oil from my hands. I spent hours in and out of this seat, burying myself in cushions, falling into books that my father had stacked in the study library. Sometimes I came here to be alone, other times because there was nowhere else to go.

"Don't you want me to say goodbye to Louis?" I asked my mother, when she arrived with the feather duster. I was feeling particularly left out. No one had asked for me in over two hours.

"Hmm?" she said distractedly. And then after a moment: "Oh. All right then, go ahead."

I slid down the hallway, polishing the floorboards with the balls of my feet. I counted the number of tears in the wallpaper, small revelations of lathe and plaster. At the top of the stairs, a glass sconce flickered and then went out. The generator was running low.

"Alice?" said my father's voice from the landing. He had emerged.

In the lobby, Marcia sat with Louis on the waiting bench. She wore her hair in a ponytail, with a fringe of bangs across her forehead. I watched as Louis handed her something small and metallic.

"Ronalda," he said when he finally noticed me. "I was just saying goodbye to your sister." He cleared his throat awkwardly and Marcia put whatever it was in her pocket.

"Where's Mum?" she asked.

"Upstairs."

"Ah," said my father, who arrived to shake Louis's hand. "Sitting out in protest." He chuckled softly to himself, happy now that Louis was leaving. "Well, better than a fistfight."

"We've had our goodbyes," Louis said, gathering up his suitcases. "That's the main thing. Well, Paul. You know where to find me if you change your mind."

"I know where to find you."

"And I sincerely wish that you would. For – " he pointed vaguely in our direction "– everyone involved."

"I appreciate your concern."

We watched as Louis went down the wooden steps and packed himself into his blue Lincoln. The other guests had already gone ahead. Soon the road would be glutted with snow, and we would have to leave our own battered truck at the opposite end of the access gate; there would be no more company until the spring. I shifted in my stockings, wondering whether or not to put on my shoes.

"Goodbye Marcia," said Louis. "Goodbye Ronalda." He climbed into the driver's seat. "Paul."

"Goodbye," said my father. He watched as Louis started the engine and manoeuvred the Lincoln around the parking lot. The car pulled out in a swirl of fallen leaves.

"What did he give you?" I asked Marcia, when the last of Louis's car was out of sight. My father had already started downhill for the generator house.

"Nothing much," she said, although her voice betrayed her excitement. I looked with some envy at a charm the size of a peanut, a pewter pine tree fused at the tip to a clasp. Marcia fastened it to her bracelet and jangled it on the end of her arm. "I think it's cute. What did he give you?"

"Nothing much," I echoed, wondering what else I should say. He hadn't given me anything at all.

Marcia and I were used to receiving presents, usually from far-off relatives who had forgotten our dress size or misspelled our names on the white space of a greeting card. These gifts usually arrived in the mail, wrapped in worn butcher paper or pressed into a cardboard box. Vinyl purses, jewelled barrettes, books and crayons, and Betsy Wetsy dolls complete with slender plastic bottles. As far as I could tell, Louis's gift to Marcia was just another part of this exchange between adults and children, an obligatory expression, although he was of no direct relation and simply a friend of my mother's.

I was able to steel myself against the disappointment of being left out. Unpleasant things happened, and they were usually a matter of chance. If a storm whipped up, a bolt of lightning might strike a tree and bring it down through the forest to land squarely on our pump house. If we visited the grocer in Shelter Bay, there might be a lack of chocolate milk. One spring day, not very long after our first full year at the lodge, I had tried nursing a baby bird back to health with doses of mashed worms and sugar water. The bird had fallen from a nest, or had been rejected, and I put it in a box of clean rags to keep it warm. Eventually, despite my efforts, I found its lifeless body curled into a chilled heap. Its beak was open in a final, silent chirp. "The great cycle of life," my father had said when I asked him for an explanation.

By the time I was thirteen, I understood disappointment. There were minor blips on the surface of life, but these could only be expected. There was an order to things, a sweet and predictable symmetry that turned the earth on its axis, that made the rain fall, the snow melt, and the skies fill up with Vs of honking geese. My place in this order was secure: I was the youngest; the most studious; the slow-growing, dark-haired daughter with skin that tanned to a brown crisp and toes that I could fan out individually, like fingers. I read books; I pressed flowers; and in the months after the tourist season, I helped my parents winterize the lodge with the acknowledgement that things were back to normal. More or less.

There were differences since Louis's departure. We continued to seal off the upstairs rooms the way we always had at this time of year, stacking the laundered sheets and heavy woollen blankets into lidded tins to protect them from mice and bugs. We closed off the upstairs hallways and returned the storm windows to their mounts. But now my father was in a frenzy, and my mother was in a silent rage. Both of them worked nonstop.

"What's wrong with Dad?" I asked one day as we gathered our things and shifted them to a downstairs bedroom. My father had been chopping and stacking wood for the past two weeks. Now he rattled around on the porch with a collection of stovepipes. I heard periodic curses rising from the clouds of black dust.

"We made a deal," my mother said. "He's got a

deadline for success, and he better meet it, or ..." Her voice trailed off as she transferred my winter clothes to the bureau drawer, arranging the socks in neat pairs. "It's only fair," she added.

I knew from the way things were going that the deal had to do with selling Raven's. I thought briefly of Louis Moss rolling down the road in his Lincoln, his shadow big enough to blot us out for good. Where would we go? What would we do? I was worried enough to imagine us cast out into the mountains, wandering from hilltop to hilltop in search of pine cones and other nutmeats like the people in my father's *National Geographic*s.

"But what if he doesn't?" I asked weakly, without wanting to know the answer. I could already see the silhouette of Raven's from the outside: comfortable and off-limits, a warm glow pressing up against the windows.

"Then we're back to where we started," said my mother with a touch of impatience. She sat down on the edge of my bed and began folding pyjamas, lining up the plaid edges from top to bottom. She had the ability to impose order on anything, and usually I loved her for it. She made me feel secure. There were times, however, when she went too far, when her flights of organization seemed to reverse everything, pitch chaos into the spaces where order once stood. This was one of those times. I knew Raven's; Raven's was home. I couldn't see any reason for wanting to take that away.

# Chapter 3

Winter came quickly to that part of the island. One moment there was sun on the lake, a canoe making its slow trek across the surface of the water. The next, clouds blotted out the sky, sending funnels of snow to coat the roofs, the mountains, the long and sloping driveway to the access road. The valley that traced the distance between the alpine ridges to Raven's Lodge stretched fifty more kilometres before bottoming out at the Pacific Ocean. While living at Raven's was pleasantly isolating in the summer, with the constant splash of the lake and the spicy wind drowning out approaching cars or overhead bush planes, winter was another matter. Suddenly the distance between Shelter Bay and the lodge lengthened. Now we had to navigate freak whiteouts, unploughed roads, and avalanches. We had to park our truck at the end of the access road and travel across the lake on snowshoes.

People from Shelter Bay romanticized our lifestyle, seeing only the pink cheeks, the knitted toques, and fur-lined leather gloves that my father ordered from a Salish woman to the south. We came into their stores, their offices, their living rooms, knocking the snow from our boots, the mud from our pant legs, and opening our mouths and pocketbooks while trying to adjust to the spike in temperature. There was always the smell of the ocean, the sluggish drizzle that spattered the truck windshield and reminded us that we lived on the coast. There were always people too, louder, bigger, more imposing than we had previously imagined. They lived comfortably in insulated houses with asphalt shingles. They had television antennas that sprouted from backyard lawns like the skeletons of trees.

To me, the lives of these people seemed easy, defined by paved streets and long afternoons in front of the television. The children were rowdy from what I imagined to be unlimited access to chocolate bars, glasses of colas, and syrupy drinks that were dispensed from the soda fountains at local cafés. When I saw them at the lodge, they were transplants, softened by their fascination with their new surroundings, but in their own environment they seemed wound-up, fractious, and difficult to entertain. Shelter Bay was not large – four or five thousand people – and everyone worked at the mill or on fish boats. Marcia and I liked our trips to town, but as the years went on, we made them less and less. When we had started spending winters at Raven's five years before, my parents made a deal with the school district. Marcia and I would continue our studies independently and send our assignments and tests to teachers in Shelter Bay, or, on occasion, all the way to Victoria. At the beginning of the 1969 school term, Marcia was in her third year of high school. I was pushing at the edges of grade nine.

That same winter, my father began to take long trips beyond the strait that separated our island from the mainland. He set out in the truck more and more frequently, always picking up whatever we needed before coming back.

I fully supported my father's attempts to drum up money and did what I could to help him. Being thirteen, I filled the wood box or ran wet clothing through the wringer washer. I kept quiet when he announced that he was going away. By Thanksgiving he was spending long weeks teaching workshops, lecturing at schools, and attending sportsman shows. I had seen him give his speeches and I knew what they were like: impassioned directives peppered with wildlife jokes. Usually he wore a baseball cap topped off with stuffed antlers. "To break the ice," he always said.

During these trips, Marcia and I spent our evenings sitting by the CB Radio listening to the weather report. Voices of island truck drivers and the off-shore Coast Guard drifted over our games of checkers or across the pages of our homework assignments. Every other night, my father radioed in a signal – *city mouse to country mouse, over* – and we took turns telling him our discoveries: rodent turds in the kitchen sink, a low supply of gasoline for an emergency generator. Cougar tracks.

"How are my girls?" he would always say. "Are you taking care of your mother?"

On weekends, he snowshoed back across the lake, hauling a sled loaded with groceries, books, and other winter supplies. He offered us apples – which seemed too waxy and red for that time of year – and chocolate squares wrapped in coloured foil when Christmas rolled around. He restocked the cold room shelves with sacks of fresh food, supplies we ate sparingly, one item at a time, from the Shelter Bay grocer. Everything else was frozen, dehydrated, or canned. Most of the time we ate salmon, with beans or macaroni noodles or Uncle Ben's converted rice. Both Marcia and I poked at the scale-flecked flesh, at the soft backbones that dissolved on our tongues as we chewed them up for vitamins.

After dinner we huddled down in front of the fire with my father and one of his library books. He favoured stories about men who spilled stove fuel onto their hands and instantly lost their fingers to frostbite, or children who fell through the ice and were hauled out by the tassels on their scarves. According to these books, the wilderness was a jungle.

"But if you know what you're doing," my father

said, "you can be prepared for anything."

Slowly darkness enveloped the landscape. Between eight in the morning and four in the afternoon, only a little light penetrated the valley. My mother slept long nights, rising after nine to look at the half-eaten mess of our breakfast, and sighed before fixing herself a cup of tea. While my father was away, my mother neglected to get dressed. Instead she walked about in her housecoat, a woollen tartan with a belt at the waist that hid the hole in her nighty. On her feet she wore threadbare woollen slippers. Leather soles flapped on the bottoms like a set of wagging tongues. I could hear her shuffle from one foot to the next as she slid them across the floor.

"You look like death warmed over," Marcia said one day, when my mother shuffled into the kitchen. We were studying at the table. Marcia picked at the pages of her home economics textbook.

"Pardon me?" my mother said.

"Death warmed over," Marcia said again. I could see the gleam of her teeth as she smiled provocatively.

I recognized the phrase. It was something my grandfather used to say when my mother's hair wasn't freshly set, when her nails weren't buffed or the edges of her slip peeked out from behind her hem. I'd heard it enough to know what it implied: not up to snuff, falling short. I braced myself for my mother's anger, which could be terrifying under certain conditions. Instead she shuffled in her slippers to the medicine chest. She cracked the seal on a bottle of aspirin.

"I feel like death warmed over," she said, a husky laugh rising from somewhere in her throat. I watched her swallow the pills with a glass of water. Up until then I had always considered my mother and Marcia to be a tribe of two, somehow rounded out by measures of grace and loveliness, which I hadn't inherited. Instead I had my father's forehead, his astigmatism. Soon I would need glasses. The only difference between that day in the kitchen and any day that came before, was the realization that my mother was getting older. Her face was sallow, the skin under her eyes as dark as plums.

"This place smells like grease and mothballs," Marcia said. "I can't stand it."

"Tell your father," my mother said, shuffling back out the door. We watched as she stumbled over the hallway rug and disappeared around the corner.

"In case you haven't noticed," Marcia said, "he's not here to tell."

⁎　⁎　⁎

A few weeks after Christmas, I heard a sound coming from the kitchen. I had already been asleep, when I awoke to a crash.

"Marcia," I whispered. "Are you awake?" I clutched at my flashlight. Light from the moon cast a blue glow onto the bedroom rug. "There's something in the kitchen." Already I was convinced that what I heard was a bear, clawing down the window screen, rooting around for buckets of flour and lard. If that was the case, I knew what to do: get out the cast-iron frying pan, the fire extinguisher. Make a lot of noise. Whether or not the bear paid attention depended on how much he had eaten.

"It's nothing," Marcia said, and by the tone of her voice I could tell she had been awake long before I called her name.

"It's not a bear?" I said.

"It's winter, you idiot. The bears are hibernating."

And so it was. I felt immediately calm, looking into the glow of the moon and the white snow outside our window. I shook off the blur of sleep and listened again to the noise. Now it was into the larder. "What is it?" I whined.

Marcia took a deep breath and ran her fingers along the bottom of my mattress, thrumming the suspension that held our bunk beds in place. "It's just Mum," she said. "She's having a snack."

I slid down the wooden ladder and pulled on my slippers.

"Christ," Marcia said, rolling over and applying a pillow to her ears.

In the kitchen, my mother sat at the table eating a tin of Christmas pudding. The glow from the kerosene lamp diffused the darkness around her head, exaggerating her features and the shadows under her eyes. She looked like a campfire storyteller attempting to transmogrify. I stood in the doorway until she noticed me.

"Oh, Ronnie," she said in a syrupy voice. "Come and sit with me. I'm all by myself."

I joined her at the table, watching as she spooned the pudding into her mouth. Even through my layers of wool socks, I could feel the floor. The vinyl chair sent a chill straight into my backside. "Did the fire in the stove go out?" I asked.

"The fire," my mother laughed, waving her hand. She pushed her hair from her eyes and continued eating. I noticed a wad of Kleenex on the table. I thought I could see my breath.

Just as I was about to get up, walk to the cook stove, put my hands in the warming oven, and possibly add a slab of wood, a sound came from my mother. The noise was garbled, like a cry but shallower. I thought she was gasping for air.

"Oh, Ronnie," she said again. "You love me, don't you? You love me."

I looked at her hands, her red, red nose; at her mussed hair and the skin creasing around her mouth. She looked orange, ghostly, sinking into her tartan housecoat and the white waffle of her long johns. There was only one answer to that question; I knew what it was. "Yes," I said. I continued to sit as she went on eating pudding, as she mumbled into her tin, leaking tears and saliva. Fear crept into my heart. Fear and disgust.

⚕   ⚕   ⚕

"What's wrong with Mum?" I asked Marcia the next day as we pulled the laundry from the clothesline. The temperature had plunged overnight. We had waded through the snow in our fur-lined leather boots.

"She sleeps too much," Marcia said, cracking a clothes peg from a set of frozen underwear.

"I think she smells," I said, feeling the thrill of my own betrayal. When had I started noticing this? Months ago. Usually it lingered beneath the stronger smell of her antiseptic mouthwash, creeping out periodically like a mouse from under a rock. Last night I had received a full blast, when my mother turned her face to me and cried *Do you love me, Ronnie? Yes*, I had said, wanting to plug my nose and run for cover. *Yes, I love you.* The blast was fetid, with all the force and sting of bug repellent. "I think she's sick."

"Sick in the head," Marcia said. "She needs to take a bath." She shrugged her shoulders and slapped another of my mother's girdles into the laundry basket. We pried the remaining clothes from the line and took them inside to thaw out in front of the cook stove. We worked our fingers into the fabric to bring out the ice. I tried not to notice, as I warmed my feet against the water chamber, that the clock said one p.m. My mother was still in bed.

When my father returned later that week, he brought with him a whirr of excitement. There was the usual clamour of boxes and paper bags, of fruit spilling onto the entryway rug as I rummaged through the produce; there was the lure of treasures, the hope that somewhere in the depths of my father's rucksack, a book, or in Marcia's case, a swatch of fabric or a velvet hair band, might be lurking; but this time there was also deliverance, a restorative calm now that my father was back to set things right, and the tentative feeling that things would slip back into their familiar grooves if only my mother would let them.

"It's good to be back," he said, shaking the snow from his jacket and hanging it by the stove. His smile was infectious, his eyes wide and unassuming. I crowded around his snow-stained socks while Marcia sat on a nearby chair with her arms crossed in expectation. My mother had risen for the occasion, setting her hair and squeezing into a skirt. There was a spot on the sleeve of her blouse.

"Especially when I have good news," he continued. "I had a talk with an investor in Washington. He wants me to come and see him to work out the particulars, but I think this time we are home free. He wants to invest in our little enterprise."

"How long?" said my mother.

"Pardon?"

"How long will you be gone?"

My father straightened as he removed his socks, allowing them to dangle from both of his hands. His exposed feet were white against the kitchen linoleum, shrivelled and moist like something that had been stored in formaldehyde. "Two weeks," he said.

"And when do you have to leave?" my mother continued. She was as expressionless as a department store mannequin. I thought I saw a faint tremor in her wrist, a tic of motion rising in small waves. She clasped her hands together.

"On Monday," my father said. "I should be gone by Monday." He looked at the floor, his smile dwindling as he considered its raised edges.

"Two days from now," my mother said. The words came from her mouth as if she was pronouncing a sentence. I felt the weight of her gloom, as dark as a winter night, as dark as the antique panelling behind the registration desk. She turned around and walked out of the room.

My father looked at us and cracked his jaw, the way he did when he clasped the leather bindings of his snowshoes between his teeth. "It's good news," he said quietly.

# Chapter 4

Over the next two days, I tried to talk to my father about my mother's behaviour. I wanted to warn him, but also to ask his advice. He was in charge, after all, and deep down I had the sense that he could take any situation and make it better. I knew from his boyhood stories that his life before Raven's was one of adventure. He had worked his way across the Atlantic Ocean on a freighter, swabbing decks and chopping vegetables in exchange for passage. In photographs he has from this trip, he looks solid, unequivocal, his oiled hair and pointed leather shoes reflecting the Protestant ethics of his upbringing: work hard, save well, and you will prosper like a well-loved horse. I knew all of these things about him, but still I had trouble voicing my concerns.

For one thing, life at the lodge had returned to

normal. Since my father had come back, the thermometer in the kitchen hovered at eighteen degrees, a comfortable enough temperature for January. The metal on the cook stove ticked with constant heat, expanding and contracting around a blaze of softwood. At night I listened for the signs of my mother, but the lodge was silent, disturbed only by the rustling of mice. More than once I crept into my father's study, watching as he reviewed the summer ledgers and moved pieces of paper from one pile to another. I tried to open my mouth.

"Not now, Ronnie," he'd say.

My father's presence held together the invisible threads of our family, but as usual, his presence was temporary. Disaster worked at the surface, running beneath everything like a river under the ice.

"Dad," I said finally on the morning of his departure. I had followed him out to the front of the lodge, my boots flapping with hastily tied shoelaces. I watched as he loaded the sled. "Mum is sick."

"She's not sick," my father said, checking over his papers. "She's just unhappy. We've been going through a rough patch. If we get this investor in Washington, everything will be fine." As he spoke, he enumerated the contents of various sacks and cardboard boxes and then began cinching his boots into his snowshoes. The leather straps were well cared for; he had treated the webbing with a fresh glaze of shellac. I watched as he looped the harnesses into place and tested the tension against the snow. *If we get this investor*, he had said. *If.*

"I don't think you should go," I said, knowing as I spoke that this was both necessary and impossible.

"Ronnie," he said, his hand moving to my shoulder. For the first time since we had been talking, he looked up at me. He spoke with certainty. "Everything will be fine no matter what."

For a moment, I let his confidence soothe me; the tightness in my lungs receded so that I could breathe without tensing up my chest. But then I realized for the second time in as many months, that I was easily influenced, easily rattled, and easily soothed. I didn't know if this was a good thing. Somehow I questioned the outcome even as I breathed in and out, repeating his words inside my head. Everything will be fine. Everything will be *fine*.

He shouldered his backpack, hitched the sled to the belt around his waist, and gave me a salute before starting out across the lake. The morning air was crisp. I watched as my breath spiralled outward from my mouth and then disappeared into the glare. All around us trees fringed the shoreline, quivering with the activity of birds and squirrels.

Ahead of me his tracks glistened in the sun. For the moment, I could hear the swish of his snow pants, the soft thump of his snowshoes throwing and compressing snow. I could see the beige of his coat topped off by a red woollen hat with earflaps receding against the lake. The pace of his travel and my own bad eyesight quickly reduced all of this, first to a moving speck, a dot on the horizon, and then to nothing. I stood on the porch steps shivering in my thin sweater. The brightness of the snow had swallowed him whole.

That week a storm ravaged the island. Waves of snow blew in from the head of the lake, hard pellets like the nutrients in fertilizer. They rapped on the roof and clogged up the eaves troughs; they temporarily blotted out the sun.

A storm at Raven's Lodge was not the big deal it could be in other places. We had a good supply of firewood and kerosene. We had rations piled up to the larder ceiling. While everyone else would be grumbling in front of a cold radiator or a blank television screen, we went on with our lives. We didn't have electricity to begin with, so we didn't miss it.

During the first few days of the storm, my mother wandered around the house in her woollen housecoat. I tried to ignore her by doing my homework. Marcia, on the other hand, took charge of the situation, scrubbing, waxing, thawing and baking, carrying out all of the tasks she had previously scorned because she was going to grow up to be a hand model for Barbie dolls.

"Eat this," she said on Tuesday when I came into the kitchen. It was nine o'clock and she had already worked herself into my mother's apron. A lump of dough lay on the counter. She was making bread to the hum of the CB radio, her hair tucked up into a headscarf. I thought she looked like the factory workers in my history textbook.

"What is it?" I asked.

"It's oats," she said. "Just eat."

I stared down into the bowl. Lumps floated in the pool of milk, as if the powder had been mixed with wallpaper paste. "There's too much," I said. "I can't eat it all."

"You eat it when Mum makes it."

"It tastes better." I said this before taking a bite.

She grabbed my bowl and inverted it over the plastic bucket that we used for food scraps. The oatmeal made a plopping sound as it disappeared. "There," she said, slamming the bowl on the counter and returning to her mound of dough. "Starve yourself. I don't care."

I stared at the empty place setting, glittering now with spilled sugar. My stomach growled. I heard the familiar shuffle of my mother's slippers as she came into the kitchen and made her way to the cupboard.

"Well if it isn't the living dead," said Marcia.

My mother poured hot water from the kettle into her teacup, keeping her back to us as she murmured under her breath. Her legs poked out from the bottom of her housecoat, white and goose pimpled like something underdone in the Shelter Bay butcher shop. "Marcia made breakfast," I offered.

"Not that anyone cares," said Marcia.

Now my mother was at the CB radio, fiddling with the knobs. The sound of the weather report disappeared.

"What are you doing?" Marcia said.

"Just turning it down," said my mother. She clutched her tea close to her chest, as if trying to warm her heart, and ambled back into the hallway. "You girls have a nice breakfast," she said.

"Where's she going?" I asked Marcia, looking after my mother as she disappeared.

"Back to her hole." My sister turned around and attacked the dough, folding it over like she was trying to wrestle something out of the grain. There was an edge to her voice, something over and above the usual irritation. I didn't like the way it sounded. Soon she started to cry. I had to put my hands over my ears to make it go away.

That evening I joined Marcia in the kitchen where she was mending a hole in her favourite skirt. She sat hunched over the table making careful, even stitches along the inseam.

"Any word from Dad?" I asked.

"Not yet."

I listened to the quavering voice of the CB radio, a man I didn't recognize calling out into the winter blackness. He was telling another man about the driving conditions on a faraway road. "What do you think will happen when Dad gets home?" I wanted to know.

Marcia lifted her head. There was a slight puff around her eyes, evidence of her earlier tears. She wore a plaid skirt and a layer of wool stockings. "If he gets the money," she said, "then we live happily ever after. The same way we do now." She looked back at her sewing, a trace of sarcasm burning the edges of her mouth. "If he doesn't, then we move and start all over someplace else."

I nodded, shivering inwardly at the notion of leaving Raven's and starting over. For a moment I tried to see the lodge as an outsider, the old carpets and cracked enamel wash basins gathering drips beneath the ceiling. I couldn't. They were all too familiar. They couldn't be taken away. "Dad will get the money," I said, but even as I spoke I could feel Raven's falling between my fingers like meltwater on the lake. Things had been badly damaged. Even my father would have a hard time putting them back together.

*   *   *

Four days later we still hadn't heard from my father. The storm was waning, reduced now to a lonely wind that swooped down the chimney and pushed smoke into the firebox. All of the stovepipes at Raven's fell short of the proper regulations. During certain conditions, a low-pressure system or a fierce wind could fill the entire kitchen with smoke.

Marcia stepped up to the CB radio and put her finger on the knob. She fiddled with the buttons. "This thing is on the wrong channel," she said with surprise. I watched as she tuned in to Channel 57 and the usual voices rang clear with the weather report. She looked at me accusingly. "Did you touch this radio?"

"No."

She grabbed hold of my wrist and twisted. A searing pain travelled up my arm. "You're lying."

"I didn't touch it," I said desperately. "Let go!"

She dropped my wrist and stomped out of the room, slamming doors and furniture before she climbed the stairs.

When I arrived at my parents' room, Marcia was tripping her way across the mess on my mother's bedroom rug. An overturned washstand littered the carpet. There were bits of broken porcelain and balled up socks spread out between the door and the window. Even worse was the rank air, trapped inside the four walls by blinds drawn against the sun.

"Time to get up!" Marcia shouted. She tugged at the blinds. One by one they retracted, revealing shafts of sunlight and great spirals of dust. "Wakey, wakey," she shouted at my mother, who lay nestled into her mattress. When my mother didn't stir, Marcia ripped off the covers with a dramatic pull. I thought of magicians unveiling a secret trick, a woman carved in half like a turkey or someone missing all of their limbs. Instead there was my mother, flat against the cotton sheets, her backside exposed through the holes in her underwear.

"What's wrong with her?" I asked, worried now that she was dead. She was still and white.

"What's wrong?" said Marcia in a voice very much like my mother's. "I'll tell you what's wrong. She's a drunk. That's what's wrong." She poked my mother viciously and I heard a small groan. My mother burrowed deeper into her pillows. "No you don't," Marcia said. She stomped back out of the room.

I pictured the men I had seen lolling on park benches with paper bags, men with crooked, rotten teeth and unshaven jowls that hung down to their moth-eaten collars. These men were drunks. "What did you say?" I asked Marcia, when she came back into the room. This time she carried the basin from the back of the cook stove. Chunks of ice still floated on the surface of the drinking water.

"You heard me," she said. She tipped the basin over my mother's head.

The groan that came from my mother's mouth was from somewhere far off. It sounded like an animal dying in a leghold trap. She rolled over and covered her head with her hand.

"Upsy daisy," said Marcia, hauling my mother to a sitting position. She whacked her gently across both cheeks. My mother clung to Marcia with the ends of her fingers.

Outside something rumbled. I felt the vibrations coming through the floor. "What's that noise?"

"How should I know?" Marcia said. She was hauling clothes from the bureau to the bed and forcing my mother's arms and legs through the openings. I ran downstairs and put on my boots.

The noise was coming from the snowplow working its way down the access road. I knew from conversations between my parents that the snowplow was a costly machine. Someone would have had to pay for this, and my parents did this but rarely. I watched as the man inside worked the controls, encased inside the glass like a figurine in a snow globe. He waved cheerily before turning around and heading back where he came from.

The thought occurred to me that my father must have been successful enough in Washington to pay for the luxury of driving all the way to our front door. But as I watched for the cab of our family truck, I had a sinking feeling. The blue Lincoln glided into the parking lot.

"Hello, Ronalda," Louis said as he stepped out from the front seat. "I'd like to speak to your mother."

Instinct told me to lead him back down the road, to the town where he had come from. His city shoes and trench coat were already wicking up moisture from the surrounding banks of ice. I noticed he wasn't wearing a hat. "She's sick," I said.

"I'm sorry to hear that, but I need to see her." There was none of his previous staring. Instead he stood before me with a look of kindness. He stepped around me and aimed for the lodge.

Due to the storm and my own neglect, the path to the lodge had not been shovelled. My tracks to the woodshed were small and light and formed a narrow passage in the snow. The minute Louis stepped off the trail, he sank up to his knees; his pant legs acted as funnels. I watched him flounder in the powder while I wondered how to help him.

Eventually we found my mother and Marcia sitting on the parlour couch. My mother had a blanket draped across her shoulders. She looked up from her mug of tea. "Louis?" she said hoarsely.

"I need to speak to your mother alone," Louis said.

*   *   *

"I don't see why we can't listen," said Marcia who was sulking now in the kitchen. I sat at the table watching as she fussed with the drafts on the cook stove. I wondered if my mother would stay awake long enough to have a conversation.

"He came a long way," Marcia went on, tugging at her skirt and smoothing out the creases in her blouse. Her former fire was gone and the haughtiness was creeping back into her cheeks. "Did I ever tell you that he said I was beautiful?"

I shook my head.

"Well, he did." She cinched the laces in her shoes as though preparing for a race. I thought back to Louis struggling in the snow, his trousers bunched up around his knees to reveal a pair of hairy shins. He had never told me that I was beautiful.

"I want to know what they are talking about," Marcia said, settling down into her chair with a sigh.

After what seemed like an hour, Louis came into the

kitchen. "Girls," he said. "Your mother wants to see you."

The mother in the parlour was only the same woman we had left in two respects: she sat on the couch in her housecoat and slippers. She looked tired. Everything else about her seemed strange. Now the blanket drooped around her shoulders. She slouched into the couch cushions, looking straight ahead. Marcia and I sat on the chairs opposite Louis and my mother. We waited in silence.

"Alice?" Louis said at last.

His words might well have been a cork unstopping. My mother collapsed into sobs. The look he gave us and the state of my mother told me he had bad news. Suddenly his eyes were wet. He put his hand on my mother's shoulder. "I'm afraid your father has died," he said.

Marcia and I watched him, this man who only ever seemed to bring bad news. He had our full attention. "On the Washington Interstate," he continued.

For a moment, his lips went on opening and closing. I could see the dark hole in the centre of his face, the black circle where air was supposed to go in and out, but I couldn't hear what he was saying over the whirr in my ears, the rush of blood that seemed to be draining from my head. I shook him off by looking at Marcia. She had crumbled into a heap on the settee.

I ran from the parlour, ran through the kitchen to the back door where my boots were piled on racks behind the cook stove. My feet inside the liners felt instantly warm, cloaked in some deceptive state of comfort that I knew would vanish the moment I stepped outside. I flung open the door. The screen banged against the doorframe, and I was back in the snow. I ran again, as fast as I could along the path to the woodshed, to spruce trees hulking along a fringe of forest and rental canoes indistinguishable under the cover of snow. I kept on running, but once I was off the path I might as well have been standing still. The snow was up to my waist.

I grasped a tree trunk and my hand came away sticky with sap. I had forgotten my mittens, had set out without a coat or hat to a part of the property considered out of bounds when travelling alone. I knew better than to hurl myself into the forest in winter, but I couldn't think. I couldn't remember anything but my father, measuring twigs by the thickness of his fingers, his white English legs clad in long pants even in the heat of summer in case he encountered a patch of devil's club; my father, outfitted for all eventualities, especially the ones including accidents, which could happen anywhere, he told me over and over, his hands feathering a strip of cedar bark like a Boy Scout making tinder. *No, like this, that's right. And when you have enough, take the knife and shave some magnesium from the bar. Now strike it; push the blade away from you and there will be sparks. Aim the sparks at your pile – it's hard, but it works – it's important. Keep trying. If you learn one thing from me, this should be it. Harder – your life depends on it. There, exactly. See, I knew you could do it.*

Above me the snow kept falling, cascading through the trees and muffling everything but the sound of my breathing. *If you learn one thing from me,* my father had said, and I had nodded, because I wanted to learn everything there was to know. But not this grief, which wasn't what I wanted at all.

# Part II

# Chapter 5

I've heard people say there is a moment when you truly grow up, a moment when you look at your childhood and find it's nothing but an old outfit that has grown too small to be of any use. The winter of my father's death, something descended on my family. It felt at first like a funnel of wind, the kind that blasts the tops of ridges, strewing mosquitoes and pollen in all directions, or the sort of dream that seizes you with grief and panic as you struggle to wake up and see whether or not any of it really happened. The week after my father's accident, I woke up to find that everything was just as I'd feared. People appeared at Raven's – strange women called Sheila or Carmen or Betty or Gwendolyn – crawling out of the woodwork and down the snowy access road to pack up our things and load them into a moving van.

These women patted us on the shoulders. They handed us handkerchiefs smelling of perfume and fed us meals of roast beef while ushering my mother into the bedroom. At the same time, Louis sat in the office running his pencil down the margins of my father's business ledgers and kneading the skin on his forehead. Once in a while he shook his head from side to side and said in a low voice, "Well, I'll be damned."

If I had a question about the way things were going, Louis was now the one to ask. I caught glimpses of my mother, flashes of her slippered feet as she passed in and out of the lodge on her way to the outhouse, but I don't remember hearing her voice. Her appearances were silent and brief, marked by whispers and the presence of a dishevelled shadow that withered against the support of the other women like a hospital patient clipped to an IV unit. A few times I made up my mind to go to her, to run upstairs and beg her to read passages from *Little Women* or *The Black Stallion*, but then I remembered the distance between our life before and the one that faced us.

The Sheilas remembered this too.

"Look how well those girls are holding up. Aren't they just the strongest?"

"They're being so brave."

"To think of what they must have been through. It just breaks my heart."

"It's not going to get any easier."

"But they're good. They're patient. Look how

helpful they've been since we got here. Sitting quietly, out of the way."

In the parlour, Marcia and I sat between couch cushions sinking farther and farther into the upholstery. All around us things seemed to be moving forward with startling momentum. Closets were emptied; suitcases were laid out on bedspreads and crammed with neatly rolled balls of socks. A woman with chestnut hair and a bow like a wing nut fastened to the crown of her head told us to gather everything we could not live without and bring it into the living room. "You can come back for the rest later," she added sympathetically.

I stared at her powdered nose, at the fleck of cold cream she had neglected to rub in beneath her left eye, and wondered about the possibility of *later*.

Louis, it seemed, had everything figured out. As the activity continued around us, he sat us down in the office and began to explain what lay ahead.

"As you know," he said with some discomfort, "your mother has been having some trouble with her nerves. Things will be difficult for her now that your father is ..." he trailed off as we stared at him. "Gone," he said with some finality. "She will need help around the house. She will need you to be patient." He took another breath. "She will also need to see a doctor –" he trailed off again.

I looked at Marcia. She was staring out the window, jiggling her foot against the cuff of her blue jeans. "Are you going to live with us?" I asked, fearing his answer.

Louis smiled, relieved now that one of us was talking. "No, that's not really appropriate, Ronalda," he said. "But we'll find you a house nearby. Someplace close to school."

"School?" I said. I didn't want his explanations. I wanted my mother's cool hand against my forehead.

Louis took a deep breath. "Now we're getting ahead of ourselves. Don't worry about that." He picked up a stack of papers and adjusted his tie. "I'm sure you will all like living in Shelter Bay. There's a lot more to do there than here."

"Shelter Bay?" I said.

"Why, yes," Louis said. "That's what I've been getting at. I'm sure you both know that staying at Raven's is impossible. When your mother is ready to go back to work, I can help her find a job in town. This way, I can help you back on your feet."

We sat for a while staring at our shoes and socks. I imagined my mother flat on her back, arms and legs flailing in wild attempts to turn over. Somewhere out of the sky, a giant hand descended and set her right again. This hand, it seemed, belonged to Louis.

"What's going to happen to Raven's?" I said, suddenly worried.

"We'll take care of that soon enough," Louis said.

The following week, more snow began to fall. Louis gathered my father's business papers and filed them into cardboard boxes. The packing women dwindled to one or two earnest faces and then disappeared. Somewhere in between leaving Raven's and driving to Shelter Bay, we attended a memorial service for my father. I remember only the feeling of a woollen skirt, the smell of my mother's antiperspirant as we rode in Louis's Lincoln to and from the park headquarters. When I thought about my father, I imagined him as lifeless as the baby bird I had tried to save a year earlier, curled into a terry cloth rag under the cover of a recycled shoebox. In reality, he had been cremated, reduced to a handful of ashes that someone scattered like grass seed across the official park boundary while my family looked on. I had been given the option to do the scattering but had refused, knowing in advance that when the time came, I would not be able to let go.

After the service I climbed into the back seat of the Lincoln. The leather interior slid against my leotards, emitting odours of cowhide and shoe polish. In the front seat, a lone air freshener dangled from the rear view mirror. I thought about our Ford Thames, the litter of dust and unpaid parking tickets stuck to the dashboard, the rubber bungee cord clamped to the glove box to prevent it from flapping open as we drove over bumps. A knot of pain and fear worked its way up my throat as Raven's disappeared behind us and Louis adjusted the knob on his car radio back and forth over nothing but static. "You don't get any stations out here," he said before finally giving up. "Isn't that a beggar?"

The air in the Lincoln was moist and suffocating. I cupped my hands, digging my fingernails into the itchy knit covering my knees. Once in a while my mother's shoulders looked as if they might be going up and down, rising and falling as if she was crying, but there was never a sound. Next to me, Marcia sat looking out the opposite window, her arms clenched across her chest. I fell asleep to the thrum of the windshield wipers.

When I awoke, we were pulling up to a traffic light. Louis had his window open. A cloud of exhaust poured over the door handle. "Are we nearly there?" I asked.

"Almost," Louis said.

The highway wound around a mountain, rising first into a flurry of wet snow and then descending again to wet pavement lined with evergreens. A glitter of electric lights lit up an oncoming hillside. The longer we drove, the denser the lights became, strung across the landscape as though part of a giant constellation. Eventually we pulled up to a small house, dark on the inside. Louis dug beneath a garden gnome and produced a set of keys.

"This is the place," he said, opening the front door. "I checked with the landlord. There's plenty of furniture. The rest of your things will arrive tomorrow." He flicked on the hallway lights and looked briefly at the contents of the house. I saw a brown rug and a glass-topped hallway table.

"Not bad," he said, answering himself. He rattled the door on the hallway closet, hanging now at an awkward angle from a loose hinge. "All in all, it fits the bill." He touched the top of Marcia's head.

"I'll check back on you tomorrow," he said. "If you need anything, let me know. Here's a number where I can be reached. I live on the other side of Main Street." He handed my mother a scrap of paper and gave us all a final nod.

I turned to Marcia who was looking back at him. "Where are we?" I said.

Slowly she removed her boots. She looked blankly at the dark rooms and then wiggled the dial on the thermostat.

Out of desperation, I turned to my mother, who stood on the brown rug huddled inside her winter coat. "Mom?" I said weakly. A pair of glazed eyes shifted in my direction.

She smiled vaguely, her reaction time off by almost a minute. Her voice was a bleat. "Thank you, Louis."

Our new house was nothing like Raven's. There were no vast hallways or winding staircases, no handmade snowshoes mounted over the fireplace. There was, in fact, no fireplace, no river rock or log purlins or any raw materials dug from the earth and fastened into place. The house might have been okay if it wasn't for the pools of water on the front lawn, if the foundation had not been slumping into the earth causing the floor to careen like the deck on a sinking boat. It might have been all right if the living room, bedrooms, and kitchen had not been coated in a hard orange lacquer that tinted the faces of my family and turned them into grotesque jack-o'-lanterns.

Every day I tried to stop things from moving forward, to halt time by staying in my bedroom and staring at cracks in the ceiling. Later, when a television appeared in our living room, I sat in front of our lone channel until the sun went down. I sat blinking and dazed before a row of coloured bars on the television screen, which signalled that the channel had signed off for the night.

By the time I had started to accept what had happened to my family, a month had passed. I looked around and suddenly saw we were living in a strange house, a war-era bungalow down the street from the Shelter Bay hardware store. We wore thin jackets instead of our usual parkas, and tennis shoes that squelched on wet sidewalks. The view I had once admired from the mountains nearest Raven's was now right in front of my eyes: there was the estuary, close-up and muddy, filled with rotting seaweed and half-submerged grocery carts. There was the Pacific Ocean, silver as a nickel and dotted with halibut boats heading up the narrows to Queen Charlotte Sound.

Despite these landmarks, or perhaps because of them, I was constantly disoriented. They were too near, looming like phantom versions of the real things with crisp edges and colours no longer muted by distance and atmosphere. I could go for days pretending things were all right, padding up and down the carpeted hallway that led to my new bedroom, but sooner or later they would catch me and bring me back. I would see with a start that everything was out of whack. This was not my life, this blurry succession of mornings and afternoons filled now with radiant heat, chocolate pudding, and the wash of light from electric bulbs. These were not my clothes, fringed kilts that had shown up on our doorstep in neatly folded packages from my mother's high school friends. I looked back on my days at Raven's, knowing I would not live on in that moss-choked valley playing in the lee of the woodpile while my father attacked rounds of cordwood with the splitting maul. Instead I would grow old and die, or I would just die. My father was not coming back. I was just beginning to understand.

Most of that first winter, I hung around in the kitchen where my mother sat in perpetual mourning. Usually she would stare into her supper, her head tilted forward, her arms extended across the place mat as if staking a claim, or else she would spoon her soup or wedge a piece of pot roast into her mouth while slowly chewing. Once in a while she would slump forward, crumpling as if her neck had given out, and I would look at her and wonder what to do. Across the table, Marcia would read the latest issue of *Tiger Beat Magazine* and ignore the both of us.

My own grief seemed to be taking me over, as if I had stepped into freezing water and was slowly going numb. I set my attention on schoolwork, and on organizing the dim chamber given to me for a bedroom, but nothing fit into place. The things I had hauled from Raven's stood out – my steamer trunk, a collection of my father's botanical notebooks and his favourite novels from the library, a chipped pine dresser, the wooden knick-knacks from my window seat – everything was out of place in the house with a paved driveway. Even the convenience of electricity wore off without much delay. I got used to the toilet bowl gleaming in the bathroom lights and the tick of the radiator as the water heated inside its painted coils. I learned to ignore the rumble of engines as cars passed down our street, remembering that the noise no longer signalled visitors or guests who would fill the empty spaces in our house with holiday requests and foreign accents.

Eventually I accepted we had money troubles. After my mother had sold the lodge to Louis, she spent a good portion of the money paying off debts. She sent half of what was left to her brother in Belgium, and used the rest to set up house in Shelter Bay. Louis, she assured us, had no plans to do anything with the lodge until he could broker a deal with the park. Apparently park officials wanted the land around the building, and so did a few businessmen. The lodge itself wasn't worth much.

"What good is the land without Raven's?" I asked more than once. I was worried that all my father's work would now be destroyed.

"You'll have to ask Louis," my mother always said.

Asking Louis proved to be difficult. When I did

manage to catch him during one of his many visits, he was usually absorbed by my family's financial business. Despite my mother's protests, he encouraged her to take charge of her own affairs. He refused to answer my questions point blank, saying, "It will all be sorted out soon."

When I came home not long after Valentine's Day, I saw his blue Lincoln parked in the driveway. I pushed against the door handle and stepped into the house. From the kitchen I could hear coffee percolating. I took off my boots and hung my coat in the closet. When I entered the hallway, they both stopped talking and looked at me – Louis with his long, reptilian jawline fixed into place by a measured smile.

"Honey," my mother said, twirling her fingers into the scarf at her neck. "Would you mind reading in your room for a while? Louis and I have something to discuss."

"I wondered if there was any news about Raven's," I said, butting in instead. "It's been almost one month now. I was thinking that maybe, if the snow wasn't too high, we could go there for a visit. I think I may have left some of my books behind."

"All of your things have been removed," said Louis. "Have you unpacked all your boxes? Maybe if you had a good look –"

Ignoring him completely, I pressed on. "We could take our snowshoes. I know it's a long, cold trip, but there's plenty of firewood and it would only take a day or two to warm up the lodge completely."

"Hon –" said my mother.

"It's been almost a month," I said again.

My mother turned to Louis.

*Let me*, he seemed to say. "Of course you miss your home, Ronalda, and you want to go back. You lived there a very long time. But you have to understand. Getting there is very difficult. The road is blocked with snow. You can't travel on your own, and your mother is trying to start a new life here. Your mother and sister have jobs. Maybe you'd like to get one too."

"I'm too young," I said.

"Ronnie –" said my mother.

"I just want to know what's going on," I said, more loudly than I intended. "Why won't anybody tell me?"

Louis sighed. "Things move slowly in the world of real estate, particularly when there's a park involved. We're going to do what's best for everyone. I want you to know that."

"Yeah, what's best for you," I accused.

"Ronnie!" said my mother.

"Never mind, Alice. I think we're finished here anyway." He started to get up.

"Just hold on," my mother said, a hand on Louis's arm. She turned to me. "Please wait for me in your room, Ronnie."

I shrugged defiantly and made my way to the end of the hall, choosing Marcia's room instead of my own. My sister had taken a job as an usherette at the Watermark Theatre. I resented her desertion, though I now had her bedroom to myself. I lay down on her quilted bedspread, smelling her perfume and scented shampoos. In front of the bed, a collection of stickers on her vanity mirror displayed the latest rock bands.

Going back to Raven's was not just a whim. I was having more and more trouble recalling my father's face, the earthen scent of him as he went about his daily routine. If only I could walk the lodge's ancient hallways, looking at places where he had kindled a fire or cradled me on his lap while reading one of his adventure books, I could bring him back in some real way. Or so I thought. At the very least, I wanted to try.

I rolled over and pressed my knees into the mattress. Across the shag carpets I could see my face reflected in the mirror, a face so empty of expression that it seemed to be patched together by features randomly snipped from the Sears catalogue. I had no idea what I looked like, whether or not I was pretty, whether my head and body were forming in a way that was good and normal. Above the crest of my eyebrows a cluster of pimples had come and gone, leaving a circle of pink in their wake. I had already been concealing the swell of my breasts beneath baggy sweaters and T-shirts for over two years. Now the fabric of my bra was worn and stretching; my hair was uneven. I was beginning to care.

Occasionally when I was in this end of the house, I

carefully opened Marcia's drawers and memorized their contents. I guess I expected to find secrets, something that would explain the way Marcia looked and acted. What I found was an assortment of hair baubles, beaded macramé chokers, lapel pins, and an eyelash curler, all arranged into converted cigar boxes. Today I was angry, so I listened to my mother and Louis speaking softly at the end of the hall. What they talked about was not interesting: financial matters, the cost of dental appointments or the need to buy a practical car. Requests were never made out loud, but after Louis's visits my mother usually clutched a cheque. I wondered how much he'd paid her for Raven's.

I stood up and walked across the hall to my mother's room, putting my hand into the half-open drawers of her bedside table. I rummaged through a stack of magazines and then turned with disinterest to the bureau.

From the open window I could smell the sulphur from the pulp mill and the moist earth odour that seemed to follow every rain. My mother's curtains hung askew, fastened by thumbtacks until we could get curtain rods. There were boxes of clothes on the floor and a tangle of belts knotted around a coat hanger. I stepped over the mess and put my hands into the top drawer of her bureau. My fingers brushed against underwear, a few half-slips and a camisole hastily repaired with a safety pin. Beneath these I found a number of plastic bottles. I popped open the lids to reveal capsules: red like blood, yellow-and-blue like Easter eggs. I was about to turn one of the bottles over when I heard the front door slam. I looked out the window. Louis was heading into the street.

"Ronnie?" My mother said, coming through the kitchen. I could hear her shoes on the linoleum. I put the pills back into the drawer and slipped into the hallway.

"Honey?" she said, more sweetly than I anticipated.

"I'm in here," I mumbled from my bedroom where I lay flat on the bed, pretending to read a book.

"We need to talk," she said when she arrived in the doorway.

I put down my book, slightly confused by her tone of voice. Wasn't I in trouble? "About what?"

"A couple of things." She came into the room and sat on the edge of the bed, crossing her legs in secretarial fashion. Her weight tilted the sagging mattress, and I started to roll as my centre of gravity shifted.

"You heard Louis. He's found me a job. With a local realty office. They'd like me to work part-time starting in June."

I turned to my book. "Oh."

"It's good news," my mother continued. "Except that if I were to take the offer, you would be home alone several days a week. I'm not sure how I feel about that."

I nodded, unsure where she was headed. For years my parents had set out in the truck or on pairs of snowshoes, leaving Marcia and me alone, sometimes over night. On one of these occasions the generator had broken down, and we were forced to take everything from the fridge and submerge it in cans in the lake. When my parents returned, they were surprised to see a row of floating detergent bottles marking the lines where the food had been sunk.

"I don't mind," I said. "I'll be all right."

She looked down and I saw again that she was delicate. Her fingers made small fans on the bedspread. I wanted her to go away, and to hug me, both at the same time. I missed the way we used to hunch together under the entryway steps, pretending we were hiding in the desert with towels flung over our heads. It seemed years since I had felt the cool relief of her hand on my forehead.

"There's more to it than that," she went on, jiggling her foot. "We had a call from the school board. The district manager. It seems they would like both you and Marcia to enrol back in the public system. They think that would be for the best. I discussed this with Louis and he thinks so too."

I stared, wondering what Louis had to do with things. The public system, as far as I remembered it, was nothing more than a bunch of shouting children, cycles of endless routine involving putting on your coat, stepping outside onto a concrete pad, and then taking your coat off again. "When?" I said.

"Not right away," my mother said. "You've been doing home study five years now. You've gotten ahead. And the school year is winding down. It's almost March and throwing you in with a bunch of strange faces wouldn't be fair."

I nodded, hooking my mind around the words *strange faces*. A series of amorphous blobs danced across the surface of my brain. Some of them had braces.

"But there is summer school, something you could do a few days a week. There are courses at the school that coincide with my workdays. I checked in at the district office, and I don't need to start until June because I'm filling in for someone on maternity." She scratched her fingernail against her pant leg. "In any case, the school board needs you both to take a test before they can figure any of this out."

I shifted on the bed. "A test already?"

"To see where you fit. You don't have to study. Don't worry, Ronnie." She put her hand on my shoulder where a knot of tension was forming beneath the skin.

"What does Marcia say?"

"She wants to go back to school in September and meet some other kids. Over the summer, she'll work at her job."

She would, I thought, feeling the stab of her betrayal. I shut my eyes and felt the imagined calm of a whole sea of books. The school library was the part I remembered best from my years in kindergarten through grade three, though I wasn't sure that it was enough. I opened my eyes and saw my mother watching me. She had been sad since my father died, but as far as I knew, she had not gotten up in the middle of the night; she had not looked at me longingly across the kitchen table and said in a slurring voice, *Do you love me Ronnie?* The way it seemed, I could do this simple thing for my mother. "OK, I guess."

# Chapter 6

The room where I wrote the placement test that spring smelled like smoked fish and fresh vinyl. My seat was made from laminated wood, topped off with a seat cover that belched like a whoopee cushion whenever I made the slightest movement. I chewed on the end of my eraser while calculating answers in my head and ticked off the corresponding boxes on my answer sheet. When I had finished the written part of the exam, a man in a tweed suit sat down on the other side of the table.

"Well," he said. "Ronalda, is it? This won't take long. Not long at all." He rubbed the crown of his forehead and a shower of dandruff fell to the table. "What we have here are a few oral problems. A little reading, a little math. You can handle that now, can't you?"

I nodded, though I had no idea what he was talking

about. All I knew was that everything about the man was creased, especially the skin on his face, which seemed too large for the size of his skull.

He started to ask me questions, commanding me to define words, factor digits, identify famous works of art, and recite lists of numbers. There was no encouragement. The man resembled a toad, with his brown-chunked hair, liver spot trousers, and wide, flat mouth that seemed as if it might open at any moment and reveal a retractable tongue.

"Twenty-five?" I said, in answer to a problem about oncoming trains.

He ticked a box on his score pad and remained expressionless.

I shuffled in my chair, trying to remain unfazed. When the clock above his head ticked round to lunchtime, he put down his pencil.

"Well," he said, scratching his chin with his thumb. "You should have the results in a week or two. I understand that you have been doing home study and that fall will be your first year back at school?"

I coughed. "My mother wants me to do summer classes."

He leaned back, taking in the view of my body from the table up: chest, chin, head. "Oh no. That shouldn't be. You see," he gave a little laugh, "summer school is for remedial students. You don't want to get too far ahead. In my opinion that wouldn't be a wise decision at all."

I must have looked sceptical, because he leaned forward and tapped the tabletop with his pencil. "You'll tell your mother I said so?"

"Sure," I said.

"All right then." He picked up his papers and stood up, waiting until I was out the door before turning out the lights. I watched him disappear down the corridor, bouncing up and down as his shoes slapped the hallway tiles. I wondered what he meant by *remedial*.

When the results came back a week later, I was in the kitchen helping my mother with dinner. When the phone rang, I was gripping the wooden handle of a paring knife, attacking the rind on a potato.

"Hello?" my mother said. "Yes, that's correct." She paused and looked over at me. "Oh, that's wonderful news." Her voice rose with pleasure. "Of course, we are very proud. Thank you very much." She made a noise of approval and put the receiver back into the handset. "That was the school board calling about your placement test. Apparently they want to move you ahead a year."

I looked up from my bowl. "What?" I said.

"They think you should skip a grade. Move on up to grade eleven. You'd be with older kids, but you might find it stimulating." She turned to her stew pot and added a ribbon of onion. "Of course, it's your decision."

According to my father, everything was my decision. Would you build a fire this way or that? Would you use this kind of wood here or that kind in that pile over there? It's your decision, Ronnie. I remember my father lining up my choices, placing them out in front of me like the doors in a game show. I always looked for a twitch in his face, a sign that might indicate left or right, this one or that one, but he was always as unflinching as a statue. My palms sweated because I knew there was still a right answer; I might miss it if I wasn't paying attention. I picked up a second potato and began peeling off a strip of flesh. I wasn't sure what to say.

"Oh," I said.

"I think you could stand to gain a lot, maybe get ahead and graduate early."

"Right," I said. I liked this idea. I had always been a good student, though at home study there was very little reason to slough off. Lessons only took a few hours a day and after that, the rest of my time was my own.

"And then there's the issue of summer school," she said. "You probably don't need to do it, but I'm worried about leaving you at home alone." She turned that look on me, the one I had seen in the bedroom. "You understand that I have to go back to work. I don't have a choice."

I nodded, because I understood. I understood that my father was dead and now my mother was paying the price. She would go off to a damp office where she would take dictation and type dry letters onto paper smelling of mildew. She would grow old and fat, her rear end spreading like those of the women in grocery stores, the ones who sat on barber stools clacking their sticks of Juicy

Fruit and working their fingers to the bone so that their daughters could get ahead. I wondered if she knew how much I wanted to help, how much I wanted to make things easier. "I want to go to summer school," I said, rotating my wrist the way my mother had taught me, holding the peeler and circling it round the potato. "I want to take a few courses on the days when you go to work."

The results of my decision were not immediate. For instance, the classes I imagined took place in a wooden schoolhouse with huge blackboards, goldfish bowls, and lunchtime snacks, not the flat-roofed factory where my mother dropped me off at the beginning of July. Inside Shelter Bay High, the narrow hallways were paved with lockers. Wooden doorways leaked the sounds of industrial-strength floor polishers and the screech of moving desks. Everything was shifting, transforming for a school year that was still two months off. The building seemed impossibly large.

On a regular day of classes, the school held one thousand students, but despite this fact, there was no map. *Nada*, the secretary told me, flexing her fingers over her typewriter keyboard. *Sorry, but every hall is colour-coded, see? Blue for arts, green for sciences.* She hammered out a letter and sighed. I did not see, but I nodded all the same and stepped back into the fray.

When I found my classes, I realized with a start that everyone was larger than I was. Most of the boys were badly in need of haircuts and wore their pant legs rolled up. Some of the girls concealed the bulge of swollen bellies, while others had pierced their ears and wore their hair half-way down their backs. Our science teacher, Mr. Turnbull, wore plaid trousers that came together in chevrons on his backside. He had hair growing out of his ears, a drooping walrus moustache, and thick eyebrows that curled over the tops of his glasses. When he talked about pollution, the hair on his upper lip moved up and down like a furry animal.

By the second week of school, I had formed an uneasy friendship with a girl named Janice Polanka. Janice had grown up on the northern tip of Vancouver Island and had recently moved to Shelter Bay so her father could work in the pulp mill. She was at summer school because she had failed grade eleven math. I had never known anyone who had failed before, and I looked at her closely to see if she was a mental defective. She was not. Instead she had large hands and feet – she pointed this out – and brown hair that she wore in shaggy layers. Her pale skin was marred by a wine-stained birthmark that crept up her forehead and took cover under her bangs, a flaw which made her both angry and repentant.

"I'm having it removed," she told me one day, looking fiercely at the ground. "As soon as my parents can afford it."

She spent most of the time talking about her four older brothers and television shows I had never seen. We still didn't have an antenna, a fact that amazed Janice.

"But what do you *do*?" she shrieked one day while we were waiting for classes to start. "There's nothing on the local channel."

"Homework," I shrugged. "Go for walks."

"Walks?" she said, with barely concealed disgust. "What do you mean, walks?"

She looked at me with her mouth open as I described my former life, the hikes to the alpine, the sleeping in tents, Raven's. She took a deep breath and held it. "You didn't have an indoor toilet?" she said, breathing out.

I shrugged again, unsure why that was important. "I can start a fire without matches," I said to distract her.

"Show me," Janice said. She drew herself up so she towered over me by a good six inches. I looked at her birthmark.

"Not right here. I need dry wood." I gestured to the surrounding lawn. Everything was soaking wet. "I need a piece of string."

"Tomorrow then," she said. "Bring what you need tomorrow and show me. I'll wait for you in front of the school." She turned and started to march away, then she asked, "Promise?"

I should have known then that I didn't have to do anything. I should have known that weirdness is almost never rewarded. But I didn't. I still believed in the power of example. "Sure," I said. For a moment, the image of my father came shimmering to mind, his thin hands wiggling sticks, his lips pursed with the effort of blowing on coals as he delivered a presentation to the Boy Scouts of British Columbia. I imagined him smiling.

The next morning, I arrived to find Janice waiting by the double doors of the school. She stood holding her schoolbag. She was not alone. I stepped across the moist lawn and tried to steady my heart as I counted the number of boys and girls gathering around her. Most smoked cigarettes and hooted in loud voices while Janice smirked.

"Here she is," Janice said as I made my way across the sidewalk.

"What's going on?" I asked her in a low voice.

"They want to watch," she said. "I knew you wouldn't mind." She raised her hand and I looked at the crowd. Whatever I was going to do, they seemed to say, it had to be better than standing in the boring schoolyard.

They followed me to a fringe of trees on the edge of school property. I made sure to pick a site sheltered from the wind and arranged a break of rocks in a knee-high semi-circle. Then I removed a piece of cedar from my pocket, attached a piece of string to both ends, and wound the centre of this bow around the middle of a stick. I placed the end of the stick in the worn groove of an old board and applied pressure to the top with a third piece of wood. When I started turning the bow, the wood squeaked.

Someone in the crowd made a farting noise with his armpit. "Good luck," he said. "We'll be here for years."

Janice shifted in her tennis shoes. "She said she could do it."

I kept turning the bow until my fingers were stiff. Within minutes there was a small puff of smoke.

"I see something," Janice said.

When a coal had formed on the bottom of the stick, I pushed harder and coaxed the embers onto a ball of waiting tinder. I blew on the tinder and it burst into flames.

"Look," said Janice.

To prove my point, I added a clump of witch's broom. The fire was the size of a fist.

"I told you," Janice said. She stood triumphant, as if she was responsible for my success.

There was a pause during which the group looked impressed, and then one of them stepped forward.

"Let's make it bigger," he said. He picked up a clump of twigs and added it to the flames. There was a faint hiss while the twigs caught.

"Yeah," said another. "Real big."

Soon everyone was adding twigs and shrubs and breaking branches off trees. The fire hissed and sputtered, sending up a column of smoke.

"Stop!" I shouted.

"*Ooga booga*," said one of the boys, dancing around the smoke like an ape. The fire continued to grow until a teacher arrived.

"What is this?" she shouted. "Who is responsible?" She looked from face to face as the students shrugged and withdrew against the fence. The smoke spiralled around and blasted her in the face. "I demand to know who is responsible."

Eventually a girl coughed, "Why don't you ask Cavegirl?" She pointed to me.

The teacher turned. "Did you start this fire?"

I nodded slowly.

"Come with me, please." She grabbed onto my coat and yanked me to my feet, and then turned to the rest of the group. "I want this fire out. Do you understand? I'm going to the principal right now, and if this fire isn't out when he gets here, you will all face expulsion." She covered her mouth with a scarf and led me away.

As we went, I saw Janice standing on the sidelines, her face white all the way up to her birthmark. She mouthed the words: "You're in trouble."

When the principal couldn't get hold of my mother, he sat me down in his office and eyed me from across a massive desk. His long nose was curved like an anteater's, and he brought the tips of his fingers together in an expression of aggravation. Beside him another man in a jacket and tie hunched against an oaken bookshelf. Already the teacher who had been on duty in the schoolyard had told both men what had happened.

"Now," the principal said. "I know you must have an idea how serious this is, but in case you don't, I've asked Inspector Lamb to fill you in. The inspector is an investigating officer with the district police detachment. He happens to be at the school today to give his yearly talk on the harms of drugs. I asked him to have a word with you."

The inspector grunted. He was a tall man, with a gruff manner that suggested lack of sleep, lack of love, or lack of proper nutrition from eating too many jelly donuts.

"Ronalda," he said sternly. "Your principal has asked me to explain the seriousness of what you did, and I'm happy to help. You see, I deal with criminals every day, some who steal, some who deal drugs, and heck, some who even break into people's houses and set them on fire. It's a known fact that most of these criminals started getting into trouble at a young age, committing minor offences before heading off to something bigger." He paused and shifted his weight. "I hope this doesn't sound familiar. I hope what we have on our hands here is not someone who looks like she is a good student, but who is slipping into mischief."

I didn't say anything. I felt a knot building somewhere in my stomach.

"If you were an adult," Lamb continued, "and that fire you started had damaged public or private property, what you did would have been considered 'arson,' and you would have been arrested. You would have gone to trial and you would have been given punishment to reflect the nature of your crime –"

He went on talking, and I thought of my father willfully blowing life into all the campfires of my childhood, his lungs swelling inside his shirt. In the few years I had spent as his assistant, I had never seen him burn himself, never seen him flinch as he manipulated flaming balls of dry grass onto a roaring fire while his friends looked on. These friends were the sorts of men prone to backyard steak pits or beer chilled in bathtubs of ice, who would douse the whole thing in gasoline if given the chance. "She's a go'er," they would say, or "That'll teach her." They never understood the beauty of my father's art, the same way that the inspector was now confusing mine. Surely there was a difference between the kind of fire I lit, and the ones the inspector was talking about? Even with my classmates' additions?

"Is your mother at home during the day?" the principal asked, when the inspector had finished his lecture.

"She works," I said.

"Then I'll call her in the evening. Will she be home tonight?"

"Yes." I didn't tell him that she wouldn't answer, that she would be in bed by seven o'clock, impossible to wake up. Her eyes would be pinched shut and her head would be tucked under the covers in an attempt to banish the light. I settled for, "But she sleeps a lot."

"Well," he said. "I'm sure we can work around that. I need this form signed. I want to make sure she gets it." He held out a piece of paper. "So she knows the seriousness of the situation. I'm afraid I have no choice but to suspend you."

"I'll get her to sign," I said.

He hesitated, considering my fate. Beside him, Inspector Lamb exhaled disapprovingly. "I'm sure that you will. You know Ronalda, I expected better from you. From the sounds of things, you are very intelligent. Your teacher Mr. Turnbull thinks so; or he did until I told him about your escapade in the schoolyard."

I considered my fingernails.

"Just a word of warning." He leaned forward; his voice bore a hint of caution. "Don't get involved with the wrong crowd. You could end up somewhere you never imagined."

☆　☆　☆

My suspension lasted five days, and although it seemed a strange system that would give days off as punishment, I didn't really worry. I was already tired of school, the drab fractions, the pie charts or equations determining the probability of selecting a matching pair of socks from a drawer of randomly mixed-up laundry. I didn't fit in with the other students and I always seemed to be saying the wrong thing. Even my initial ability to dazzle my classmates with freakishness had waned: no one cared about the meat-eating plants sketched to a fine detail in my notebook; no one wanted to know how to track.

I spent the first few days of my suspension watching soap operas on the local television channel. The house was dim and quiet, filled only by the ticking of the kitchen clock and the rumble of cars passing by our otherwise empty street. For two days in a row, I had hung back in the doorway, telling my mother and Marcia that I had forgotten my textbook. As they headed down the walk clutching purses and shopping bags containing half-baked lunches, shrieking about being late for work or arguing over the state of the refrigerator, I snuck into the living room and lay on the couch. I waited for a full ten minutes before turning on the television.

On the afternoon of the second day, as I was prying another wad of tomato soup from its tin, I felt a wave of sickness rising in my stomach. The soup fell into the pan with a slurping sound and lay there quivering. I stood dazed for a moment before I ran to bathroom and threw up into the toilet. Then I started to cry.

By the time I had finished cleaning up the bathroom linoleum and the spilled soup, I wanted to see Marcia. I put on my coat and walked the five blocks to the Watermark Theatre.

"Hey," said a boy seated in the ticket booth. "Two bucks for the matinee."

I stared at his face, large and clever-looking, which peered out at me from behind a rim of spectacles. "I don't have any money."

"Sorry. Then I'll have to ask you to shove off.

Unless," he added, leaning forward and pressing his nose against the glass. "You want to sit on my lap."

I blinked back incomprehension. "What?"

"You know," he said.

"Ronnie," said a voice. I felt Marcia grab me by the wrist and tug me into the lobby. "What are you doing here?"

I looked at the floor. Now that I had found her, I didn't know what I wanted to say. The purple carpet was patterned and looked like a solar system. I felt the orange and yellow planets zoom in front of my eyes. "I thought," I hesitated, "that you could let me see a movie."

"You're supposed to be at school."

I kicked my boot into the rug in an attempt to stall. "I'm sick."

She sighed, exasperated, and waved her flashlight. A crimson bow tie nested in her shirt collar. "All right. But don't get me into trouble." She led me to a door at the end of the lobby and pushed me inside. "And stay away from Stephen. He's a creep."

I nodded as the black consumed me.

The inside of the theatre was nothing like I had anticipated. Instead of a vast auditorium hung with velvet curtains and braided tassels the colour of cranberries, Marcia had led me to a small room, box-like in structure, with low-slung ceilings and exposed metal pipes. A collection of office chairs dotted the room's interior. As my eyes adjusted to darkness, I saw several people staring out – women mostly – clutching bags of popcorn, cans of cream soda, and looking through what appeared to be a pane of glass. One of the women rocked a bundle at her feet, jerking her knee with a nervous tick. When I sat down I realized the bundle was a baby.

The movie was something forgettable, a love story perhaps, or an allegory involving men and women with hairpieces and sprayed-on, steadfast grins. It is the experience I remember, the feeling of escape. The room, I later found out, was sealed off from the main theatre by soundproof glass. Through this glass, women with noisy babies could watch Robert Redford frustrate Jane Fonda; they could watch the wonders of life in stereo unfold before their very eyes without bothering a soul. A low wattage speaker pumped sound into the black.

Besides the chairs, the room had a waist-high iron railing to protect anyone from falling through the glass. I sat behind this railing listening to the movie and the rustling of paper bags and purses.

During those hours in the crying room, I felt safer than I had felt in months. Crouching beneath the sloping ceiling that covered me like a tent, I heard cooing and whispers, even the burps and passing of gas, while the mothers discussed everything from hemorrhoids to formula.

"My poor back. Every half hour and I can hardly stand up."

"Mine eats like a hound."

"My husband has no idea."

"I feel like twenty going on fifty-four."

"This one's a vacuum cleaner."

Comfort, tenderness, and safety, each one in bigger quantities than I had ever known. When the show ended and the mothers spilled out into the lobby to collect buggies, prams, and carts filled with blankets, I crept quietly out behind them, avoiding Stephen, slipping out the back door where I had come in. I had the briefest of feelings that some order had returned to the world.

Despite my newfound comfort, I still had to get my mother's signature to prove she knew about my suspension. After the movie, Marcia yelled at me as we walked home.

"You could have got me fired."

"I'm sorry."

"You're supposed to be in school."

"I told you, I was sick."

"You don't look that sick to me."

"Well," I said. "I threw up all over the bathroom."

Marcia winced. I didn't know whether or not she believed me. I wanted her to.

"Does Mom know?"

I hesitated, wondering whether or not I should come clean. By now rain had started to fall and I pulled up the collar on my coat to protect my neck. Useless. I felt the drops dribble down my spine. "No. Please don't tell her."

Marcia stopped and laughed. "Why would I?"

"I don't know."

"She doesn't give a shit, Ronnie. If you're in trouble, she probably won't even care."

I had a hard time believing her. "I need her signature on a form. I don't want to ask her."

"What kind of form?"

I dug into my pocket and pulled out the piece of paper. The edges of the folds were worn and pulpy. She read the paper and snickered.

"Geez Ronnie, this isn't Raven's. You can't just go around burning things."

I tucked my chin into my coat. "I didn't do it by myself."

She started up again. "Don't worry. I'll take care of it."

That evening, we waited until dinner was over and my mother was sitting with her feet on the ottoman drinking a glass of lime seltzer. I lingered nervously in the hallway. From where I stood, I could see the holes in my mother's stockings. The pale pink of her toenails looked vulnerable and innocent.

"Has she taken her pill?" Marcia asked, coming in from the kitchen.

"What?" I said.

"The red one," she hissed. "In the little bottle. She takes it after dinner to help her sleep." She peered around the corner into the living room. "Sometimes she takes two."

"I don't know."

"She has," Marcia said, stepping onto the carpet. I

watched her move briskly as if heading out on an errand to buy postage stamps. I tried not to flinch. My mother stared at the photo album.

"Mom," she said. "I'm going on a trip and I need your signature for permission." She held out the form – supported now by the hard surface of a book – and a ballpoint pen.

"What?" said my mother, then, "Of course." She scribbled her signature on the paper without reading it, and then handed it back to Marcia. I thought I saw her head waver on her neck.

"Thanks," Marcia said.

"Marcia." My mother turned slightly. Marcia was almost at the hallway.

"Yes?"

"Where did you say you were going?"

Marcia didn't hesitate. "To the zoo," she said. "With the Girl Guides."

My mother nodded and turned back to the photo album, fully satisfied. "You girls have a good time."

I let my breath out and watched Marcia make her way to the kitchen. For a moment my mind was numb, overwhelmed by relief. Marcia was a star and now I would owe her one. Then the ridiculousness of what she'd said hit me. There was no zoo in Shelter Bay. On top of that, both my sister and I were too old for the Girl Guides. I watched my mother as she stood up and clutched her temples.

"I'll see you in the morning," she said hoarsely as she headed for her bed. "I have a terrible headache."

*　*　*

After my fifth afternoon at the Watermark, I sidestepped Stephen and headed out the back doors toward the river. By now it was four o'clock. The sun was peaking high in the sky, casting shadows onto uneven ground. I felt suspiciously free, rattling a handful of coins in the pocket of my shorts.

The river that drained into the estuary at Shelter Bay was the same one that ran from the lake at Raven's. As I walked through a maze of streams and lily ponds, I half expected it to look familiar. I had walked that same trail with my father to watch the salmon spawning. Now the forest was like a tomb, cool and silent. I sat for a moment alone with my grief, with my father's memory and the flash of his charming smile. Overhead an eagle called, pursued by a crow with an attitude.

I was about to go on when I heard twigs cracking. The boy who stepped into the clearing looked startled, and then relieved. He cleared his throat. "Hey. Do you know the way back to the marina? The moss here grows on all sides of the trees."

I didn't know what to say. I stood in the sunlight looking over his unruly hair and wide, mud-stained pant legs.

"Do you talk or what?" he adjusted his jacket, staring at me. For the first time I remembered my low neckline, the outer layer I had stripped off on my way up the river and tied around my waist. I crossed my arms over my chest.

"Look," he said. "I got turned around somehow. I've been wandering around for a while and I keep coming back to this spot." He gestured with his hands. "I know I can't be far from the turnoff to town, but for some reason I keep missing it. If you know how to get back, it'd be great if you could share the secret."

"That isn't true," I said eventually. "About the moss. That's an old wives' tale that gets just about everyone who believes it lost."

He tilted his head and blushed. "So I noticed."

"I'm going towards the marina," I said, turning to set foot on the path. "You can follow me if you like."

We walked in silence for nearly half an hour. I could hear his steady breathing and the slop of his pant legs. His worn running shoes weren't suited for the slippery ground, but he kept up, sliding once or twice on wet river rocks. Eventually he said, "So, you just hang out here by yourself?"

I recognized this question. Janice Polanka said the same thing.

"I was taking a walk," I said. "Getting some air."

He followed me for a few more minutes until we reached the junction between the stream and the main fork in the river. When I started across a fallen log spanning the stream, he called out. "I don't remember this from the way here."

"You probably took another route," I said, putting my foot on the log. "There are lots of branches. They criss-cross the estuary all over the place. This one is the fastest way back."

He looked at me sceptically and then relented, inching his way onto the log and out over the stream.

I watched him briefly, wondering why he was so unsteady. The log was only four or five feet off the ground and the stream below was knee deep. I waited until he made his way towards the middle, and then I crossed back to help him. "Here," I said, holding out my hand. "It's good for balance." I didn't say whose balance. If he went over, there was a good chance that I would too. Still, my treads were good, and I usually landed on my feet. He looked at my hand. "Come on," I said.

We made our way to the other side and stepped onto a junction. I pointed across the flats to the marina. "This path will take you to the main road. Turn left when you get there and follow it all the way. You can't miss the smell of fish."

"It smells pretty bad already."

I shrugged again. "You get used to it." I turned around to go.

"Wait," he said. My eyes moved to his hands, tugging at the zipper of his coat. He was struggling with something. "I don't like heights. It's hereditary, I guess. A product of my liberal education."

I didn't say anything.

"Look," he continued. "Do you live around here? I've got this place if you ever need anywhere to crash. Some friends of mine come around to talk and eat. The food is fresh. They grow their own eggs, salt-of-the-earth and all that."

"Thanks," I said. "But I should be going."

"I don't even know your name."

"Ronnie," I said. "But I probably shouldn't have told you that."

"Why not?" he asked.

"Because I don't even know you."

He laughed. "I don't know you either but I let you lead me out of the deep dark woods." He paused and looked down the length of his nose. "You're not still in school?"

For a moment, I recognized something in his look, something that brought to mind the way Stephen stared at me every time I passed his ticket booth, but I knew I was running out of time. I had to be home before my mother. "I should go," I said, turning on my heel and slipping down the path. The last thing I remember was the crunch of his footsteps heading toward the marina, the feeling of my heart as it gave a little flip.

# Chapter 7

If I had thought that things would get better after my suspension, I was only partly right. At home things went on as ever. Arguments, half-baked meals, voices barking from the television set. My mother – rattled now by her three days a week at the real estate office – continued to go to bed at seven o'clock. She had been to see the doctor, she told us. He recommended rest and more rest. Marcia continued to let me into the Watermark, as long as I went to classes and did my homework. On the days when no one turned up for a showing, she even snuck me popcorn and cream soda.

I returned to school on a clear day. The winds had shifted and smoke from the pulp mill drifted south. I skulked up the sidewalk in a pair of Marcia's tennis shoes, stopping only for a moment to look at a wildflower crushed between a pop can and a brick pried from the schoolyard flower garden. When I rounded the corner I saw Janice Polanka conferring with a boy in a baseball cap. The boy and Janice had their backs to me.

I knew by Janice's posture and the look of the boy that they were exchanging important information. Janice kept her hands in her pockets. She cocked her head to the side. "Of course I know that," I heard her say. "I'm no dummy."

The boy stepped back and said something in a low voice. I thought I recognized him from a group that hung around outside the school in the morning before classes. He was large, with slicked-back hair and a hulking stance that reminded me of a bear in search of a scratching post. As he stepped back, the bell rang, and I saw him point a finger at someplace behind the school. He turned and walked away.

"I'll give her the message," Janice said.

"You'll never guess," she squealed when I found her in front of the garbage can.

"Never guess what?"

"What happened while you were away. What I have to tell you."

I thought for a moment about my week off. For some reason it felt like more than that. "I don't know," I said at last.

"One of Moose's friends came over to talk to me, first on Friday, and then again this morning. He asked me about you."

"About me?"

She smiled a toothy grin. "He'd heard about your suspension."

"What did he want to know?"

Janice shifted. "Everything. Where you came from. What grade you were in. I told him you moved from the mainland, and that before you came to Shelter Bay you lived in a regular house like everyone else."

"Why would you do that?"

She drew back as if scalded. "To make you sound normal, you numbskull. If I didn't make something up, he might have found out that your parents couldn't afford electricity."

I stared at the ground. As far as Janice was concerned, I was the *poor* in *poor people*, the kind her mother had pointed out lining up in front of the food bank in downtown Shelter Bay, wearing only track suits and dirty caps. *It's not the children's fault*, Janice had quoted her mother saying. *They can't help what their parents are.* I had tried to correct her, to show her snapshots of my smiling family in our snowsuits, but eventually I had given up. I started to fear she might be right.

She lowered her voice and bent down to pull me closer. "You know what this means, don't you?"

"No."

"That Moose picked you. That's what his friend told me this morning. Moose wants to take you *behind the warehouse.* You're supposed to meet him there after school."

I shrugged and considered this bit of news. "What for?"

Janice hissed. "You idiot. Why do you think? To make out." She straightened and readjusted her bangs so that they covered her birthmark. "This will make you part of his gang."

I stared at my tennis shoes, which were planted on someone's discarded homework. In my short time at Shelter Bay High, I had already heard stories about people going behind the warehouse. I don't know what I imagined they did – kissed perhaps, or held hands – but whatever the case, I didn't think I wanted to do that with somebody called "Moose." The boy from the estuary flickered briefly in my mind's eye. "What if I don't want to go?" I said.

Janice's eyes widened. "Then everyone will find out. And probably," she continued, "you'll ruin our chances of ever being popular."

I looked out to the schoolyard where crowds of people gathered in clusters. A long and impossible list of things determined the territory they occupied and how much power they wielded over the masses. Somewhere at the top of this hierarchy were Moose and his gang. Beneath them, various groups of homogenized, flat-faced teenagers ran a close second, clumping together in the schoolyard like the cells of an amoeba, moving *en masse* and splitting only when there was enough of them to venture out over the vast and unknown terrain of the schoolyard. After those two groups, things became unclear: there were the penny-loafers, the grease monkeys, one or two oily-haired boys known to sniff paint from paper bags; then there were the hippies, a handful of well-meaning, browbeaten potheads who drifted around in a haze of patchouli oil and spiced cigarettes, chanting verses and saying how *absolutely cool* everything was and wouldn't it be *absolutely cool* if we could all just love each other?

Somewhere at the bottom, Janice and I stood like sentries on guard for the losers of Shelter Bay. Neither of us knew why we were stuck where we were, but most of the time it bothered only Janice.

"You're going to do it, aren't you?"

When the afternoon bell rang, I walked with Janice to the edge of the wood.

"Over there," Janice motioned.

I took one final look and headed toward the meeting area. The air was hot. I felt a trickle of perspiration work its way down my rib cage and wished that someone had warned me to wear deodorant.

When I arrived at what I thought was the spot, I saw no one. A patch of shade huddled under a clump of ravaged fir trees, and I stepped out of the sun for some relief.

"Hey," a voice said.

Immediately I understood why they called him

Moose. He was nearly twenty feet away, but even at that distance he looked taller than six feet. A grease-stained baseball cap nested on his head, flattening his hair and pressing down on the tops of his ears so they stood out. He wore tight pants, a black T-shirt, and a worn jean jacket with embroidered patches stitched across his biceps that read *Motorola* and *Hot Rod*. I watched as he pulled something from his pocket – a bottle – and then took a long, hard swig.

"Here," he said, handing me the bottle.

My first thought was to wipe the mouthpiece with my sleeve. Instead I took a sip. The sting of the liquor brought tears to my eyes. My throat seized and then relaxed. I knew the taste – I had sampled my mother's before, but never straight. We passed the bottle back and forth, the noise of our swallows outdoing the nearby clang of the warehouse forklift. Eventually I felt a slow burn travelling up my spine.

"Loosens ya up," he said. He took the bottle and recapped the lid, returning it to the inner folds of his jacket pocket. Then he turned to me and took my head in his hands.

His mouth, it seemed, was larger than the lower half of my face – for a moment, I thought he might disconnect his jaws and swallow me whole like a boa constrictor – and his slurping brought to mind the mating rituals of bugs: praying mantises or centipedes. My brain settled on deer tongue – a delicacy my father had insisted we eat at least once a year because of the protein. I struggled to stay upright, pressing my feet into the dirt and gnarled tree roots as he worked his way into my mouth. There was a cold and callused hand working its way up my back, the thumb fiddling with the clasp on my bra.

Afer some time he withdrew. "See you tomorrow," he said, and stalked off.

I stood for a moment, adjusting my field of vision. There were lights in front of my eyes, pinpricks of heat that danced back and forth. My face felt sore and wet, and when I shifted my weight, a breeze from the pulp mill wafted over me in a wave of sulphur.

I walked to the edge of the wood and made my way to the parking lot. As I was heading toward the boundary of school property, I ran into Mr. Turnbull.

"Ronalda?" he said with the raise of an eyebrow. "What are you still doing here?"

My head swam as I tried to think of an excuse. Suddenly I became aware of my crooked T-shirt, my mussed hair and the roar of alcohol on my breath. I pulled down the back of my jacket and said unconvincingly, "Looking for mushrooms."

"All by yourself?"

I nodded.

Mr. Turnbull stared, giving me a look of disappointment. He didn't have to say any more, but he did. "You'd better be getting home. Your mother will be wondering where you are."

I thanked whatever god appeared to be watching over me at that moment and slipped past Mr. Turnbull and onto the sidewalk. Exercising immense concentration, I walked in a haze all the way home, counting the steps as I went until I found the front door to my house. I made my way into the kitchen – feeling the sway of the floor beneath my feet – and over to the chesterfield where Marcia's usherette uniform lay crumpled in a heap. The feeling of the cushions beneath my head and the weight of my body on the upholstery was bliss. I lay still for a moment, watching the smoked-glass light fixtures whirling out from the spattered stucco ceiling. I thought of jellyfish and what it must be like to explore the ocean in a submarine. I thought: how simple, this bottled numbness, this prescription for taking the pain and making it slowly drain away.

I woke up some hours later, wildly disoriented. Light from the living room window slanted across my face, scorching my cheek. I sat up in a flash of panic and shook my head when I realized where I was. Television, patterned tweed sofa, Marcia's polyester bow tie wedged between the couch cushions. Someone was knocking on the front door. I fought to get free of my schoolbag, which had become tangled around my ankles.

"Hello?" The door inched open. Louis walked slowly into the hall. "Ronalda? Is that you?"

"Yes," I croaked, surprised by his impromptu visit. Since my mother had started her job at the real estate office, his visits had become less and less frequent.

He stepped into the living room and paused, looking around. "Where is everyone? Are you home alone?"

"Yes," I said again, and then revising, "I don't know. No one was here when I came home from school. I fell asleep on the couch."

He looked at me, expressionless and then sat down on the chair. "Are you feeling all right?"

I nodded. "I'm just tired."

"Well," he said. "Would you like a glass of lemonade? I could use one. It's a particularly hot day."

I nodded again, wondering how long I had been asleep. "Sure."

He stood up and walked to the kitchen. I heard him rummaging through the cupboards and then a low pop as he opened the refrigerator. Too late: in a flash I remembered the layers of green fuzz coating the vegetables in the crisper, the dried-out carrots wizened to resemble chopped fingers. Marcia and my mother had argued for days about whose job it was to clean the kitchen, buy groceries and wash the dishes. Eventually the house had settled into a deep neglect.

After awhile, he came back and handed me a glass of water. "There doesn't seem to be any lemonade," he said, taking his seat.

I took a sip, thankful for the cool liquid, and watched as he fingered the tassel on a pillow. His hands were beefy and covered in freckles. Thick hairs sprouted from his pale wrists. "I went round to the Watermark," he said with a quick swallow. "Marcia wasn't at work."

I glanced at the mashed usherette uniform to my left. I felt a sudden surge in my bladder. "No," I said. "I think she said something about a date."

Louis raised a single eyebrow. "A date?"

"Yes," I said.

"Well," he said, "she didn't mention it to me." He ticked his glass with his fingernail.

"Maybe she forgot," I said, fidgeting now with discomfort. I wasn't sure why Marcia would tell Louis if she had a date. I didn't think he had any jurisdiction over what she did.

"Maybe." He took a deep breath and stood up for a second time. I heard him walk back to the kitchen and put his glass in the sink. I took the opportunity to go the bathroom.

The pressure released from my bladder was like air pressed from a balloon. I sat still for a moment, tinkling against the sides of the bowl, before finishing and returning to the hall. Through the window I could see the sun falling behind some fir trees.

"I'd better be going."

I turned to find Louis standing directly behind me. He looked tired, his thinning hair and sharp features honed to a flinty grey by the sunset. "I came to see your sister, but since she's not here, well –" he rattled his keys, "– maybe you can just tell her to call me when she gets in." He was about to step out the door when he reconsidered. "Ronalda," he said, turning to face me. I felt the pressure of his hands on my shoulders, two weights clamping down. I wondered if he had detected the liquor. "Is your fridge usually this empty?"

I didn't know what to say. I didn't want to lie in light of my rumbling stomach, but I certainly didn't want to betray my mother to Louis Moss. What sort of power did he have anyway? Was he capable of taking us away? "No," I said, looking at the ground. "My mother gave me the grocery money because she's been working late. I guess I forgot to go shopping."

He took a step back and looked at me. "I see." There was a long pause. "I'm counting on you to be grown up, Ronalda. Things must seem difficult right now, but I know you and Marcia are responsible girls. You need to pitch in and do your part. That's not just cooking and cleaning. That also means letting me know if you can't cope." He didn't straighten until I had given him a sure nod. "Just call me if you need anything," he said, and then he was gone.

As soon as Louis left, I returned to the bathroom to wash my face. My reflection in the mirror was grim: knit brow, splotches of red creeping over my cheeks. Something was pressing into my lower back and I lifted my T-shirt to find a bunch of pine needles. It was like waking up in a tent with my father, the same foggy sleeplessness – chilled limbs, the feeling of something dead in my mouth – only this time I couldn't shake it off.

I leaned into the stream of water and let the tears fall into the sink. Steam rose, and my sobs mingled with whatever minerals were coming through the pipes.

I stuffed a wet face cloth in my mouth to stop the crying and then pulled it out again. Back in the mirror I looked like the poster child for thyroid disease: wet and miserable, my throat swollen and shuddering from the rain of tears. Briefly I recalled Moose's hand as it made its rough way across my back, my rib cage, and up to my nipple. He had been hard and impersonal. I didn't know whether I cared.

In the kitchen a spider was spinning a web across an open window. I washed the dishes. Then, when I was finished, I turned my attention to the refrigerator. I started with the crisper. There was a hard lump of something in the bottom of a paper bag. A beet? A parsnip? I didn't know. I tossed it into the garbage and found a wood-handled bristle brush. Slime moulds – I knew – were some of the most sophisticated creatures on earth. I wondered if the fuzz in our refrigerator was related.

After an hour or two, I had thrown out everything close to expiring. That left a tin of sardines, two potatoes, a jar of sweet butter pickles with free-floating herbs; also some raspberry jam engraved with the tracks of someone's peanut butter sandwich, and a rubbery but still edible stalk of celery. I put a half-open box of baking soda on the top shelf – because I had seen someone on television do the same thing – and closed the door.

When Marcia came home, I was sitting on the chesterfield eating from the tin of sardines. The flavour was strong: old shoe meets salted rubber. She walked by me into the kitchen. "Mom's not home yet," I hollered after her.

She came back into the living room. "Where is she?"

"How should I know?" It felt strangely pleasant to talk to her this way: snidely, with my nose in the air. I dipped my fingers into the tin and sucked back a tailfin. She stared down at me without moving.

"Well, do you have any idea?"

"Sorry," I said.

She was about to leave when I remembered the message. "Louis came by here looking for you."

"What did he say?" she asked, sitting down in a chair.

"Just that he went by the theatre and you weren't at work. He sounded worried."

"Damn." She considered her usherette uniform. "I forgot all about him."

"Were you out on a date?" Now I wanted to know what she had been doing, but I couldn't get the sarcasm out of my voice.

"Yes," she said, "for your information. Not that I had a good time. The guys here are full of crap. One lousy drink and they're all over you." She stretched out her bow tie. "He wanted to see a movie. Can you believe that? I told him, I can see a movie any time I like – big hint – but he took me to the drive-in all the way over in Saratoga. Some fun: sitting in the car with a case of beer. God," she thwacked her bow tie against the armrest, "it's like summer at Raven's all over again."

"You did that at Raven's?" I asked.

"No," she said. "Not exactly. But those summer guests – their kids – they had the idea that they could feel you all over, just because they'd never see you again. Like that's any fun. I might as well be dating Stephen."

I looked into my sardines and thought about my summers at Raven's: long afternoons spent in swim trunks, the thrill of wildflowers poking through a retreating crust of snow; huckleberries, fresh fish, games of backgammon with people from Texas who said things like "Thanks y'all" and "You bet." Marcia was three years older, but we seemed to be talking about different places.

She must have seen my bewilderment, because she looked at me and said, "You wouldn't remember. You were too busy taking notes."

I didn't say anything.

"Did Louis want anything else?"

"Just for you to call him."

Marcia cursed again.

"Why does he care?"

"Because," she said, "we were supposed to have dinner. He was going to take me out and talk about some things."

"What things?"

Now she was irritated. "I don't know what things. We haven't talked about them yet. I just forgot."

For a moment, I imagined Marcia and Louis chattering over a restaurant tablecloth, canned music in the background, a sickly carnation stuffed in a vase between them. "He didn't ask *me*."

"Yeah, well." She straightened. "That's not my fault."

We were both silent. As if on cue the door creaked open and my mother stepped inside. She was busy muttering to herself when she saw Marcia and me looking in her direction.

"Hello girls," she said. "What are you doing still up?"

"It's only nine o'clock," Marcia said flatly.

"So it is," my mother said, taking a quick look at her wrist, but then realizing she wasn't wearing a watch. Her speech was dull; her pale eyes darted to the window. "I hope you had a nice dinner."

"As a matter of fact, Ronnie here was just finishing off the sardines. How were they, Ronnie?"

"Good," I said.

"And there's a jar of pickles in there for dessert," Marcia added. "Unless Ronnie has polished those off too."

"Now, Marcia," my mother said. "Don't start. I've had a hard day and I just need to get some rest. You know that you are perfectly capable of buying groceries."

Marcia fumed. I could see the flare of her nostrils. "With what money?"

"With the money you make at the theatre."

I heard a snort. "You mean the money I spent on the phone bill? Or the money I was saving so that I could fix the leak under the kitchen sink? You've seen all that mould, Mother. It doesn't grow there for nothing."

My mother stared blankly. A flush had risen to her cheeks. "We all have to pitch in," she said, her lower lip trembling. "We all have to do our bit. I'm sorry if things are hard for you girls, but sometimes it works out that everyone has to take responsibility."

"Responsibility!" Marcia said. "What responsibility do you take, Mother? Tell me, because I'd like to know. And I'd also like to know another thing. Just when, exactly, did they start serving booze at your realty office meetings? Because I can sure as hell smell it from over here."

I thought my mother was going to cry. Her voice came out weepy and slow, as if depressurized by sadness. "I work hard," she said. "I work in that office so you girls can have a decent life. You don't know what it's like, so soon after being a housewife. It's not something that I can just wake up and step into – presto – like a genie. I'm doing my best –" she stopped short, and her voice caught on something. "It's the best I can do –"

"We had a deal," Marcia said, seething now and on the verge of what seemed like implosion. "You promised."

"– the best I can do," my mother continued, crumpling into a heap on the stairs.

I couldn't stand it: my mother was as limp as a

rubber chicken. She sat with her face in her hands. Her collar was inside her coat, turned inward. Marcia took a step toward the door.

"Where are you going?"

"Someplace away from here." She put on her shoes and slammed her way out.

I sat for a moment listening to my mother, to her sobs rising above the entryway. Slowly I stood up and felt sparks of pain in my legs. The sun had gone down and only a meagre light crept into the living room. Outside Marcia was headed for who knows where in nothing but her jeans and a T-shirt; I just wanted to go to bed. I turned from my mother and inched my way across the carpet, pausing for an instant to retrieve my tin of sardines.

*   *   *

I don't know what time Marcia came back, but when I woke up in the morning I found her standing in front of the bathroom mirror.

"Where were you?" I said crankily. "I need to use the bathroom."

"Nowhere important," she said. "Hold your horses."

I watched as she applied her makeup. Cheeks, nose, forehead. She paid careful attention to her lips, whipping up her white lipstick in a little enamel pot and applying the whole mess with a paintbrush. When she was finished her eyes looked permanently astonished. "Aren't you going to be late for school?" she said at last.

"Maybe," I said.

The clock in the kitchen said 8:00 a.m. I had to be ready for classes at eight-thirty. With lightning speed I plugged in the kettle, combed my hair, slipped on a pair of trousers and a stomach-hugging polyester halter top; then I ran around the house looking for my math homework until I remembered my nap on the sofa and the tangle of straps at my feet. After I had located the schoolbag, my geometry set, and a stub-nosed, chewed-up pencil, I turned off the kettle and made myself a cup of tea. My mother and Marcia came into the kitchen at almost the same time.

"Good morning, girls," my mother said cheerily.

Marcia gave her a look, followed by a loud harrumph.

"Is everyone doing well this morning?"

No one responded.

"What is it?" my mother said. "Is something wrong?" There was such sincerity in her voice that I wanted to shake her.

"Girls?" she said, passing around a heartfelt, worried stare.

"Just drop it," Marcia said. She took a bite out of one of the sweet pickles, fishing first around in the jar with a dessert fork and then pinching the round with her thumb. She put on her jacket and headed out the door.

"Ronnie?" my mother said. "What's wrong with

your sister?"

I wondered why now, of all times, my mother had decided to show concern. I was already late, coming in two days after a suspension; I had almost allowed someone to suction off my face. When I got to school there was the distinct possibility that Mr. Turnbull would put me in with the students working off misdemeanours (stolen cars, break and enters) or the girls who conceived children while standing up in bars. There was also a chance that Moose and his gang would poke me full of cigarette holes. I had no idea what awaited me when I got back to school, and I didn't have the time to stick around and offer comfort. "She's fine," I said lamely, throwing my bag over my shoulder. "Talk to her when she gets home."

"Well," said my mother with a little grunt. "I will."

I reached the double doors three minutes before the morning bell. Janice was standing by the garbage can, her bright red slicker glimmering like a candy apple in the rain. Around her clusters of boys and girls huddled, smoking cigarettes and cursing the rain. I stepped up to Janice and tried to catch my breath.

"Well?" she said. "What happened? Where have you been? I've been waiting for a half an hour."

"Sorry," I said. "I woke up late."

She shook the moisture off her coat. "It doesn't matter. Tell me what happened."

"When?" I said.

"Yesterday," she hissed. Her whispers were loud

enough to hear from across the schoolyard. "With Moose."

"Oh," I said. "That." I knew what she had been referring to. I just didn't feel like talking about it. "We kissed, that's all."

"What was it like?"

"He drooled a lot."

Janice withdrew with a look of distaste. "You didn't tell him that, did you?"

I shook my head. "Of course not."

By now people were milling about us, stubbing out cigarettes, shouting brief and final curses into the mist. A boy pushed by with an armful of textbooks. Janice stomped the rain off her tennis shoes. "Well," she said, after giving me a relieved stare followed by something that looked like awe. "I have to go, but I'll meet you outside at recess."

I watched her back up into a stream of bodies – fogged glasses, a blur of nylon and leather, the odd team jacket with the name *Whalers* embroidered in fancy letters – and gave the skyline a final glance. Clouds had absorbed the mountains. A watery haze clung to the landscape, blotting out buildings, forest, and sea. How quickly I had forgotten the elements, their power to disorient, remove landmarks with a shift of the wind.

# Chapter 8

My morning class was long and wearisome. The hours passed in a numbing blur of blackboard diagrams. Every time Mr. Turnbull said the word "reproduction" a snicker erupted from the back of the class. Eventually he turned around – chalk poised, moustache quivering – and said in a gruff voice: "Surely, boys, you can get through this lesson without too much excitement?"

When the bell rang, I put away my diagram of an onion root tip and stood to leave. Mr. Turnbull stopped me.

"Ronalda," he said, "would you mind staying back for a moment?"

I sat back down at my desk and watched as the rest of my classmates filed out the door on their way to pick fights, vandalize toilets, and blacken their lungs with hand-rolled cigarettes. Who knew whether my tryst with

Moose had elevated me among their ranks? At this rate I was never going to find out. I didn't even know if I cared.

When everyone was gone, Mr. Turnbull closed the door. He turned and put his enormous foot on the seat in front of me. I looked up into his chest. The outline of a white undershirt pressed against his sleeves, making small half-moons above the perspiration gathering in his armpits. "The reason I asked you to stay," he said, "is that I need a little favour."

This was not what I had expected.

"You may have noticed that there's a lot of work to cover this term. Some of the teachers have students that help them along. Someone to take care of the details and keep things on track."

I nodded. I had seen these student helpers standing in line at the mimeograph machine. Most of them were older teenagers who spoke in complicated sentences about grade point averages.

"Now," Mr. Turnbull went on. "I've noticed that you are a good student. Except for that unfortunate mistake with the campfire," he paused again and fondled his moustache. "Your record is spotless. Your grades are high and you work hard."

I shifted in my desk. This wasn't exactly true. Since the third or fourth week of school, I had grown progressively apathetic. I had completed my homework, but with none of the initial relish that I used to have when I saw a blank white page before I found out that all I had to do was memorize the facts for twenty-four hours. Once the tests were over, we moved on to something else.

"To make a long story short," Mr. Turnbull continued, "I'm looking for a helper. I wanted to ask if you would take on the job."

I studied my fingers and weighed my options. What he was offering me was the chance for salvation: no more recesses, the briefest of lunches spent dribbling crumbs over stacks of pop quizzes and scientific reports.

"Will I work by myself?" I said.

"That can certainly be arranged."

I found out soon enough what my new position meant to my friendship with Janice. After our chat in the classroom, Mr. Turnbull led me to the supply closet where he proceeded to load me down with glass beakers and lengths of rubber tubing. He asked me to wash out the instruments and dry them again, and then bring the whole lot to the classroom. "We have some interesting experiments ahead of us," he said pleasantly, leaving me to struggle with the taps in the janitor's closet. "I just haven't had the time to get things in order."

By the time I returned to the classroom, I knew Janice would be wondering what had happened. I poked my head out the window. She was waiting by the garbage can, nervously fidgeting with her slicker.

"What are you doing in there?" she said impatiently when she approached. "Did you get in trouble?"

"Mr. Turnbull asked me to help him."

She drew back and frowned. The intensity of her raincoat seemed to deepen the stain on her forehead: it looked like a splash of raspberry jam. "For how long?" she said.

"Probably for the rest of the summer."

She didn't talk for a moment. "Does that mean you won't be coming out for break anymore?"

"I guess not," I said.

There was a long pause, after which I said, "I guess I should be going."

"Sure," said Janice. "I guess." She turned and walked away. I felt guilt, followed by an immediate stab of rage. The rain had stopped, but Janice had found a way of looking sodden. Her hair was damp, separated into thick clumps that whipped her in the face as she walked. I didn't know if I owed her anything: we weren't friends exactly, but rather, two people thrown together by circumstance. If there had been someone better to hang around with, I was pretty sure that she would have given me the slip. My only real *friends* were children from the lodge whose parents visited two or more consecutive summers: Susan of the painted toenails; Marjorie of the seersucker bathing suit; Alison and Deacon, fraternal twins with matching inflatable seahorses who took to biting each other to make a point. Last but not least, there was Everett – digging for frogs, excavating stones – frying under the summer sun until his skin peeled and his nose was covered in boils. I had spent an entire childhood learning to let go – the mainstay of my friendships was not constancy – and now I had no idea what was expected. I didn't think I owed Janice; so why did I feel so mean?

I turned to my beakers and looked at myself in their stretched-out, glossy surface: buggy eyes, hideous grin warped around the bottom. I stood with my hip against the desk until I could no longer call to mind my father – his white skin, the way his features came together in unexpected agreement – and could picture instead only Janice's disappointment hovering like an anvil over my head. The classroom was silent, and except for the noise of distant footsteps, I could only hear my breathing, a flat *in*, *out* bordering on a wheeze. Everything was quiet, rigid, and antiseptic, undisturbed except for a lone player, me.

*   *   *

More than a month went by before Marcia and I went back to school for regular classes. In that time, the landscape made startling shifts toward autumn: fog, midnight rain, gusts of wind and blackouts caused by branches on the lines. Maple and alder trees dropped their leaves, clogging the sewer grates and exposing trunks thick with moss. Almost immediately, humidity infiltrated our house, clotting the table salt, softening the lone box of Girl Guide cookies that Marcia had purchased from a pigtailed scout peddling in front of the Watermark. Every few hours the foghorns sounded, echoing across the harbour like the honk of a lone goose. A week before Labour Day, I celebrated my fourteenth birthday. My mother brought a cake home from the grocery store, and we sat in companionable silence eating Chinese take-out for supper. For a brief moment, we were like a normal family, sparring over the last packet of plum sauce. Save my father's absence, I almost felt whole.

"You will be lucky in love and money," my mother said, after we had each taken a turn reciting the contents of our fortune cookies. She gave a whoop of delight, and then sobered a little. "I'll take the money," she added. "The love I can do without."

⋇ ⋇ ⋇

At school the hallways swelled with returning students. Groups that had formed over the summer reconfigured. Somewhere along the line, the scope had widened, grown to include other people who looked more or less like I did – smallish, bereaved – and I wondered if Janice hadn't been wrong about our place in the world. Before classes I caught a glimpse of her clinging to a group standing just outside of school property. I recognized most of them from summer school, including Moose who lurked in his denim jacket like the alpha male of a wolf pack.

The first day back began with a general assembly. Teachers herded everyone into the gymnasium, pushing us into wooden chairs that screeched on floor tiles and creaked beneath the collective weight of the entire student body. I had heard rumours that the year always started this way: students and teachers crowded together into a single room, the smell of floor wax and deep-fry grease wafting in from the nearby cafeteria. The principal – whose name was Jim Brower – liked to gather everyone together in the style of a pep rally. I knew from Mr. Turnbull that Brower had come to the school two years ago and had almost immediately begun to change things. Due to his absence over the summer, I had met only his stand-in. I had, however, heard stories. Jim Brower was a madman, a genius, a wacko from the USA; he was someone who once walked across the Sahara desert in nothing but a kerchief; he had served in the Peace Corps; he had supplied the Canadian government with the recipe for Agent Orange; he was a staunch advocate of music therapy (he had composed symphonies at the age of eleven) and had once ran for the leadership of the provincial New Democratic Party on a platform of free love; he had also sired children in the backseat of his Oldsmobile. Whatever the truth about our high school principal, it must have been good: everyone cared enough to show up for the general assembly.

When he came out onto the stage, Brower seemed like a normal man who had just come back from vacation: skin tanned, eyes flashing with rest and innovation. His thick hair was peppered with white, and he wore a wide belt with a buckle that flashed in the stage lights. Then he began to speak.

"Friends," he said explosively, holding his arms in the air. "I would like to take this opportunity to welcome you to Shelter Bay High. I can see by your many faces, even more than last year, that we have a large and important job ahead of us." He paused and surveyed the room. There was a muffled snort from the front row.

"I consider our task one of the most important tasks on the planet." He paused again. "The task of learning, of helping a future generation such as yourself to move through this stop-over we call high school. As you well know, the world is a changing place. Things are happening that, every day, move us closer to the possibility of improvement, of efficiency and stellar learning. For those of you who were here last year and in previous years, you will already know that changes are afoot, changes that will take us in the direction of these improvements. Some of you may question these changes. Allow me to explain." He walked forward on the stage and opened his hands, a gesture that reminded me of the travelling evangelist who stopped for a holiday at Raven's Lodge.

"You are not factory workers, cranking out cars on an assembly line. You are individual people with individual needs. But so far in your life, you may not have been treated as such. So far in life, you may have had experiences that made you decide that school wasn't worth your time. Well, as part of your educational system, I have let you down. We have all let you down!"

There was a chastening silence. I saw Mr. Turnbull scratch the balding patch on the back of his head. Beside him Morris Roper coughed.

"The tragic irony," Brower continued, "is that we know how to make learning better and easier, yet so many times we do not; so many times we continue to teach as our grandparents were taught." He raised his hand in the air. A low hiss that had been building at the back of the room stopped short.

"No more. No more, boys and girls, men and women, future astronauts and world leaders, doctors, lawyers, nurses, teachers, funeral home directors, veterinarians, mothers and fathers. I say all that because that is what you are. In this room, there is undoubtedly all those things. In this room is our future."

I looked around the room and caught a glimpse of Marcia sitting cross-legged on the floor in front of the water fountain. A cluster of girls surrounded her, each one with long hair and a rapt face. Briefly I imagined them, ten years down the road, packed into nurses' uniforms or space suits, their adult faces alert and confident with the prospect of success. For a moment I allowed something to well up inside of me – excitement, perhaps, or hope – the way I felt watching my father talk about plants. But then I heard the next part.

"Parents," Brower said, "have a unique role here at

Shelter Bay High. Together you and your parents will design a 'Plan of Innovation.' Together you will use this plan to achieve your goals." He went on to explain the rules as they existed at Shelter Bay High, rules that would enable each and every one of us to fulfill our dreams. No skipping, no loafing, no smoking, no irresponsible behaviour. And for teachers, no yelling and no punitive disciplinary measures. School would be open until eleven o'clock at night and all students in the upper grades could work at an accelerated pace if they so desired. On top of all this, students maintaining an A average did not have to attend classes.

"Show us what you are worth and you will always be rewarded," Brower said. "No one fails at Shelter Bay. If you don't participate, you will simply be marked 'incomplete.'" A murmur went through the crowd. Brower raised another hand in a gesture of silence.

"Together we will create a vision of education that will help you to go on with your life. Together, we will create a vision that will help you to change the world. So I ask you: are you ready for the changes that are coming? To explore the wonders of the galaxy, the mysteries of history, the challenges of math, English, and other languages? Are you capable of stretching your mind, observing the world and other people in it? Of exercising tolerance, equal rights, and taking responsibility for your own life? Because if you are, Shelter Bay High is the place for you."

There was a momentary silence and then a cheer went up from the audience. A number of teachers sat blinking in the lights, clapping or shouting to one another over the din. I saw Marcia stand up and stretch her arms, then shoot her friends a look. I wondered what she thought about the part of the speech that required our mother to participate in a way that almost surely meant coming to school. I was about to ask her when a girl turned to me and murmured something about Mr. Brower being a dream. When I turned back, the crush of bodies pressing toward classes had swept my sister away.

My first class was the same as summer school in every respect, except that Mr. Turnbull asked us to call him "Barry."

"I'm obliged to tell you," he said with a weary glance around the room, "that those of you with A averages are not required to stay for this class. Instead you may –"

There was a screech of desks, a clatter of book bags and pencils being filed hurriedly into pencil cases. Mr. Turnbull stopped talking. A brief and guilty silence followed.

"I see many of you know the rules," he continued, moving up to the front of his desk and waving a piece of paper. "So if your name is one of the following, go on ahead to the library. You can collect your study topics at the door."

He proceeded to read through the list and the clatter resumed. When he had finished, he noticed me still in my seat. "Ronalda," he said. "Aren't you going to join them?"

I shook my head, silent now that all eyes were trained on where I sat. I still considered myself his helper, and though I no longer had any formal duties, slipping away seemed something close to betrayal.

"Very well." A smile flickered beneath his moustache. "Let's get started."

Two hours later, my head overrun with the life history of the foetal pig, I sat in my second class while a blushing woman in a pink midi stammered out the very same announcement.

"Will all of the following students –" she read. This time I saw no reason to stay. I gathered my things and quietly made for the library. As I went, I saw Janice in the far corner, her birthmark gleaming under the fluorescent lights. She rested her chin on a bent wrist and looked up at me with something like loathing. There were only four or five other students heading for the door, but each of us was the subject of momentary jealousy.

The library during second period bustled with activity. Discussion groups, stacks of reference books piled into leaning towers; tables littered with slide rules and balled-up Kleenexes. Students hunched in study carousels, their necks craned, their backs bent and frozen. Laughter and groaning burst forth from whispered conversations, girls in corduroy skirts, boys with hair combed haphazardly over protruding ears. Somehow Brower's system had whittled down the students of

Shelter Bay and given them free reign to lounge and discuss. I claimed a seat in a study carousel and opened my biology notes. After reading twelve long pages, I wondered if I might be in over my head. Skipping grade ten had put me at a disadvantage. I decided to start with something less intimidating.

"Can I help you get started?" a librarian said when I approached the desk

"All right," I said. I listened half-heartedly as she described the system, her fingers counting off – Dewey decimal, card catalogue, microfiche, periodical, abstract, *and don't forget the World Encyclopaedia* – and then I followed her to the stacks where she left me in front of the reference books. The first study topic on my history list was "The Protestant Reformation." I settled down with a book on Martin Luther and began to read. From the corner by the magazine rack I overhead two girls in conversation. The whispers of nearby groups reduced their dialogue to fragments.

"– the new girl in Form One, with the long blonde hair. She's supposed to be from up north someplace."

"I know the one. She works at the Watermark."

"– really nice but,"

"– supposedly seeing older men."

"How old?"

"Old. Old enough to be her father."

"How gross."

There was a burst of giggles and the librarian

passed, her finger to her red lips. "Girls," she said with an air of infinite patience, "you know the rules. Unless you're doing homework, you go back to class."

The girls returned to their texts, glancing up only to wink at one another and giggle softly.

☆　☆　☆

Several days later I packed my text books into my locker and headed across the greens to the turnabout. I made my way across the lawn – sticky now with the rising autumn muck – and watched the ground for land mines left behind by the janitor's miniature terrier. When I was halfway across the greens, a voice called out from behind me.

"Hey, if it isn't Cavewoman. Run out of things to do for the teacher?"

I swivelled around to see Janice, cloaked in her father's rain jacket, staring out at me from a group of teenaged girls. Another girl was doing the talking, someone with long hair and a cigarette pursed between her lips. As far as I could tell, we were off school property so her smoking wasn't really an issue; all the same, she made a point of drawing the air in hard and eyeing me up and down. "No one waiting behind the warehouse today?"

I was about to answer when I heard Janice pipe in. She looked larger somehow; fierce. She spoke in a low voice. "So stuck up she can't even talk to us. That's a laugh, when everyone knows she's easy."

"Behind the warehouse with every guy who wants her." The other girl clapped Janice on the back and gathered her into the circle. A shriek went up. I looked at a wall of sneering mouths. Janice's face was twisted; her forehead bulged with hard-won satisfaction.

"That's right," hollered the other girl. "You just keep on walking. Our boys have better taste than girls with hand-me-down underwear."

Their laughter echoed across the greens. I walked quickly, hands clutching my school bag, remembering this sort of cruelty from guests at the lodge: children with glass eyes or missing fingers, whose parents introduced them with an embarrassed grumble; children teased and chased, run into the woods by other children because they were not smart or quick enough to form alliances.

I continued home, shouldering the weight of my library books. The streets were wet and the town had a ghostly emptiness. High in the trees, lone leaves rattled on drying stems. I trudged up the steps, stopping to glance at the windows of my house, blackened and smudged from the inside. I knew what I would find if I went in: musty, vacant hallways; sour milk and hollow light. The blue glow of the television drowning out my father's voice as it rang, quizzical and disappointed, in my ears. *Ronnie? Are you doing your best? Is that the best you can do?*

If I hurried, I still had enough time to catch the

matinee at the Watermark. I turned around and sprinted down the street.

I hadn't visited the Watermark in over three weeks. The comfortable darkness and the smells of the concession seemed like a far-off memory, but I knocked on the back door, suddenly desperate to be let in. There was a pause before the door opened and a sneakered foot stepped out.

"Can I help you?" It was Stephen.

"Is my sister here?"

"She's busy at the moment," he said, considering. His eyes squinted slightly behind his glasses. "Maybe I can help?"

"No," I said. And then, because I had heard Marcia speak in the same way, "Aren't you supposed to be working at the ticket booth?"

Stephen shifted and cleared his throat. There was the rattle of something – flu or asthma – before he coughed his way out again. "Aren't you supposed to be paying like everyone else?"

I fingered the holes in my pockets, filled now with elastic bands, gathered pebbles and one or two flattened pennies that I had discovered along the train tracks. As usual, I didn't have any money.

"Or," he continued, "you could do me a favour instead."

I looked around. I was about to come up with an excuse when Marcia stepped outside.

"What are you doing out here?" she said to me. She stood with one hand clamped on the doorknob, the other perched on her hip.

"Unfortunately, nothing," Stephen said.

"I thought I told you to let me know when you were coming," Marcia hissed.

I stared at the ground. "I was bored."

"Get inside." She grabbed me by the wrist and tugged me through the door. The lobby was vacant except for a lone man scurrying to the bathroom. The smell of popcorn filled my nostrils.

"You owe me, Marcia," Stephen grunted, smoothing his hair and making his way slowly toward the ticket booth.

"You're dreaming," my sister said.

Apart from the usual furniture and one or two discarded drinking cups, the crying room was nearly empty. Only one other person sat inside. When I entered, he continued looking straight ahead.

The movie was something childish – *Born Free* or *Elsa Returns* – but despite that, I felt tears running down my face. Once in a while the guy ahead of me shifted in his seat. When the credits rolled, I stood and stretched my legs. I looked up and jumped.

"Some movie," he said. His light hair rose from his head as if badly in need of a washing, and he had started to sprout a beard. Still, there was no mistaking him: here was the guy I had led out of the woods.

Suddenly I was flushed by the idea that I had helped him at all; that, for the past few months I had thought about him, recalling the softness of his hands. I turned my face to the wall, but not before he recognized me. I fled into the lobby and out the back door.

Once outside, I trudged out along the estuary. Slowly the sounds of the river replaced the din in my head. The air smelled of wetted earth and skunk cabbage. Roosting crows above my head nestled down in bare branches. Suddenly I heard twigs cracking behind me, and I swivelled to find Stephen, panting into the clearing.

"It's about time you took a rest," he said, clutching the opening on his coat.

His face was red, wet with perspiration and the smudge of dirty fingerprints, and his chest heaved. "Is this where you spend your time? Really, Ronalda, I would have thought you could do better than this – muck, and rotting salmon." He winced with distaste, and then paused to wipe his glasses on the front of his T-shirt. While he was preoccupied I reached into the shallows for a stone.

"Now," he said when he was finished. "About that favour."

"I don't owe you any favours."

"No?" He snickered. "I don't see why not. I have, after all, been letting you get away with free entry to the movies. I could tell the manager, you know. He wouldn't like the fact that you've been scamming. He might even fire your sister."

I stood silently, the rock concealed behind my back. "That room is never full. I'm not taking up any space."

"That's for him to decide," he said calmly. "Of course, there are other reasons too. You've been granting favours to every other boy in school. I think it's only fair that I get my turn."

I blinked.

"The warehouse? Or didn't you know that nice girls don't do that sort of thing? People might get the wrong idea. Well," he frowned, "maybe it's like I thought. Maybe you're not a nice girl. Maybe you're like your sister, someone who likes them older?" He took a step forward.

"That's not true," I shouted. "About Marcia. None of that is."

"But I've seen them myself," said Stephen, "driving around in a blue Lincoln, eating in restaurants. He takes her to dinner, you know, and to the docks. Your sister, a regular escort service."

Anger surged to my temples. I saw Louis in my mind's eye – his freckled skin pallid and wet in the dim light of our living room, leaning forward to offer me a glass of lemonade. That he should be there instead of my father made me blind with fury. I flung the rock and watched it bounce off the centre of Stephen's forehead.

"Aagh!" Stephen gasped, clutching his head and lunging forward. A stream of blood trickled down his face. There was a momentary skirmish, and then the feeling of fingers pinching down on my forearm. I don't know how long we struggled before a voice called out behind us.

"Is everything all right here?"

I felt Stephen's fingers loosen and then let go. He swore under his breath, dabbing at his head. We both turned around. "Just fine, thanks," Stephen screeched.

"I don't think it is." The guy who spoke was the same one from the movie theatre, the same one I had led from the clearing, a month before. "I think you'd better get out of here," he said to Stephen.

Stephen looked at me and swore. He pushed his glasses back up to the bridge of his nose. Blood had trickled into his eye; he wheezed into the handkerchief and dabbed again at his forehead. I watched as he lumbered out of the clearing, throwing back a final, hateful glance, before I took a breath and allowed myself to cry.

"Who was that guy?" he said when I had gathered myself and we had been walking by the river for several nondescript minutes. So far we had only gotten as far as introducing ourselves – *"Lee." "Ronnie." "Right, I remember." OK now what.* "He sure has problems."

"He works with my sister at the Watermark," I said. "He's a creep." The path was too narrow for us to walk abreast; this gave me the disadvantage of having to go ahead and aim my words over my shoulder.

"I kind of figured that. Nutcase," he said as he

made a circle with his finger next to his earlobe. "Did you do that to his head? He was bleeding."

"Yes," I admitted.

"Cool. A woman with a temper. Tempers can come in handy. I've been working on mine. Maybe you can give me some lessons?"

I didn't know what to say. Was he serious? We rounded the oxbow and walked out over the estuary.

"Well," he said after we had come to a junction in the path. "At least have coffee with me? Sometime?"

My face burned with excitement. "Sure."

He put his hands in his pockets and wiggled his boot in the muck. "You can find me at the marina. I hang out there most of the time. When I go out it's usually for groceries or the movies or something like that. Come whenever. I should be home."

*Whenever* sounded at bit vague, but I didn't want to let on that I had no idea how these things worked. Dates, dating: is that what we were doing? "Should I call first?"

"You can try," he laughed. "Except I don't have a phone."

This confused me, but I thought for a moment about my life at Raven's, our lack of connection to the outside world.

"Just come by," he said. "I'll be hanging out there all weekend. My boat is called *The Minstrel*."

# Chapter 9

I took up Lee's offer the following Saturday. The Shelter
Bay marina hunkered down behind a jetty at the north
end of the estuary. Schooners and fish boats cluttered the
docks, rising and falling with a groan of wood against
wood as the tide swept in and out, washing slicks of oil
and rust against lurking hulls. In the shallows, white and
orange anemones filtered a stream of bilge water, waving
through the murk like sets of feather pens.

The Minstrel sat moored between two aluminium-
hulled fishing boats. My first impression was a good one
– the boat was long and graceful, fit with brass and
sullied only by salt spray – but then I noticed the patched-
up deck, the dregs of paint peeling back to reveal aging
timber. I knew as much about boats as I did about dating,
but I understood the need for upkeep. Parts of the rails

appeared to be rotting. I guessed that Lee was on a budget, the same way my parents had been with Raven's.

I stepped onto the deck and felt the boat sway. Before I found my way to the door, a hatch opened and a face looked out.

"Who are you?" a man said. He was older than Lee. His brown skin was weathered.

"I'm looking for Lee," I said.

He peered at me through the hatch opening. "Lee who?"

I remembered that I didn't know Lee's last name. "I'm not sure," I said. "I met him down by the estuary. He told me he lived on this boat."

The man squinted. "Don't think I know any Lee."

At that moment, laughter erupted from the quarters below: a man's and a woman's. The first one sounded a lot like Lee.

"He told me to come by for coffee," I said rather lamely. "Are you sure that he isn't here?"

The man considered me for a moment, before grunting and turning into the blackness. I waited for several minutes before he came back.

"Well," he said. "Come on if you're coming."

I followed him down into a tunnel that led from the hatch to a living area. The space was small, lit by candles jammed into wine bottles and a single kerosene lantern. Through a haze of smoke and incense I could make out a kitchen nook fitted with a gas-powered stove; two small seats upholstered in Indian print scarves; a plastic toilet fixed into the corner, visible on all sides to anyone who cared to look; and a low V-berth, sloping down at the end of the tunnel. Every available space seemed to be taken up.

"Ronnie," Lee said from the end of the boat. There was an uncomfortable silence.

"I can come back later," I said.

The man who answered the door leaned against the counter, his arms crossed at the chest. He looked at Lee with a raised eyebrow.

"Hang on," Lee said. "I want you to meet Alex and Bo. These two are my comrades, my guardians. They help keep me in line."

Alex – the man – nodded curtly, and grunted a second time. Bo gave a quick smile. "Hello, Ronnie," she said.

"I was just telling them where we met, that you helped get me out of a nowhere situation."

I flushed, remembering the log crossing, and then the way Lee had helped me get rid of Stephen.

"I told them all about the way you can navigate the river with your eyes closed. I'm not sure they believed me."

"Not with my eyes closed," I said.

"But pretty well," Lee said. "She didn't use a map. She lives sort of back in the garden, like that Joni Mitchell song."

Bo looked into her drinking glass. Alex stared at the

flames in the gas stove, his shoulders hunched. Suddenly I felt the urge to defend myself.

"I grew up on the river," I found myself saying. "Farther upstream, but my father used to take me to see the salmon. He liked to make sure we spent most of our time outside. He was a bit of a survivalist. He did a lot of work for the National Park."

I went on to tell them – in as complete a story as I could muster – about my family life at Raven's, about our move to Shelter Bay after the death of my father. The details seeped out fake and disconnected, as if I was telling a story about somebody else's life. "It wasn't that bad," I said, apologizing. "We came to town once in a while."

Alex and Bo looked at me with renewed interest. I heard the clearing of throats, the shifting of bodies in chairs. I wanted desperately to sit – my legs felt weak with exhaustion – but all the seats were taken. Eventually Alex rubbed his beard and sighed deeply. Bo leaned forward and said, "Lee, why don't you let Ronnie sit down?"

That first evening on *The Minstrel* reminded me of home: dim light, pots on the stove bubbling with stew and water for tea. Lee handed me a glass of sharp liquid, and only a few moments had passed before I felt that familiar melting sensation. I looked at him through a stream of incense, perched now across the table. He was older than I was by three or four years. His thick yellow hair hung low in his eyes, and he brushed it away with a gentle sweep. When he spoke, his voice held the traces of an almost imperceptible twang.

The drinks went around again and I started to feel grateful – for these strangers who had taken me in, for Lee. I sat in silence with the ocean beneath my feet, until the conversation turned.

"Alex and Bo live on a farm," Lee said to me. "They raise chickens and trade lumber to local builders. They're bona fide societal dropouts, the scourge of the establishment. Everywhere they go they're walking picket signs demanding instant confrontation."

"Hard honest work," Alex said, blushing a little.

"Work?" Lee said. "Work is something you do for money. It's a dirty, four-letter word. I never work. Not that way. Life should be free."

A life without work was directly opposite to everything my father had taught us, and at first, Lee's words made me cringe. But eventually I realized what he was getting at: living free meant standing up for your ideals. "That's like doing what you believe in, right?" I said. "My father always did that."

Alex smiled and explained how he used to live in Seattle, work in an office overseeing factory workers who were all as bored as he was. "Then I had my epiphany," he added, rubbing his hands into his beard and taking a swig. "Sold off everything and came up here to fourteen acres of paradise. Sort of like your family, Ronnie, only a little less wild."

Bo agreed. "No more nine to five. Now it's five to

nine." She winked at Alex. "Get up with the sun and watch it go to bed."

I nodded. They seemed impossibly happy, pink and weathered like the Amish farmers I had seen in my father's *A History of Agriculture*, their cuffs unravelling, their hands criss-crossed with cracks. "How did you all meet?" I asked.

Alex cleared his throat and looked into his mug before speaking. "That's a long story," he said. "One best saved for another time."

I waited, but when no one spoke, I took another sip from my glass.

Bo leaned forward and patted me on the arm. "Just think of us as the welcome wagon," she said. "It's really not that interesting."

The conversation turned again, this time to politics. Apparently the Americans wanted to test nuclear bombs off the Alaskan peninsula. Both Lee and Alex had strong opinions on the subject.

"We should be a part of the protest," Lee said. "Not sitting pretty in a small town. I've got the boat and I certainly have the time." He stared sullenly into a candle. "I can't believe I'm not doing anything."

"We've been over this before," Alex said, swallowing hard. "You know all the reasons."

"Sure," Lee said. "While the U.S. exposes us all to earthquakes and radioactive waste. While everyone thinks they live in a wonderful free-speaking country just because they have cars and television sets, their kids are getting brainwashed in school." He jabbed his finger into the wax. "Those seem to cancel out my reasons."

Alex sighed.

"All the revolutions in the world happened when Marx or Fidel or Mao or whoever showed the people how repressed they were. You have to let them see, brother to brother. Here they haven't woken up."

Bo jumped in. "There's a group going from Vancouver. They've chartered a boat and they've got the media on board. They plan to head out soon enough. The government can't set off a bomb with people in the test site."

"What if they don't make it?" Lee said. "*The Minstrel* could get there faster."

"And get you a whole lot of attention," Alex added, with some finality. There was another silence, during which Alex and Bo exchanged meaningful looks. I watched Lee, wondering how old he really was. He seemed very worldly compared to the boys of Shelter Bay. I was pretty sure none of them cared about politics. Until I met Lee, I hadn't cared much about them either.

"I might as well be growing chickens," Lee muttered.

Alex raised another eyebrow. "I think it's time for us to leave." He picked up his woollen jacket and helped Bo to her feet. "Ronnie," he said, "can we give you a lift?"

I nodded politely, thanking Lee for the visit. Behind us I heard him mumble: "Screw this. It will be different when our generation takes over."

The drive home was bumpy and short. Alex's truck rattled along the estuary road, protesting the curves in much the same way as my father's Ford. When Alex and Bo let me out in front of my house, I stepped dreamily to the pavement and thanked them for the ride. They had only just pulled away when Louis's Lincoln glided up to the sidewalk.

I crept behind a tree and watched as Marcia slid out and walked to the front door. Louis waited inside the Lincoln, his body a dark cut-out in the car's interior. He stayed there idling the engine until she stepped inside.

The whole episode took less than thirty seconds, but my brain insisted on replaying the sequence in slow motion: the Lincoln, Marcia stepping from inside and feeling for the sidewalk, Louis lurking in darkness like some vampire in the night. I left my hiding space behind the tree and followed the path of his taillights to the centre of the road. Cones from nearby evergreens crunched underfoot; I cursed their inconvenience and kicked them into the gutter. Down the street I could see only trees, houses dissolving against a watery night. A swing set in a neighbouring yard creaked back and forth with all the ghostliness of an abandoned schoolyard. The road was empty, and save the cry of a distant cat, I was alone.

My head felt suddenly heavy, and for the first time I felt direct and terrible malice for another human being. "Go away," I said through clenched teeth. "Leave us alone." Somewhere farther down the highway, Louis sat smugly in his Lincoln, humming along to the sounds of late night radio and nestling in to the leather upholstery. His air of benevolence had dwindled away, and in its absence I could see only deception, a force so disruptive it was tearing my family apart.

# Chapter 10

From the moment I first stepped on board *The Minstrel*, I began to hate going home. I did not want to go back to the orange walls and dusty carpets, to the state of obvious neglect that was now beyond embarrassment or covering up. My mother's headaches had become horrific. With shaking hands and a vaguely described ringing in the ears, she stumbled off to work in a haze of Seconal and other pills, her hair moulded into a sort of fisherman's cap by a friend from school who owned a beauty parlour on the waterfront. Heels wobbling and tissue in hand, she made her way to the real estate office on legs jammed into twisted hose, wincing all the while against bracing winds, street noise, and shafts of light that streaked down through the trees.

I tried not to think of Marcia, who avoided me much

of the time. I especially tried not to think of Louis, who didn't seem interested in what I did, not that I would have told him if he'd asked. Since designating Marcia as our official family contact, he hadn't come around as frequently to talk to my mother. Even so, I cultivated a secret hatred for everything about him – details which came at me when I least expected them. My greatest fear was that a neighbour or a teacher might decide to show concern, so I learned to keep a handful of excuses ready in case anyone should accost me in front of the school or neighbourhood park and say in a pinched voice, "Ronalda, is everything all right at home?" To my relief and astonishment, no one ever did.

There is nothing lonelier than being an outsider, but in the places I was used to – the woods around Raven's or the trails that led up to the alpine or down to the lake's edge – I never felt alone. There were always birds calling, the whisper of wind as it passed through the branches of evergreens. My father had liked to stress the importance of sounds in nature, the rustlings and peeps so often missed by hikers. *Listen*, he would say. *You are not alone.* There would be a moment of silence, filled by the burble of a creek or a raven cawing. *He's right*, I would always think. *I am not alone.*

Among kids my age, loneliness descended. As the days grew short and the cold weather arrived, I found myself back at *The Minstrel*, drawn to its hollow interior full of cast iron pots and wax drippings. Usually I would find Alex or Bo in a state of transit, hands wrapped around a basket of eggs (still warm, with bits of mud and feathers glued to their surfaces) or a cluster of herbs yanked from the garden. By turns the cabin smelled of rosemary and sage, of meadow rue and fall harvest vegetables simmering in a pan meant to keep Lee in vitamins. At these times I tried to ignore the rumble in my stomach, to concentrate loosely on the conversation with the hope that they might ask me for dinner. Alex reminded me of my father. Every seam on his shirts and trousers showed the mark of obvious repair. Bo was less imposing, small save a pair of sturdy hands that were usually slipped into work gloves several sizes too large for her body. She always wore dresses, bleached to a dull print by too much time on the clothesline, and wrapped herself in layers and layers of old jackets. Her flyaway hair was usually woven into a complicated twist, skewered on the end of a pencil or a whittled twig. "They can't make me do what they want," Lee said more than once, in the months that I was getting to know him. "But usually I do it anyway to make life easier."

The relationship between Lee and his guardians did make me curious, but when I asked him about the subject, he didn't have much to say.

"Friends of my dad," he said. "He asked them to keep an eye on me while I'm up here ... to keep me out of trouble. He probably wants to make sure I won't wreck his boat."

"Your dad owns *The Minstrel*?" I asked.

"My dad gave me *The Minstrel*," Lee corrected. "But he wants to make sure I don't do anything radical, like sail into a hurricane."

At face value Lee was someone who had taken time off school to drift about in the academy of life. His attitude about society was the topic of frequent rants, and he was anxious to get involved politically. From discussions I overheard between Lee and Alex, and from our walks along the riverbank – which happened now almost every other night – I gathered he had once been involved in a number of protests: war, big oil, civil rights, or the advancement of what he called "the revolution." He read copies of newspapers called *The Morning Star* and *The Fire Next Time*, which he carefully burned afterward in the galley stove.

"No offence, Ronnie," he said one evening, as we walked along the trails to the estuary. "But you really shouldn't be in school. There's no way of being in that scene without being co-opted."

"What do you mean?" I said.

"School turns you into a robot. They don't even let you grow your hair long if you're a guy. Don't they know that man is descended from apes? Jerry Rubin says we're supposed to grow our hair and smell like men."

I stared at the ground. I didn't know who Jerry Rubin was, or why he would encourage people to smell bad. I did know that I liked Lee, and that hearing him talk was the closest I'd come to feeling included. He was the only person who cared whether I came around or not, and I wanted to learn everything he knew. I listened as he carried on.

"In Vietnam, the U.S. uproots peasants from their homes and puts them into compounds surrounded by dogs and barbed wire to keep out the Viet Kong. The school board does the same to high school students. Have you ever wondered why chain-link fences surround your fields? You're prisoners of the system. They're trying to keep you in by telling you it's for your own good, when really what they're doing is keeping you down."

I nodded, though strictly speaking, I didn't really understand what he was talking about. Since our first meeting, I had started watching the news, but these stories only took me so far. In Lee's eyes the planet was marching toward some horrible destination, much different from the one my principal Jim Brower promoted. I just wanted Lee to like me.

"We have to make people aware of how unhappy they are," Lee went on. "We have to show them that we can't be bought, because nothing they can give is worth the freedom of a people. The revolution is happening Ronnie, but everyone here is still asleep."

In comparison to other towns, Shelter Bay did seem sleepy. There were a few women clogging down the sidewalk in dirndl skirts, one or two men with broad moustaches and wig-like hair who wiggled like fleas in their tie-dyed T-shirts, but nothing approaching the state of revolt Lee sought.

"What about Bo and Alex?" I said. "They live a life different life than most people. They care about all those things."

Lee rubbed his chin, shaggy now with an untrimmed beard. "They do," he said. "But I mean more than talk and delivering flyers. Getting involved and taking things right to the top. The goal of the revolution is to open all doors and break all locks. Alex and Bo may have avoided the establishment, but they're not doing anything real. Look at those guys in Quebec. They were willing to do something drastic to get rid of the democracy of the rich. Those guys are *real*."

This time I knew what Lee was talking about. A month before, a separatist organization called the Front de Libération du Quebec had taken two politicians hostage in Montreal and then released a list of demands for their safe return. Lee had listened to their manifesto on the radio. When Trudeau invoked the War Measures Act, he nearly hit the roof.

"The fascist capitalist prick!" he said, his face turning red as a beet. "Doesn't he know that sometimes people have to die to bring about change? No ruling class in history has ever given up power voluntarily."

Back at the estuary he pranced on, pawing the hair from his eyes and staring at me with intensity. I loved the look of his eyes when he was on the verge of a rant – his passion reminded me there were things worth fighting for. "We're not protesting issues," he said. "We're protesting civilization. We don't want to resolve war or corruption so that we can go back to normal life. Normal life is nowhere. Normal life is *shit.*"

Eventually I started to notice things about Lee. For instance, he had a habit of overdressing, donning a bulky jacket and even a toque when the air was warm. He also wore a pair of mirrored sunglasses whether or not the sun was shining. There was also his preoccupation with his CB radio, and the cryptic messages shared with Alex and Bo at the beginning of their visits.

"Heard from Daddy?" Lee might say, casually inspecting his beer.

"Not yet," Alex usually replied. "Daddy's still shopping."

I put down this weirdness to Lee's heritage (American). At the same time I concentrated on other things: Lee's lankiness, his laugh; the way he could sit for hours by the river watching a ladybug climb a blade of grass and then turn to me with wonder in his eyes.

"You know what I like about you?" Lee said one day.

"What?" I said.

"You don't ask questions. You're happy to just let me be. That's the way everyone needs to act."

I blushed, remembering that I liked the same things about Lee. So many times I had prepared myself to tell a story about a mother who worked too hard, a sister who was saving for college, and a house that was being renovated to explain why I was alone. But I never had to.

He reached his hand across the space and gently touched the side of my face. "I trust you, Ronnie," he said. "You're special to me."

Around us the evening faded. I didn't stand up until my backside was completely numb.

In those first few months after I first stepped on board *The Minstrel*, Lee and I met after school; we took walks along the rising estuary, and visited the Watermark, where Lee always paid and insisted on sitting in the crying room. Back in the boat, we played games of hearts or canasta and drank homemade wine. *The Minstrel* seemed safe, just as the Watermark had seemed safe, only this time, I wasn't alone.

Even Alex and Bo accepted me into their lives, inviting me into the cabin for dinners of roast chicken and freshly dug potatoes – which I devoured while trying to hide my hunger – raising eyebrows when I told them about plants that lived in the alpine. They found my knowledge of the natural world a bonus and said that more people should have my kind of childhood, poised on the brink of wilderness; pure, clean, and absolute. I began to see myself as someone other than who I had become in this town.

On those evenings when I was not with Lee, or

during those times when our meetings lasted only one or two hours, I sat down in a pigskin library chair at school and read until my eyes crossed.

After darkness had fallen and blackness pressed up against the windowpanes, I usually felt too hungry to go on. I had already been living off the salvage from my mother's refrigerator for over three months, meals that I pieced together from the groceries either she or Marcia had remembered to buy. Mostly this was peanut butter sandwiches on white bread, but on days when the cupboards were entirely bare, I eyed other people's lunches at school. If I was really hungry, I avoided walking past the school cafeteria. The torment of hot soups and fish and chip grease spilling out the doorway was enough to turn my stomach.

Eventually I became light-headed, constipated, my stomach wracked with cramps. I hid out in the library or the dead-end hallway, a book under my nose and my hand clutched around my waistline.

One Wednesday during the second week of November, I made my way down the sidewalk and through the double doors of the school. Light streamed through a second-floor window, illuminating fingerprints on the walls and graffiti scrubbed to a hazy shroud. Students passed; one pair of girls giggled over a bag of potato chips. A slow ache had already started building in my cheeks when I ran into Mr. Turnbull.

"Ronalda," he said. "I haven't seen you in a while.

How are you doing?"

"Good," I said.

"I'm looking forward to reading your paper, the one on the pollination of alpine flora. I hope you haven't forgotten about the due date. The end of this week?"

I shook my head and tucked my chin into my turtleneck. "I haven't forgotten," I said, lying through my teeth. Remembering anything, I had noticed, seemed to be harder and harder. Lee's criticisms of school reached me enough to justify slacking off, but I wasn't ready to drop out all together.

"Good," he said. "I knew you'd keep on top of things. Our school system offers a lot of freedom to students who deserve it, but sometimes, people get left behind. There are a lot of distractions for students who are looking for them."

I nodded lamely.

"Are you sure that you're all right? You're looking a little white. I hope you're not working too hard." He regarded me with a look of concern and then patted me on the back with a single motion that almost sent me sprawling. "I'll see you in homeroom?"

"Pardon?" I said.

"For the Remembrance Day service. There's a short ceremony down at the cenotaph. We're going together as a class."

*　*　*

We reached the cenotaph after a ten-minute walk from the school, in a small park surrounded by dormant flowerbeds and knee-high wire fencing. We arrived close to ten thirty, huddling in our coats, avoiding puddles, which were scattered through the park.

By some stroke of luck the sun was shining; the sky shimmered blue and clear overhead. I found a spot to stand alone, away from the clusters of shrieking girls and the boys who poked them in the backs with their fingers. After a briefing by Mr. Turnbull on the meaning of the armistice, we waited in broken silence, whispers rising and the smell of cigarette smoke carrying across the green. Eventually several hundred students amassed around the cenotaph.

When the veterans arrived, marching down the streets in their navy coats, sporting medals and uniforms and tilted berets, any chatter that had been stirring in the crowd fell away to the drone of bagpipes. I watched them file in, these older men of my father's and grandfather's age, their allegiance to the First or Second World War evident by the number of lines in their faces. All of them were silent, shadowy figures, standing with their arms at their sides and casting eyes that had seen Germany, France, and Belgium down to the moist-packed earth. I thought briefly of my paternal grandfather, a man I had never met but who was known to me as someone who searched for bodies in the weeks following the first armistice.

When the bugle sounded signalling the start of

eleven minutes of silence, I noticed a tear on the cheek of the veteran closest to me. I shifted, uneasy in my wet shoes, and my stomach let out a loud growl. As the minutes stretched on, I started to sway, first my hands, gently against my sides, and then my shoulders. When the teacher in front of me stepped ahead, I fell forward into a puddle.

When I finally came to, I looked around slowly, surveying the nurse's desk, weigh scales, jars of tongue depressors and Q-tips. The paint on the walls was a horrid pink, the same colour as the illustration for the inside of the ear canal hovering on pins above the desk. The acrid smell of rubbing alcohol wafted across the bed. A nurse came forward and put her hand on my forehead. "You're back at school," she said. "You fainted at the Armistice Day presentation and we wanted to make sure you were all right."

I noticed one side of my face was numb, and when I raised my hand I found, to my surprise, a gauze bandage.

"You grazed your cheek," the nurse went on. "Nothing serious, but I didn't want it to get infected. You can remove the pad tomorrow, providing you put some antibacterial ointment on the sore every day for the next week." She handed me a small silver tube.

"Now," she said. "People faint for a number of reasons. We have at least two or three cases every year and usually it's from a short-term virus or a skipped meal. There are other reasons as well, and it's only to make things easy that I'm going to ask you this question. Could you possibly be pregnant?"

I flushed and answered quickly. "No."

"I didn't think so," she said. "Your symptoms are more characteristic of poor nutrition than pregnancy, but I needed to ask."

"Symptoms?" I said.

"The spots on your arms. Your pale skin that looks a little too yellow." She stepped toward her desk and pulled out a coloured leaflet. "And you have some bleeding along the gum line. That's a bad sign and we're going to have to do something about it."

I felt with a start my swollen tongue.

"I know you students work hard. This new system lets you stay up at all hours with your nose in a book. It's good to keep on top of your education, but you have to remember that you need a certain amount of vitamins to keep you going. You can't forget to eat."

I nodded weakly.

"I'm very serious." She handed me the leaflet. "This is Canada's food guide, and it tells you everything you need to know. Following these recommendations will make sure that you get enough protein and carbohydrates, and enough iron which is most likely your problem." She began to explain, in a quiet voice, the ratio of grains to meat, of fruits and vegetables to milk and other dairy products that I needed to eat every day so that I didn't wither away and die. The list of foods danced before me like a buffet in an exclusive restaurant: beans, molasses, cabbages and carrots, bread with fortified margarine and the occasional serving of liver, soup stocks, chicken breast, a stuffed pheasant on a bed of rice. I watched her speak, reeling off a list of ingredients that existed only in other people's refrigerators.

"Does that make sense?" she said at last, sitting back and regarding me with a look of gravity.

"Yes," I said, "only –"

"Only what?"

I gulped. "Will you be telling anyone that I fainted?"

She put down her food guide. "Aside from the entire student body who saw it for themselves? I'll be making a call to your mother."

I peeled off the bandage and floated down the street, trying to decide whether to go to the Watermark or all the way home. Since my run-in with Stephen I had not visited the theatre by myself; I hadn't cared enough to sit and listen to the rustlings of hungry babies now that Lee had relieved me of my loneliness. I chose the route home and opened the front door. I was surprised to find Marcia at the kitchen table, eating the tail end of a bowl of popcorn. We hadn't talked in ages, and I was angry with her for leaving me out of her affairs. I thought briefly about the rumours I heard at school. What was she up to anyway?

"Don't you get enough of that at work?" I said, taking a seat and helping myself.

She turned her head in my direction but looked past

me with glazed eyes. I wondered, for an instant, if she had been crying.

"What?" she asked.

"I said, 'Don't you get enough popcorn at work?'"

She looked at me more closely, and then said, "What happened to your face?"

"I fell down."

She nodded and continued looking through the unpopped kernels. "Have you seen Mum?" she said eventually.

"No." I knew today was one of my mother's days off, but if she wasn't lying in bed or sitting here at the kitchen table, I didn't know where she was. I was tired of trying to keep things together. I was even more tired of being left in the dark. Taking a deep breath, I said point blank: "Why are you spending so much time with Louis?"

For a moment she stared at me. "Who says that I am?"

"Everyone. Everyone says that. Girls at school. Janice."

"Don't believe everything you hear."

Not wanting to let her off that easily, I gathered my evidence. "I saw you in Louis's car just after school started. You were coming home late at night."

"It wasn't late," she said.

Her carelessness infuriated me, but just as I was about to get mad, she straightened and looked back at her bowl. When she spoke her voice was level and distant. "He's trying to help us. I know some people are talking –

stupid people. You can just tell them I'm his assistant. I'm helping him out at work." She made a flick with her hand, and then added, "He thinks Mum should go to the hospital. She doesn't agree. He says he can't really help her anymore if she's going to be like that. That's why he's stopped coming around."

I stiffened at this news and felt my throat close, my anger against Louis flaring. "What about us? Where are we supposed to live if she goes away? We can't stay here and take care of ourselves. People don't let you do things like that."

"That's what he's trying to figure out."

"I won't live with Louis," I said. "I hate him."

"Ronnie," Marcia said. "You'll do what he tells us. You're just a kid and you don't have a choice."

"I won't!" I shouted, and stomped to my room.

I had been avoiding my room for so long – creeping in after dark to collapse on the heaped up covers – that the mess surprised me. Piles of tossed-off clothes sat in the corner beneath my mirror. Someone had opened the window and the pages of my homework were drifting across the floor. I sat down on my bed and rolled over onto my back; a water stain was inching its way across the ceiling. I lay there for a long time listening to the noise of a tree branch as it scratched against the window pane and then quietly fell away.

I hadn't expected to sleep, but when I woke with surprise, the sun on the carpet had shifted and my head felt heavy and weak. I heard a clattering in the kitchen. I walked down the hallway and found my mother.

"Ronnie," she said. "I'm so glad you're home. I wanted to talk to you, but I didn't want to wake you up if you weren't feeling well. I know how you need your sleep. You've been working so hard. I'm so worried that you will wear yourself out."

I could tell by her stance and the dull fluidity of her movements that my mother had been drinking; how much, I didn't know. She smiled in my direction, and I noticed the cupboards were full. "Where did all this food come from?" I said.

"I bought it at the supermarket. I went to see old Albert – you know, the nice grocery man who bags produce and always adds a carnation for the ladies."

I saw the single flower on the table wrapped in coloured paper. Around it were the deflated carcasses of several grocery bags, a sack of potatoes, dried beans, and something that looked like a cucumber but wasn't. The refrigerator door remained open, and I could see a rainbow of vegetables inside.

"He's always cheerful, and his jokes make me laugh," she said.

I had a momentary vision of my mother chuckling with the produce man as she emptied the contents of her purse onto the checkout counter. She never could find her wallet, and her attempts to locate it embarrassed me even when she was sober.

"Did anybody see you?"

She gave me a look. "Of course people saw me. What do you mean? The grocery store was full of customers. Women, children, nice gentlemen saving their wives from the chores by picking up the meat."

"I mean people who we know. People who you work with, or one of my teachers. People from the neighbourhood."

She thought for a moment. "Well, there was Mrs. Rice from the bank, but she hardly gave me a nod, she's so terse. And she wore an awful hat – the feathers!" My mother let out a laugh.

I cringed at the name, imagining Shelter Bay's biggest gossip watching with satisfaction as my mother fumbled with a jar of molasses, leaning in close enough to take a sniff. Liquor: something to tell the ladies at the bank. "I wish you wouldn't go out," I said, suddenly angry. "Why do you have to go out?"

My mother's smile wilted, and she let the last of the bananas fall to the table. Then she sat down. "You don't want me to be seen," she proclaimed quietly to herself. "You are ashamed of your mother." She turned her wavering head slowly downward; a tear spilled off her cheek.

"Forget it."

"I'm a bad mother."

"No," I said. "You're not. I just –"

She raised a tissue to her eyelids. "You're ashamed."

I didn't know what to say.

"The school nurse called today," she said, changing the subject.

"What? When?"

"She told me that you fainted. She said you need to get better nutrition, and that your new schedule is allowing you to forget meals. I know things have been hard around here, with me back at work and then sick a lot of the time," she sniffled a little. "But I can do better." She drew herself up. "There's a lot of nutritious food in there." She motioned to the cupboards, the refrigerator. "And I want you to eat anything you want. I can't always make your lunches, but from now on, I will put dinner on the table. You and me and Marcia will eat a proper meal together. How does that sound?"

I nodded, though I didn't see how I could eat anything now with Marcia and my mother at the same table.

"Good," she said, sniffing again. "I know we can do this. We just have to try. We have to be strong. Your father would want us to be strong." She stood up and wiped her hands on her apron, and then pressed a hand to the scrape on my cheek. "Oh, Ronnie. You're so young. I wish things were easier, but I know they'll get better for you. When you get older, you'll be a smart woman. You won't make the same mistakes that I did."

I sat in silence.

"Well," she said eventually, and withdrew her hand. I felt reality flood back and along with it, all the things I wanted to tell her; but I wasn't fast enough. She turned around and headed for the hallway. "I'm going to take a little nap," she said. "I'm going to lay my head down and make myself feel better. And after that, I'll get up and make us all a nice dinner."

But my mother did not get up and make us all a nice dinner; she went to sleep and snored on, burrowing deep into her pillows despite my attempts to wake her. She breathed in deep and sonorously, her skin pale, her eyes frozen and shadowy, as if trying to outdo the dead.

And so, rather than wait for Marcia – who could have been out with Louis or working an extra shift at the Watermark – I ventured into the kitchen. I had already eaten a raw apple and slice of processed cheese, but I now needed something with more staying power.

True to her word my mother had stocked the shelves with food of all shapes and sizes, but as I looked, as I moved heads of lettuce and sorted through drawers of onions and tomatoes, I realized I didn't know where to begin. Where there might have been bread, there was now a cake of yeast and a pound of enriched flour. Where there might have been boxed cereal, there was slow-cooking, whole grain oats. I stared at the refrigerator, at the cupboards and countertops whose contents reminded me of the displays in whole foods stores: dry beans, little nuggets of radishes and rice; everything colourful, vital, and raw.

I had never taken a home economics course. I had

never done more than boil an egg without instructions. Marcia was the helper, the blonde Betty Crocker; I was the one usually out gutting fish. I settled for an egg – which burst when I lowered it into the water – and Uncle Ben's converted rice.

The meal was a sad one, with an explosion of dirty dishes and the smell of burnt rice rising in a cloud of starch from the stove element. I sat in depressed silence, spooning the meal directly from the pan into my mouth, and watched the light waver on the horizon before ducking behind the trees.

After scraping the pans and leaving them in the sink to soak, I went outside and headed along the sidewalk in the direction of the marina. By the time I reached *The Minstrel*, cold air was spilling out of the valley and raising hairs on the back of my neck. I stepped from the dock to the starboard side and felt the boat give beneath my feet. "Hello?" I said, the way I always did.

The fact that Lee did not have a phone meant that finding him at home was hit and miss. This time I heard voices: both Lee and Alex. The door on the hatch was halfway open.

"I don't see that you have many choices," Alex was saying. "You've used up every available avenue and you know what's left. It's not an easy decision to make, but I'd hoped you would make the right one."

"The right one," Lee said. "And which one is that?"

"We've been over this."

"Screw the system. I'm not going back," Lee said, and to my surprise, it sounded as though he might be crying.

"Well, I guess you've got some planning to do. You can wait things out a little longer, but you know the outcome doesn't look good. I'll help you in any way I can, Lee. You know that. I just want what's best."

There was a long silence, and I suddenly felt like an eavesdropper. At the same time, I was afraid they might be talking about me. "Hello?" I said again, more loudly this time. I knocked on the door and stepped in.

The interior of the cabin was darker than usual, as if both Lee and Alex had decided to forgo the candles and kerosene lamps in an attempt to save fuel. I could see the outline of their faces, two solemn expressions. Perhaps I had been wrong about the crying: I didn't see a trace of tears. Alex fidgeted with his fisherman's cap and stood up as if to leave.

"Hello, Ronalda. I was just on my way out." He gave Lee a final glance. I let him step around me and ascend the tunnel to the fresh air.

Our walk to the estuary that night was surreal and unpleasant. Lee straggled several feet behind me, poking his boots in the mud puddles and mumbling about the hopelessness of life. I worried that he was angry, that he had found out about my mother or the fact that I wasn't anywhere near the age he thought I was. I kept a few steps ahead.

Eventually he said, "There's no use."

"No use to what?"

"To anything. The struggle, the hiding. That's the whole point. People don't want to be any better off than they are."

I didn't know what he was talking about. Halfway back to the marina – feeling anxious and self-conscious – I wheeled around to face him. He was bent down over the water, looking intently into the murk.

"Lee?"

"Yes."

"Why did Alex try to stop me from coming on board your boat, the first time I came over? He told me he didn't know any Lee, but then later, he pretended like it never happened."

He gazed at his reflection for what seemed like a minute, long enough to suggest he'd missed everything I'd said. I hoped that he hadn't; I didn't know if I could say it again. Then he straightened and tucked his hair behind his ears. He said in a rather stern voice, "I thought you were someone who didn't ask questions."

Back at *The Minstrel* we stood silently on the dock. Waves lapped against the hulls of moored boats, rising and falling with the pull of the moon. In the silver evening Lee's skin gleamed like a salmon's; a tendril of hair lolled in the centre of his forehead.

"I'll see you on Friday?" I said. "For our usual walk?"

"Actually, I'm going to be busy. I have some things to take care of and I won't be back until late."

"Saturday then?"

He turned and shuffled his feet. "Sure. In the afternoon."

We stood quietly for a moment.

"Lee?" There was more I wanted to say, but he seemed suddenly distant, even though I could have reached out and tweak him on the nose.

⁎ ⁎ ⁎

The idea that I had done something to make Lee angry consumed me. I spent the next two days drowning myself in television, in books and magazines that had nothing to do with my homework – most of which had drifted to a standstill on my bedroom rug. I combed over the preceding evenings and afternoons for a clue or detail to see what I could have done differently. At one point I found myself in front of Marcia's vanity mirror, contemplating a puzzling array of cosmetics that – when applied – made me look more like a fraudulent Cleopatra than the sophisticated woman I knew I had hidden inside. Eventually I collapsed, sad and exhausted, and passed several hours flat on my back.

In the middle of the second night, while rain pounded the roof and sent the gutters running with overflow, I determined that the clue must lie with Alex, that gruff version of my father who welcomed and terrified me, both at the same time. Perhaps I had been too open in my adoration of Lee, and Alex had concluded I was simply too young. But I wasn't too young; I was practically taking care of myself.

On Friday, after a late night at the school library, I came home to find the house empty and the rooms ringing with silence. I headed into the kitchen and opened the refrigerator where most of my mother's groceries had begun to rot. Lettuce wilted on wire shelves; a pair of tomatoes speckled with brown dots melded together in a puckered, sour kiss. I took out a package of processed cheese and made my way through the wrapped slices. Each piece was as smooth as tile, glazed and orange like a rubber boot. I ate one and then another. I was working my way through a third when the front door opened.

I knew by the sounds of things in the entryway that my mother had come home: first the slide on the linoleum, then the heave of balance as she attempted to remove her shoes without falling over. Slide, heave, step. I could hear her measured intakes of breath, the weight of her body as it sagged against the wall.

"Ronnie," she said, when she rounded the corner. "Shouldn't you be in bed?"

"I'm having something to eat first."

"Good for you," she said, and crossed over to the kitchen sink where she poured herself some water. "You were always so smart."

I watched as she raised the glass to her lips and took

a long messy slurp. I resumed eating until she said, "Have you seen Louis?"

"No."

Water trickled down the front of her raincoat. She took a step back and leaned against the counter. "He's been avoiding me."

I thought back to my conversation with Marcia. "He's probably just busy."

"No," my mother said and gave a little laugh. "I've been trying to see him all week. I've been calling him since last weekend."

"Maybe he's busy with Raven's," I said. "Maybe the sale finally came through and he's been away getting things organized."

"If that were true," said my mother, "it would have been in the papers. Besides, I know things are still on hold. The government needs to approve new zoning in order for him to sell. I work at his real estate agent's office, remember? "

I took in this information about Raven's with a sigh of relief. My father's legacy was still intact. At least for now.

My mother laughed again. "Which doesn't explain why his Lincoln was still in the parking lot when I went to see him today at his office. His secretary tried to tell me he was out at a meeting, but I know better. If he was at a meeting, he would have driven. I guess she hasn't noticed that Louis never walks anywhere."

"She was probably mixed up," I said, returning to

the conversation.

"What does she think I am? I saw his Lincoln plain as day."

I stared at my pile of cellophane wrappings. My mother's voice was dangerously close to cracking, and I didn't want to witness another weep session. If she didn't know why Louis was avoiding her, I wasn't going to tell her. "Maybe she made a mistake."

My mother laughed again, and I saw that she was angry, not sad. She took another sip of her water and watched as the clock ticked on for one painful minute after another. Before long the door banged open and Marcia walked into the kitchen.

"Having a party?" she asked. "You didn't invite me."

"Marcia," my mother said.

I watched as my sister crossed the floor and draped her coat on the back of a kitchen chair. Her hair was drawn into a ponytail, exposing a face that was stained with tears. The charm that Louis had given her, a long time ago, jangled on the end of her wrist. "Ronnie," she said, "I want to speak to Mum alone."

I made a motion to get up when I felt my mother's hands on my shoulders.

"Ronnie is having something to eat. She has every right to be in the kitchen like the rest of us. She needs her vitamins."

"I want her to go," Marcia said.

"Well, Marcia, you can't always have what you

want. Or haven't you noticed? Life sometimes turns out differently than you expected."

"Yours certainly has."

"What's that supposed to mean?"

Marcia took a step forward. "You know exactly. I saw Louis tonight. He told me everything. I guess he's been trying to tell me all along."

My mother's mouth made a small O. Her voice came out slurred and indulgent.

"Marcia, I don't know what Louis told you, but he must have been joking. I'll have to talk to him and straighten things out."

"No you won't. He doesn't want to talk to you. He's tried talking to you. But you always lie."

My mother shrugged, making the exaggerated motions she always made when she was trying to command respect but was having trouble. She stepped forward and pointed her finger at my sister. "Listen –"

"I won't listen. I'm tired of listening." Tears were streaming down her face, but she continued to speak, her voice rising. "You're just a drunk who doesn't care about anybody. You've been lying so long that you can't even tell the difference anymore."

There was a crack, and in the silence that followed a red welt sprung to Marcia's cheek. I saw with surprise the imprint of my mother's hand.

The shock of the slap must have been less for my sister than the idea she had been hit. In all our days at

Raven's, my parents had never hit us. Better we should carry a heavy pack up the alpine trail or clean the stovepipe with a toothbrush than get spanked. (I had felt like a packhorse often enough to know.) My sister ran down the hallway and locked herself in the bathroom; my mother slumped to the floor.

"What is she talking about?" I said, in the moments following the slap. "What did Louis tell Marcia?"

My mother looked at her hands and a cry escaped her lungs. "It's his fault," she said morosely. "He's the one to blame."

# Chapter 11

If anything could convince me that my family was going crazy, it was that image of Marcia standing in the kitchen with tears rolling off her chin. I didn't know why my mother was suddenly blaming Louis for our situation, but I certainly agreed with her. Why had it taken her so long to see his true colours? Angry at everyone, I ran down the street in the direction of the marina.

The air was brisk, and the moon shone clear into the night. I thought of Lee, of our strolls on similar moonlit evenings when stars twinkled and the glow of distant planets reduced everything to silhouette. This time, clouds of shallow breath steamed from my mouth, and I was surprised to find myself shivering. Again the weather had deceived me; again I had stepped from the house in nothing but a spring jacket thinking that the absence of snow meant higher temperatures. After nearly one year I was not used to the climate. I hustled along the sidewalk, keeping my arms close to my body.

It must have been eleven o'clock and the streets were empty. I stepped onto *The Minstrel* and opened the hatch. The cabin was dark, lit only by the flickering of the wood stove.

"Who's there?"

"It's me. Ronnie." I groped my way down to the bunk, working my hands along the wooden trim and kitchen table until I could feel the bed. The stove threw off a steady heat. I paused for a moment to warm myself.

"Ronnie? What are you –"

"Don't worry." I shushed his questions, put my fingers to his mouth in the way I had seen actresses do on television.

His body felt hot. In an instant I felt him reaching for me, moving his hands across my face and neck. He pulled the covers out of the way.

"What are you doing here?" he asked more softly.

"Don't worry," I said again.

I wasn't sure I knew what I was doing, but one thing is for sure: Lee wasn't Moose. He wasn't aggressive or greedy, and he didn't smell like gin. He kissed me on the bridge of my nose, softly, and then he wrapped his arms around me.

Around us the details swirled: warm air, the sway and tilt of the boat, and the occasional crackle from the CB radio; shadows rising from reflected light and the dregs of fruity incense. I was quietly thankful that he wanted me. Nobody else did. I was grateful to be needed, but I was also shocked by his touch.

"Lee?" I said, shaking in the darkness. Unprepared and inexperienced, I didn't know what came next. Thankfully I didn't have to. He lay beside me, silent as the night. *If only we could stay like this*, I thought to myself, wishing for the impossible.

He didn't answer. I could hear the soft breath seesawing from his lungs. He was asleep. That made what I wanted to say easier.

"Lee, I love you."

☀    ☀    ☀

In the morning, I woke to find him rummaging through his things. I saw with a start that he had chopped off his hair.

"What are you doing?" I said.

"I'm packing." He moved about the cabin, selecting a spoon here and a sock there, picking up items from his spice rack before shaking his head and returning them to their nests. His chin gleamed without his beard.

"Why?" I asked, suddenly terrified. "Why are you packing?"

He said nothing for a moment, and then leaned against the table. "This is going to be hard for you to understand, Ronnie, but –"

I didn't let him finish. "Did I do something? Did I make a mistake?"

"No, you didn't do anything. This had nothing to do with you."

"But you're packing," I said. "You're leaving to go somewhere. You're running away from me." I felt a catch in my voice, followed by the embarrassment of tears. "Is it because of last night? Because I didn't – "

"Last night?" He approached me and sat on the bed. "Listen. You're sweet. And I'll admit that the timing doesn't look good. But the thing is, I was always going to leave. The question has only ever been, *when*?"

I tried to contain myself. "But why?"

"That's a long story, full of a whole lot of stuff you don't need to worry about."

"But I want to worry about it." I clambered out of the V-berth, covers drooping around my shoulders.

"Look, Ronnie –"

I started to cry. I was horrified, inconsolable. In my mind, last night had been the start of something new and wonderful. I couldn't just forget.

"Listen," Lee sighed. "I'll tell you what I can – you're probably going to find out sooner or later anyway – but I want you to promise you won't pass this on. I trust you Ronnie, but I've been wrong before."

I nodded.

"I'm serious."

"I know." I tried to sound convincing, but I was shaking again.

"O.K. You've heard me talk about some groups I used to be associated with, in the states?"

"Yes. I remember."

"We organized bail funds to help people get out of jail. We set up crash pads for runaways and gave everyone food and clothes who came around with their hands out. People were dropping out, but they had no idea where to go. We organized festivals and gave them something to do."

"That sounds good."

"It sounds good," Lee echoed. "But it was *shit*. It didn't get us anywhere, except stoned, which was good for a while, but eventually we realized they had us right where they wanted us. Pacified. We were all so busy dancing and celebrating that we couldn't see that things kept right on marching forward around us."

"What kinds of things?"

"The war. The government. Everything. Vietnam kept on raging; people kept right on buying leaded gasoline from the Standard Oil Company of New Jersey." He paused to grit his teeth. "So I joined a group of people who were willing to take direct action. We wanted to push youth culture toward the kind of revolution they needed." He stopped and took in a breath. "To make a long story short, things went a little bad. We weren't supposed to get caught, but somehow we did; or I did.

And now they want to put me in jail."

"What did you do?"

"You don't need to know."

"You keep saying that, but I want to know. How can I understand if I don't?"

He sighed again. "I blew something up. Which isn't as bad as it sounds – nobody died – and it really would have gotten us a lot of press if bourgeois society didn't own all the newspapers in the universe."

"What did you blow up?"

He clapped his hand to his forehead. "What difference does it make? I didn't do that much damage, not half as much as I had planned, but the government still chased me all the way up here. I've been hanging out in la-la land waiting for my appeal. Now that it's been rejected, I can't wait any longer. They're not going to let me off, and I won't spend the rest of my life moldering away in a state prison. Survival is the first goal of the vanguard. I can't go to jail. It's my duty to escape."

We sat in silence for a moment, before I said, "Can't your dad help you?"

Lee snorted. "He paid for my lawyers, and let me tell you, he wasn't that happy about it. You'd think I was asking for the world the way he went on, *no son of mine* this and *no son of mine* that. The guy's got 'sell-out' written all over him."

I waited for him to continue.

"If you ask me, those lawyers are the problem. They

may be the best that money can buy, but they're still a bunch of bumbling idiots. Personally I think it's sabotage. He wants me to pay for all the times I disappointed him, by not cutting my hair and putting on a suit. Do you know what he said the last time we spoke? *Son, if the appeal fails, I think you should turn yourself in.* Can you believe it? He wants me to go to jail with all those Hells Angels and child slayers. I'd be meat loaf in less than a week."

I stared at him. I couldn't believe what I was hearing. "Are you making this up? Because Lee, if you're telling me this to get me to go away –" a tear slid down my cheek.

"What?" he said. "Ronnie, no." He sat down beside me and put his hands on my shoulders. "You don't think I could come up with something like this unless it was true, do you? Do you really think I'm like that?"

"No," I said. I didn't, and I desperately wanted to believe him. Even if the truth was as horrible as he said it was, at least it meant he wasn't trying to get away from *me*.

He continued, dropping his hands to his sides. I reached out to touch him but he pulled away. "Alex agrees with my father."

"What does Alex have to do with this?"

"After I lost the trial and came up here, and the whole lousy process began to ship me back, some bleeding hearts down in San Francisco put me in touch with Alex and Bo. They're members of some affinity group, some overage hippies who like to bake meals for the soon-to-be deported. They're in with the draft-dodging bunch. I guess it makes them feel better for doing nothing else."

"Then how do they know your dad?"

He looked at me blankly. "What are you talking about? Alex and Bo don't know my dad."

We sat for a moment, blinking in the sunrise, while I wondered what else Lee hadn't told me. I wanted badly to run my fingers through his hair. I settled for taking his hand. Eventually he roused himself. "That's why I have to get out of here."

"But where are you going to go?"

"I'm still working that one out." He stood up and tossed a sock into his army issue duffel bag, the same kind my father lugged around to his presentations for the Boy Scouts – over-washed with bottomless pockets, musty and smelling of kapok. "But I'm going to get off the boat. It's too obviously linked to my father. As far as I'm concerned, I'm an orphan of America."

"Do you have to go far?"

"I don't know. I'll figure that out as I go. There are crash pads all over the place south of the border. There's got to be a few around here too."

"But you can't just take off. You need some kind of plan." I was feeling desperate again. I couldn't just let him disappear.

"Chill out, Ronnie. I intend to make one. I'm not going to walk out into the street and turn myself in."

I looked at his face, his pink chin and underwashed, close-cropped hair. He was dappled in sunlight, in the scents of leather and hops that rose from his skin like a perfume. Whenever I thought of Lee, I immediately thought of forests: dense tangles of branchlets, Indian wickiups or earthen rabbit holes stuffed with feathers and arrant leaves. He was the man in all of my father's survival books: dimly lost, but with a hope for rescue. I wasn't ready to give him up.

"I know a place," I said.

He turned and focused his still green eyes. "Listen, Ronnie. It's best that you don't get involved. I've already told you too much and I really can't involve you any further. I'm not really sure why I said as much as I did. I guess it's a relief to talk about it, even if Alex is constantly telling me not to." He pivoted back to his bag and continued talking, planning his escape as he filled the compartments with socks.

"But I know somewhere. Somewhere no one will ever find you."

We took down Lee's map of Vancouver Island and I pointed out the location of Raven's. The National Park stretched its way around the lake, a vast series of ridges, valleys, and alpine peaks. In the distance lurked a number of caves, ridge routes so remote people traversed them less than once a year. I knew them inside out.

"You'll have to walk up an access road to the lake," I said. "But once you get there the lodge is visible in this small bay." I put my finger on the map. "The door might be locked – it probably will be – but that doesn't matter because there's no locks on any of the windows. You can remove the storm coverings with a chisel – they're just hook and eye latches – and get inside. There's got to be firewood, and probably enough fuel and food to last you a month. If you don't mind eating pancakes."

The words poured out, unchecked and excited, as I tried to imagine the state of the lodge: there would be pots and pans, bedding and kerosene, sacks of unused flour slumping into the black. Mice would have infiltrated the pantry – it was winter after all – but my parents had made a point of securing all dry goods in mouse-proof tubs. Louis, I knew, had purchased everything we left behind as a sort of bargain basement package deal, which he planned to sell to the National Park when the permits came through. According to my mother, this was taking longer than he'd anticipated.

Lee remained quiet for a long while, eyeing the map and my moving finger. "How do we know no one is going to be there?"

"It's winter," I said. "Louis closed everything up when we left earlier in the year. No one will be back until spring. It's just too out of the way."

Lee looked sceptical.

"I can check with the real estate agent just to be sure, but my mother said yesterday the sale was still in limbo. She said we'd know as soon as anything happened because the papers would report it. This is a small town. Word gets around."

"That's what I'm afraid of."

"Not that kind of word," I said. "There's no one out there. Not in the winter. My mother used to think we were crazy for spending the season out there, because we were so isolated from other human beings. We were really alone. Sometimes we didn't hear from anyone in months."

Lee rubbed his chin.

"The slog across the lake will be tough of course, because there's bound to be snow. But once you get out there you can get a pair of snowshoes from the storage shed. You can stay out there for at least a few months."

"Until things die down," Lee said.

"Right," I said.

There was a moment of silence, and then he said, "OK, thanks Ronnie."

I waited on the boat while Lee finished packing. He was moving quickly now that he had dispatched Alex and told him of his plans. Alex would make the necessary call to the real estate agent, and then, if everything was in place, he'd come to pick up Lee despite his misgivings. Lee listened only half-heartedly as I reeled off a list of what sorts of things he would need. Sun streamed in the portholes, high in a sky that had recently threatened rain.

"Lots of warm clothes," I continued. "Because it takes days for the lodge to heat up once you get the fire going. And there's usually tinder next to the stove in an old liquorice tin."

He turned and looked at me. "Geez, Ronnie, I'm not going to light the fire."

"Why not?"

"Because people will see the smoke."

"Oh," I said. "What about at night?"

"Then they'll smell it. I'm not taking any chances."

"Then you'll have to dig out the sleeping bags. There's a set of Arctic Three Stars on the upstairs landing, stored in a garbage tin. My father used them for sleeping outside in winter under the stars. There's also a whole lot of blankets. We only took a few of them when we left."

Lee sighed. "That's great."

"The kerosene lanterns are scattered here and there. The gas is in the back shed and you won't be able to use any running water. The pipes will be frozen. You'll have to bucket from the lake."

"I'll be fine," Lee said.

"But it's really cold. The high ceilings suck up heat, and it's better to stay in one of the bedrooms than hang around in the dining hall or living room." I pictured Lee, teeth shivering, surrounding himself in a fort of blankets.

"It's OK, Ronnie. I've got it. You can stop worrying."

Was I that obvious? Of course I was. "Lee," I said excitedly. "I just had a thought."

He sat down on at the table. "What is it?"

"Raven's has a CB radio. I can call you from

*The Minstrel.*"

Lee raised his hands, and I noticed for the first time that they were thin and narrow, like a girl's. A coat of downy hair covered his knuckles. "Oh, God," he said. "Don't do that. Don't ever do that."

"Why not?"

"Because they can track those things. Do you understand? If you radio me you're sending out a message to the universe. Lee, come in Lee." He made a nasal sound with his hand over his nostril. "You might as well call the police."

I quieted.

"Ronnie, do you understand that you can't tell anyone where I'm going? Not your mother or anyone. I'm in trouble and I've got to lie low. I'm trusting you here, and I need to know that I can count on you to keep your word."

"I won't tell my mother," I said. "Or anyone else."

"Good," he said, but he didn't sound convinced.

"Lee," I said. "I won't tell anyone. Ever."

He straightened, and I felt the dip of someone stepping onto the upper deck. The utensils bobbed back and forth against the ceiling, indicating that Alex had arrived. "Good," he whispered, looking into my eyes. "I trust you, Ronnie. You're the best chance I've got." He moved in an instant to the hatch. "Alex, is that you?"

Alex popped his head into the cabin. "It's me. We're ready for takeoff. Everything is just as Ronnie said. Now,

Lee, are you sure you want to do this?"

Lee looked back at me with something like relief. "Yes," he said.

I felt proud for a moment. I crossed the room and gave him a kiss.

☆  ☆  ☆

Afterward I sat quietly, listening to the sway of the boat and the sounds pouring in from outside: seagulls, the blast of engines revving up to a steady thrum. I ran my hands through the remains of our hasty breakfast, which lay scattered in an arc across the kitchen table. Lee had eaten a piece of toast and then swilled down a cup of coffee. I was still hungry and sat down to finish my oatmeal.

When I was done, I wiped everything down with a clean cloth. I walked home via the estuary, and then along the waterfront to the movie theatre. Just past the gas station, I had the strange sensation that someone was following me, but I ducked behind some trees before determining the feeling was just my mind playing tricks.

At home the television was running, and my mother snored on despite its blaring. I sat down and watched for an hour or so as the woman gutted a chicken. I had never seen such a demonstration: smiles and hot ovens; glaze and maraschino cherries. The woman's jubilation was more than I could bear, but I was too tired to change the channel. Beside me my mother snorted, and then rolled over, her raincoat falling to the floor.

For the rest of the weekend, I didn't see Marcia. My mother got up from the couch only long enough to stumble into bed, and I spent one lonely night and much of the next day watching a film marathon on the public television network and trying not to think of Lee.

In the middle of Sunday night I woke to a crash. I sat up with a start, and then put my feet on the carpet. "Lee?" I whispered.

There was a bang, followed by a series of loud curses, coming from the far end of the house. "Where is it?" I heard my mother yell. "What did she do with it?"

I groped blindly for my slippers. The noise was coming from the bathroom. More crashing followed – the sound of objects being thrown at the floor.

"You girls," she bellowed. "You don't care about anyone but yourselves. You don't know how hard life is without something to – I just need one little –"

I stood up and feebly closed the curtains, worried that she would wake the neighbours. I also didn't want her reported to the police.

"Ronnie? Can you help me? Do you know what she did with it?"

Suddenly her footsteps were coming down the hall. I sprung to the door and wedged my trunk under the knob.

"Ronnie?" she said again. She rattled the door, slamming it against the trunk in an attempt to get inside.

After a number of tries her voice collapsed into a wreck of unbearable sobs. "Ronnie? Hon, don't you want to help your mum? Don't you want me to feel better?"

I didn't say anything. Inside my bedroom was a mess of unwashed covers, dirty clothes, magazines open and discarded along the heat vent; hand-me-downs smelling of mothballs and someone else's body odour spilled out of the closet in black plastic bags. I stared for a moment, unable to recognize any of it.

At length the sobs receded. I went back to bed and lay awake for a long time, thinking of Lee, the cluster of hairs at the crown on his forehead, the way his mouth lifted into an easy smile. I wondered if he had found Raven's, and if he had, what he thought of the dark hallways and cedar-scented interior. Was he warm enough? Did he have enough to eat? Mostly I wondered if he was as lonely as I was.

In the morning, my mother did not get out of bed. I checked on her briefly. Her breathing was shallow and her mouth was frozen into a slack grin. If I had been thinking straight, I might have remembered that today was Monday. My mother worked Mondays, and usually she was already halfway to the real estate office by now. But I had other things on my mind. I walked down the sidewalk thinking of Lee. It seemed impossible that I would not see him again, yet equally impossible that I would.

Concentrating at school was difficult. Heaters hummed; teachers and students moved back and forth like a network of ants on a hill. I walked aimlessly through the chaos – to the lobby and the cafeteria, past the smoking area where Janice Polanka had taken to smoking Virginia Slims – trying to act as normal as possible.

By the time I reached the library, I was starting to seriously consider the idea that Lee might freeze to death. Hypothermia, I knew, was obvious to the outsider – the shivering and shaking of the limbs, slurred speech and sometimes convulsions – but for the victim, the illness came quickly, deranging judgement, transforming reality into a bleak and blurry euphoria. I had once heard my father describe a friend's behaviour as "insane" when he had gotten himself a little too wet on a snowshoeing expedition. I prayed that Lee would remember where to find the winter sleeping bags, and that if the weather was bad, he would take the chance and light a fire.

When the noon bell rang, I went to my locker. I was rummaging through my school bag when Marcia took me by the elbow.

"Ronnie," she said. "Come with me."

I felt nothing for a moment before filling up with rage. "Where have you been?" I shouted, shaking myself loose.

Marcia looked over her shoulder and spoke again in a whisper.

"That doesn't matter," she said, hushing me with her voice. "Get your books and come on. We've got to sign you out and go somewhere. We should go now."

"I'm not going anywhere with you."

She looked hurt but not surprised. "Listen," she said. "Mum's in the hospital. I found her this morning, unconscious in her bed. Louis is waiting in the lobby and he'll take us both if you want to see her. We're going in a few minutes, so if you want to come, you might as well come now."

The ride to the hospital was a long one. Shelter Bay General was located only ten minutes from the downtown spit, but Louis drove slowly, nosing the Lincoln along the road as if testing the engine. The last time I had been in the Lincoln, I had been leaving Raven's for good. The smell of leather and *Old Spice* reminded me of that day, almost a year ago, when I had said goodbye to my father. I felt my stomach sicken with grief. Eventually I realized Marcia was talking.

"– I was at the house to pick up some clothes, and I thought I had come at a time when Mum would be at work. But then I heard something coming from her bedroom, something quiet. I went in and found her. Around the far side of the bed were her pills, but this time, they were empty. I'm not sure where she got them, because I had thrown them all out two days before."

Her voice faded, and I heard her murmur something about an overdose. Marcia had been staying with Louis over the weekend, and she ran out to get him from the car. They called the ambulance together.

"After we found out she was going to be all right,

Louis suggested we come and pick you up. She's not in danger anymore, but she isn't all that alert. Still, he thought you'd want to see her."

"That was nice of him," I said with as much hatred as I could muster.

People who think hospitals are white have never visited Shelter Bay General. On the outside, the hospital was a horrid brown. On the inside, the building looked like a paint warehouse. Colours drifted by: yellow for maternity, pink for intensive care, green and blue for geriatrics. A clutch of elderly patients hunched over wheelchairs and transport carts, watching with interest as we passed through their lobby. I kept my neck bent, my eyes following the granite tile imprinted with small specks, until we stopped in a ward uniformly painted turquoise.

The nurse at the desk smiled. "Good afternoon, psychiatric ward?"

I stared for a moment.

"Marcia," I said eventually. "Where is Mum?"

She turned around and silenced me, a thin finger held to her lips. "We're almost there."

We found my mother in a shared bedroom with a curtain drawn halfway around her bed. The scene was grim: zero flowers, the unmistakable smell of urine rising from a bedpan. Through windows bare of everything, save a thin grate obscuring the view, a wash of pale light leaked across the speckled tile. At the edge of this light lay my mother, her eyes closed in an expression of peace. A nurse fumbled with a blood pressure cuff.

"Hello," the nurse said to us. She touched my mother's arm. "Alice, you have visitors."

My mother opened her eyes and took in Louis, my sister, and me. She forced a weak smile, and then she closed her eyes again. "Hello," she whispered.

"She's heavily sedated," the nurse said. "Don't let that bother you. She can't have a full conversation but I'm sure she's glad to see you." She touched my mother again. "Aren't you, Alice? Your lovely daughters? I always wanted daughters. But you never know what you're going to get. You're a very lucky woman, in more ways than one. See how many people you have depending on you?" She turned to us and smiled. "The doctor will be around in a minute, if you'd like to have a word."

We waited in the lobby. The air felt close, and patients wandered in and out – barefoot or in housecoats – across the boot-chipped tile. I was fingering absently through a medical journal when a picture caught my attention. The advertisement showed a tired housewife, her hair rolled into curlers, looking demonically at a sink full of dirty dishes. Across the picture ran the bars of a jail cell. "You can't set her free," read the text. "But you can give her something to help her cope. Diazepam."

The doctor greeted us with a nod. He was a thin man with the beginnings of a moustache. He wore beige slacks and a wide, unavoidable tie. "Louis," he said. "I'm glad that you could make it back. As you can see, we are out of the woods in terms of emergency. Alice's stomach is clean and we've got her on a solution that should see her fluids back up in no time. All the same, we're going to have to keep her here for observation."

Louis nodded and fidgeted with his keys. "Thanks very much, Phil. I appreciate your directness. Alice has been going through a rough time. We'd like very much to get her well again as soon as possible."

Phil nodded. "Of course you would. But there's some other issues to deal with – at least, we think there might be." He went on to talk at length about things I didn't understand: blood levels, a shortness of breath that seemed somehow related to my mother's eating habits. He was also concerned about her sensitivity to light, her lack of nutrition and her incessant need for sleep. He talked directly to Louis, but Marcia and I listened in. At some point I became impatient.

"What's wrong with her?" I said at last. "Why is she here?"

The doctor turned and looked at me. Louis piped up. "Phil, this is Alice's other daughter, Ronalda. She just saw her mother for the first time. She's worried, obviously."

Phil nodded. "Hello," he said. "Well, I've already explained this to Louis and your sister, but it seems as if your mother took too much of her prescription medication. What we need to find out is exactly how that happened."

I stared at the doctor. "What do you mean?"

He cleared his throat uncomfortably. "These are

difficult issues. I knew your mother because she came here a number of times. She complained about feeling unwell, and we always referred her to her doctor, who, of course, knew her complete history. In the absence of any real illness, that is our job."

We waited for him to continue.

"Now, I don't like to point fingers. Your mother has been suffering from considerable nerves over the past year. Her grief, I understand, is enormous. And these prescription medications are supposed to help keep that under control, help her get some sleep and cope with her life as a working woman. But when we have accidents like these, we have to look seriously at what's best for the patient. For now we'll just have to play it by ear. Keep her on regular meals, and then we'll see. Eventually she'll be well enough to go back home."

"How long will that be?" Marcia asked.

"Could be a few days." The doctor said. "A lot depends on how quickly she responds to treatment, but we'll know more in the coming hours. I understand Alice is a strong little woman. She's just gotten off track."

After the doctor had left us, I turned to Marcia and said, "What did he mean about Mum coming here before?"

Marcia remained silent. Louis coughed again and looked at me. "From what I understand," he said, "your mother came here a number of times but the doctors weren't able to help her. They gave her a good stiff coffee and sent her home to bed, which was really all they could do, considering the circumstances."

I ignored Louis and talked only to Marcia. "What circumstances?"

Louis continued. "She wasn't really sick."

"I was talking to my sister, thank you very much," I said to Louis. I remembered my mother's absences, the evenings and afternoons that she spent who knows where. At the time I had thought she was at work, or maybe at a bar or the liquor store. I had never expected her to be loitering around the hospital waiting room. I said to Marcia: "If she wasn't sick, then why did she come here?"

"She was drinking, Ronnie," Marcia said. "They think she wanted attention."

From inside one of the rooms, the disturbed hollers of a woman erupted with a shriek. There was a clatter of dishes, followed by a cry for help and the scurry of orthopaedic shoes. By the time the orderlies had subdued whichever patient had been making the fuss, Louis and Marcia had already walked halfway down the hall and around the corner.

We drove home in silence, passing the scenery we had regarded one hour before. It was like a movie on rewind: hospital parking lot, shady driveway lined with alder trees; then down the highway to the golf course, past the old row houses where children hung around before heading back to school. But the movie stopped too soon. I wanted it to go all the way back to Raven's.

I stared coldly at Louis's head, trying to recall the

exact moment he had come into our lives. The back of his hair was slick and layered, cut to the nape of his freckled neck. His ears stuck out at odd angles, and as he turned to offer Marcia a Kleenex, I saw the flash of his profile, his heavy jaw and pointed nose. Like all of his gestures toward my sister, his offering unsettled me. I wanted to cause him pain.

When the car ground to a halt, I was surprised to see our Shelter Bay house at the end of the sidewalk. Louis turned around and put his arm on the back of the seat. "I don't like leaving you both alone at a time like this, but as I've told Marcia, it's not really appropriate for you two girls to stay with me. People are already talking about your family, and we want to keep things as private as possible. I'm arranging to have someone come and stay with you as soon as possible. And you know that I'm only a phone call away."

Marcia nodded. "How do you feel about that, Ronnie?"

"Fine," I said coldly.

Louis paused and jangled his keys in the ignition. "You know, you'll have to listen to your sister, Ronalda. She's older, and she has a good head on her shoulders. By tomorrow we'll make sure you have some help."

I stared at the back of his elbow, which was draped over a plush seat cover. At some point Louis must have refitted the benches with these wraparound protectors. I twanged one of the elastics with my thumb. I wanted to shoot it at his head.

"Well then," he said. "We're agreed."

There was nothing more to say. I waited while Marcia gathered her things. I needed her to release the catch on the door so that I could get out of this two-door rattrap.

"You don't mind," Louis went on, "if I have a word with you, Ronalda?"

I watched as my sister slithered out the door and made her way up the sidewalk. I had demonstrated that I wasn't speaking to Louis. Unfortunately, he kept right on talking.

"I'm a little worried about your visits to the marina."

The skin on my back prickled with nervousness. There was a gaping hole of silence as I attempted to gather my wits. Louis waited until I responded. "What visits?" I said defensively.

"Ronalda," he said. "I saw you walking down the road one day. I was going to offer you a lift when you turned into the marina." He sighed and jangled his keys. "And I know you went there again, just the other night. I know you didn't come home until morning."

I tried to bite my tongue, but my arrogance was overflowing. "What did you do, sleep in your car?"

"No," he said in a measured voice. "After her fight with your mother and after your mother had gone to bed, Marcia waited for you to come home. She waited until midnight, and when you didn't return, she called me and asked for help. Naturally I told her to calm down. You were probably taking a walk the way your mother used to, trying to clear your head. Still, we were worried about you. Fourteen and out at night. I took Marcia back to my house so that she could get some rest – I invited her to stay for the weekend – and in the morning I followed a hunch to the marina. There's a small café, not very far from the docks, with a good view of the water. I eat there quite regularly, as a matter of fact, and this time I happened to see you climbing out of one of the boats." He paused, and let the full effect of his discovery sink in.

I sat quietly for a moment, wondering what to say; a sickening guilt passed over me now that my carelessness had endangered Lee.

"I know things haven't been easy for you at home," Louis continued. "So I'm thinking you have found yourself an understanding friend. You visit the marina as a sort of escape from reality. Is that true?"

"Maybe."

"And would this friend be a boy?"

I paused, gauging how much he knew. "I don't have to tell you that."

"No," he said, "you don't, though I had hoped you would feel safe enough to confide in me. Ronalda," he leaned in to the upholstery. "You are young. It's easy to make mistakes, and I just don't want to see you get yourself into trouble."

With a relief I saw the kind of trouble he was talking about. Janice had mentioned it often enough: young girls, dropping out of school after conspicuous bouts of first period vomiting in the women's washrooms; young, stupid girls, swelling up like melons after a series of ill-planned trysts.

"I know more than you think I do," I said with disgust. "I don't need your advice."

"For everyone's sake," Louis said, "I hope that's true."

# Chapter 12

It rained all week, the driving, torrential kind that comes down in sheets from a dark grey sky. Drains clogged; gutters overflowed. The drone of sump pumps started to fill the air. Everywhere I went – to school and back again, down to the corner store – people complained about the weather, sharing a common grumble or shaking their heads in disbelief over how it *never rained this much* in as long as they could remember.

I spent the week living in fear that Louis would find out about Lee, that he might corner me, force me into another round of questions. I tried to avoid him, to ignore the stare of his cool eyes, which seemed to watch me even when he wasn't around, and I moped in my bedroom while rain pounded the roof. I became surly and mean-mouthed, glowering at Marcia and speaking only when I could cut her short. I had so much dirty laundry that I pulled the plastic bags of hand-me-downs from the back of my closet. I wore a pair of blue jeans and an old sweater and walked around smelling of mothballs.

In my mother's absence the situation at home had gone from bad to worse. Louis had hired a live-in house-keeper, a stout woman named Mrs. Cunningham who spent her days ransacking cupboards and stealthily bemoaning the mess. She cooked up plates of boiled vegetables – soggy and wilting in puddles of stew – and served them with slices of rubbery meat.

"You girls," she would say. "You need your three square meals a day. I don't know how you expect to grow into mothers if you don't get your vitamins. Nobody's going to look at you twice if you look like sticks."

In theory, I knew she wasn't to blame for our circumstances, but I was embarrassed and furious that a stranger should be allowed into our private affairs. Mrs. Cunningham was thorough. She had an industrious, military efficiency, and more than once I found her bent over the dust mop, straining against her apron strings as she attempted to whisk something from under my mother's bed. I didn't know what my mother stored under there, but I was fairly sure she kept more than dust balls.

Whatever it was, it bothered Mrs. Cunningham. She refused to sleep in my mother's room and lay down instead under a thin sheet on the living room sofa in a filmier version of the housedresses she wore during the day. She was up before dawn and asleep long after midnight, though once, when I tiptoed to the refrigerator to get myself a snack, I saw the gleam of her curlers in the moonlight. I noted with some satisfaction that Mrs. Cunningham snored, just like my mother.

One day, when both Marcia and I were in the kitchen, Mrs. Cunningham clanked her way in, carrying an armload of bottles. She set them down on the table and made a loud harrumph.

Marcia raised an eyebrow. "Where did those come from?"

Mrs. Cunningham pursed her lips. "I found that one in the toilet tank, and that one," she said as she pointed to an empty gin bottle, "behind the hot water heater."

I looked at Marcia as she calmly wiped a hair from her eye. She was quiet for a moment before saying into her cereal bowl, "Thank you, Mrs. Cunningham. I didn't know about those ones."

I didn't know what Louis had told Mrs. Cunningham about my mother. A story about a burst appendix had been making the rounds among some people, but Mrs. Cunningham wasn't likely to believe that. Before she discovered the bottles, she had avoided me in the hallways, talking to me only when a meal was on the table. Now I felt the weight of her glances, of her roving eye that peeked out from beneath a severely coiffed hairdo and whipped away when I turned around to face her. She was obtrusive and menacing, preoccupied with rooting around our house. By the end of the week, the kitchen shone; appliances sparkled with crisp reflections and the house smelled of Spic and Span. The rooms took on a ghostly quality, a sense of disuse and order that I had seen only in the houses of old ladies, and when I walked too close to the windows I was assaulted by the smell of vinegar. I couldn't shake the feeling that something was wrong. Eventually I realized Mrs. Cunningham had erased my mother.

Since our first visit to the hospital, both Marcia and I had returned twice. My mother lay in her bed leaking the same brief smile, raising her hand in a limp gesture that looked something like a salute. She didn't seem to be getting better and, until I could have her back the way the doctor had promised, I preferred to stay away. Instead I thought of Lee.

I had no idea if he had made it safely to Raven's, or whether or not he was freezing to death. Several times I considered hitchhiking to Alex and Bo's farm, but I had only a vague notion of where it was located. Frantically I cobbled together an image from conversations I had overheard on *The Minstrel*: cedar barn, clapboard farmhouse on a wilting foundation; a John Deere tractor marooned in fields full of rain; dying sunflower stalks. There didn't seem to be enough to go on.

I went to school and pretended to be absorbed in my homework assignments, a few of which I actually completed. My grades were slipping, and these papers should have been an embarrassment, but at that point I could not have cared less.

One Friday, while sitting in the library next to the magazine racks, I overhead two girls discussing an article from the local newspaper.

"I think it's exciting," one of them said, "that someone as cool as that might turn up in Shelter Bay."

"Susan," the other one said. "You're such a flake. He's a criminal. He's wanted by the police."

Susan straightened her shoulders and pouted. "He's not really a criminal. So he blew something up, big deal. He did it for a good cause, didn't he? He was trying to make a difference."

"He paralysed somebody."

Susan quieted. She picked at her cuticles and blinked. "I think it's brave."

"You would."

I waited with impatience as they returned to their homework. The air in the library was painfully hushed. I could hear my heart beating and the noise of a distant pencil sharpener. By the time they stood up to leave, my palms were moist. I slunk over to the table and grabbed the paper, rifling through the mismatched pages that were scattered in a heap. *The Gazette* was a small town rag, one my father used to criticize because of its slanted editorials. Today it was full of advertising supplements, notices about hydrant flushing and amendments to the burning bylaws. I found the article the girls had been discussing plastered across the bottom of the front page.

SHELTER BAY- A California man could soon be on trial for the 1969 bombing of a university campus in Los Angeles, California, after a judge issued a warrant for his arrest late yesterday. William Arnold Passchier, 19, is wanted in connection with the bombing of the ROTC building at the University of California, which paralysed a sanitation worker and disrupted operations at the Officer's Training Corps. He is believed to have entered Canada aboard a 30-foot sailing vessel in the vicinity of lower Vancouver Island, where he was awaiting an appeal to his extradition on charges of arson, aggravated assault, and attempted murder. Passchier had been free on bail with the condition that he surrender his passport and not leave California. He went missing last April. Anyone with information concerning his whereabouts is asked to contact their local detachment of the RCMP. Passchier is five feet eleven with brown hair ...

Beneath the article, a snapshot of Lee emerged from the bleeding ink. Eyes pinched and chin heavily bearded, he peered out from the mug shot like a debonair version of Charles Manson. I didn't know he had ever been a brunette.

I slipped from the library and ran down the street, ideas jostling through my head. Most of my thoughts didn't make sense. I couldn't believe Lee was guilty of anything. He was not the longhaired freak staring out from the photograph with bug eyes and a mouth worked into a snarl. He was an entirely different person, soft on the inside, with principles and a heart. He was also the only person who really cared, and I had to warn him. I ran down the sidewalk with my school bag flapping against my legs. I turned in the direction of the marina.

Lee had warned me not to use the CB radio, but this was an emergency. I was pretty sure he would want to know about the warrant and get himself as far away from Shelter Bay as possible. In the back of my mind, I was also planning to go with him.

When I arrived at the marina, two squad cars were parked in front of the café. A cluster of police officers consulted each other around the hood ornament before separating and skulking down the docks. The one in the yellow jacket was heading right for *The Minstrel*. I didn't know what he might find inside. Fingerprints; the crumbs of Lee's breakfast. Who knew what evidence could be gleaned from a half-finished piece of toast and a coffee cup? I turned around and headed in the direction I had come, walking as briskly as I could without breaking into a run. Things were worse than I'd thought.

When I reached the house, I ripped open the front door. Inside my closet, on a set of upper shelves accessible only by footstool, my winter clothes lay parcelled into cardboard boxes: goose down jacket, mildewed waterproof pants, toque with the earflaps. I couldn't find my winter boots, but I stuffed what was left of my clothing into a khaki knapsack. I lurched down the hall.

"Ronalda? Is that you?" Mrs. Cunningham emerged from the kitchen, a dusting of flour covering her nose.

"Yes."

"What are you doing home early?"

I held up the khaki knapsack, ballooning now with layers of old clothes. "I forgot something that I needed for a homework assignment."

Mrs. Cunningham frowned. "All right then, I'll see you after school."

I stepped down the front walkway, breathing in the cool air to calm my racing heart. Leaves littered the sewer grates, and overhead clouds threatened. I had been walking for five minutes when I passed Marcia on a cross street. Cursing my bad luck, I remembered she had a free period this afternoon.

"Ronnie?" she said. "Where are you going?"

"Nowhere," I said. "I have to do some research at the public library."

She eyed my knapsack sceptically. "Why do you have all that stuff?"

I paused for a moment, trying to think of an explanation, but I was taking too long. Anger rose to my cheeks and I felt my logic blur with frustration. "Look, I just have something to take care of, that's all. Why do you always have to go nosing around everywhere? I wish you would leave me alone for once." I turned around and headed down the street.

"Ronnie?" she called, but I kept going.

I had never hitchhiked before, but I knew from my drives down the highway in our old Ford Thames that hitchhikers usually walked to the cut-off and stuck out their thumbs. Here they waited while rain came down and cars sloshed by, pinching a cigarette between thumb and forefinger and trying to look worthy of a ride. My mother had guidelines about hitchhikers: no smoking in the truck, and if they smelled like fish, she pitched them out on the shoulder of the road. I had been standing by the cut-off for almost ten minutes when a transport truck ground to a noisy halt.

"Hullo," said the man inside. "Where to?"

"Over near Sealers," I said.

"Hop in."

I climbed up the running board and into the cab.

The trip was brief. I had no intention of going all the way to Sealers, so named because of the sea lions that congregated on the docks. I had been there only once before, and remembered the burned-out bars, the strings of camp houses, boxy and identical, like something out of a comic book. In the absence of a sidewalk, rough-looking children had been playing on the road, a game involving a broken bottle. I still remembered their thin arms, the way they squeezed their eyes into a gritty look of warning.

Now I sat in the massive passenger seat while the

truck driver talked.

"Shame about them Americans, eh?"

"Pardon?" I said.

"Buying up our hockey teams like they was hotels in *Monopoly*. It ain't right, I tell you. The game won't ever be the same."

I nodded silently.

"That there's our national game. Without home teams, how're we supposed to support 'em?"

I didn't know.

"You got that right."

As we climbed over the pass and gained elevation, snow began to gather on the sides of the road. The bleak afternoon light filtered through the trees, catching droplets of moisture in beams of sun.

"Can you let me out here?" I said, as we neared the entrance to the access road.

"Here? Wha? In the middle of nowhere?"

"I'm meeting someone for a ride the rest of the way. They told me to wait at the yellow gate. I know they'll be along soon."

"O.K." He sounded unconvinced. "Sure hope they don't take long."

. Snow was falling outside the truck now. I waited until he pulled away before turning around and heading down the access road. My shoes in the snow made a rhythmic crunching. With some care and difficulty I could walk on top of the frozen crust without sinking. This saved me a bit of energy, in addition to the icy discomfort of getting snow in my shoes. I walked on in silence, watching the changes that had occurred since my family had left: a locked access gate; one or two trees fallen across the road. I noticed with some excitement a set of human tracks beneath a layer of snow. The tracks went in, but not out.

When I rounded the corner and emerged from the woods almost an hour later, I saw Raven's in the distance – alpine drift and Scandinavian rooftop, siding brushed with a layer of ice. The generator house and boat shed were barely visible from beneath a mound of snow, and the surrounding trees slouched under the weight of early winter. With a pounding heart, I stepped off the road and followed the shortcut across the lake, keeping my eyes ahead, my thoughts focused on home.

The snow at the end of the lake was moist and puckered and filled with depressions. When I got closer, I noted that the depressions were actually holes, a network of breaks in the ice that Lee must have been using to fetch water. The effect was of a lacy tablecloth, white drifts surrounding dark voids, the cavities so closely grouped that the spaces between became unusable, even dangerous. Beneath the crust the lake dropped off to a depth of fifteen feet. A skim of ice covered the patches of open water.

I circled around the area and climbed up onto the bank. In the snow surrounding the lodge, boot tracks made their journey to the lake and back again. I saw their tread on the steps and up on the porch in the wide arc of the front door. Then I saw another set; and another.

Immediately my heart went cold. The second and third sets came from the opposite direction, somewhere over by the trailhead. These were more recent than the ones leading from the access road, and they made me nervous. At one point they blended together in a confusing skirmish. Alex? Bo? I took a step inside and listened. "Lee?" I said. "Lee, it's me."

There was no answer; the lodge was silent and cold.

"Lee?" I said again. This time my voice echoed across the wide expanse of the entryway. As my eyes adjusted to the darkness, I saw the shadows of furniture: dark wood and oiled sideboard, my grandmother's Queen Anne side table. I walked farther into the living room until my foot stepped on something soft. On the floor, scattered next to the fireplace, lay a heap of Hudson's Bay blankets. Around them two kerosene lanterns were broken and seeping into the wool.

The smell was overpowering – the same smell I remembered from the afternoons my mother spent refilling lamps, trimming and replacing wicks with a pair of sharpened scissors. I tried to imagine what must have happened, a skirmish, a careless nap; Lee sitting in blankets, dozing when a noise outside startled him, or huddled down in the cream wool of the Hudson's Bay trying to get warm. Then he rises, a boot kicked into a lamp, the police or Alex arriving to deliver some news.

"Lee," I said again, moving through the rooms with the kind of desperation I had felt only once or twice in childhood when I had gotten myself lost: panic, a wild and furious clenching of the throat. The water in the wash basin was frozen solid, and my breath came out in icy blasts. I covered the kitchen, the parlour, my father's study; I looked inside the empty linen closet.

"It's me, Lee. Ronnie. Don't worry. There's no one else here but me. I have a message for you. You have to come out."

Nothing but the ticking of snow against the outside walls and a hollow emptiness.

Eventually I came back to the living room, to the fireplace and the fuel-soaked blankets to piece together an explanation. I righted the lamps, gathered shards of broken mantels; then I dropped them again and sank to the floor.

I'm not sure how long I sat there feeling my feet buzzing with cold, but the shadows cast by the furniture lengthened in the light of the doorway, and then disappeared. I found a bottle of half-finished vodka – something I assumed Lee had left behind – and drank it until I felt numb all over. I went to sleep.

When I woke up, I saw a man at the door.

"Who's there?" I said. "Who is that?"

The figure took a step forward and stumbled into the room. I saw with a start Louis's profile. He wore a thin pair of trousers, leather shoes and a jacket that hung to his knees. His neck glistened with what must have been sweat. I watched as he moved to the fireplace, convulsively, as if hurling himself at the hearth. His hands reached for the mantelpiece, knocking over a number of wooden carvings.

"What are you doing here?" I shouted.

He ignored me, concentrating instead on the box of matches he had taken from the cast iron matchbox holder. He pulled a folded piece of newsprint from his pocket and flattened it with his palm.

In the flare of the first match, I understood a number of things: Louis's face, half-crazed and smeared with dirt, was not sweaty but wet. His entire body was drenched with water, and I realized then that he must have fallen into the lake. He was also missing a shoe, and the gleam of his foot was like something shrivelled and dead: a plucked, decapitated turkey waiting to be cooked.

"What are you doing here?" I asked again, and this time when I spoke, he turned around and handed me the piece of paper from his pocket.

My horror grew as I glanced down at the newspaper clipping and saw the same article I had discovered that morning in the high school library on the front page of *The Gazette*: the article about Lee.

"You knew he was here!" I shouted, furious now with bottled-up rage. "You've been following me all the time and you knew! You told the police about the boat at the marina, and then you told them about Raven's because you knew this was a safe place, the only safe place left. You're the reason he's gone!" I shook my fists in his direction, but he only shuddered briefly and murmured.

"You're the reason my father is dead," I said, "the reason everything is falling apart. If it weren't for you, we would still be living here. My family would still be together!"

He lit one match and then another. Each one burned for a moment before he blew it out. By the third strike he was lighting the matches and letting them fall to the ground, tossing them away in a haste of fear and confusion. Some of them went out, but others flared for a moment on the floor.

"What are you doing?" I asked. My stomach growled, and in the dimness of the living room, I heard Louis mutter. I couldn't make out what he said, but I could tell something was wrong. I watched as the matches kept falling, as he stepped nearer to the fuel-soaked wool. With each strike his agitation grew. I stumbled to my feet, swaying in a hazy drunkenness toward the entryway. Louis muttered again, his shoe on the Hudson's Bay blankets.

In an instant the symptoms of hypothermia came flooding back to me, the hard shivering, the confusion and unexplained behaviour. My father's words, *"People do strange things when they're cold,"* echoed through the night. Louis was out of his mind with cold, and he needed my help to get it back again.

"Louis," I said, suddenly trying to reason. "Stop lighting those matches. Don't you see what you're doing? Those blankets. There's been an accident. I don't know what happened but someone spilled kerosene down there. Do you understand what I'm saying? Can you hear me?"

But Louis didn't hear me, because he turned his head like an idiot and shook his neck as if trying to clear his ears. He said something I couldn't understand, and I was closer than ever to the door. Outside the snow was falling harder. I shivered and took another step toward the flow of cool air.

"Louis, don't!"

The next match flared, and Louis dropped it into the blankets. The roar that followed was astonishing.

Somehow I was already outside, already on the porch and into the crisp new snow. I remember looking up at the stars, at the clouds moving around the moon. The sky was black, and the limitless universe – which I now knew to be cold and inhospitable – felt temporarily welcoming. I wanted to float up, to fly away; leave my body behind.

By the time I reached the highway, I was verging on hypothermia. My head and shoulders were coated in snow, and my eyes bulged beneath eyelashes frosted with ice. A car loomed out of the blackness, and in an instant I was waving my arms.

"I need to get to Shelter Bay," I said, warming my

hands in my armpits while trying to stop my shivering. "It's an emergency."

"Ya, sure," said the man in the front seat, who sputtered out a string of poorly pronounced words before coming around to, "Vee can take you. Can you help us find our way to the ferry?" He looked at his wife, who smiled and nodded vigorously.

"Do you two speak English?" I asked, before climbing into the back seat. "Do you understand what I'm saying?"

"Me, not too much," said the man pointing to his chest. "Her, not at all."

I clamped my knees together and prayed for heat. The inside of the car was better than where I'd come from, and I removed my hat to shake out the snow. "There's a man back there," I said, pointing behind us. "I think he needs help. I don't know what just happened."

The man looked confused and turned to speak to his wife in a string of exclamations I couldn't understand.

"I think I should call someone," I added, mixed up now about who I should tell, "but the nearest phone is miles away. I think I should do something, but I don't know what to do."

I heard my voice rising, and the man's face went from concerned to frightened. His wife was asking rapid-fire questions in what sounded like German. Slowly the feeling in my limbs started to return. I rubbed my hands together and slapped my thighs to get the circulation flowing. I needed to focus on where I was and what I was doing. The trouble was, what I was doing didn't make any sense.

"What ferry did you say you were looking for?" I said, suddenly wanting to divert the couple's attention from my distress.

The man looked immediately relieved. "Port Hardy." He paused and gathered himself. "I'm thinking we can make it by morning."

Port Hardy was the place where ferries left regularly for the Inside Passage. Somehow this couple had gotten turned around and had ended up driving in the wrong direction, or so I gathered. I calmed my thoughts and tried to think about directions and getting myself as far away as possible from the man who had turned Lee over to police. My presence at the lodge could only incriminate Lee further, if indeed he hadn't already been captured. I needed to get back home and find out.

"What you want to do is turn left after you drop me off," I said. "Head north for three hours. The ferry leaves first thing in the morning. You can stop at a hotel along the way. There shouldn't be snow when we get off the mountain pass."

Around nine o'clock they let me off in front of the sign proclaiming *Welcome To Shelter Bay, pulp and paper capital of the world*. I trudged the final mile to our house and crawled in the door, past the glow of the television set. Mrs. Cunningham sat upright on the couch, her head lolling forward on her neck.

My bed felt glorious even though the covers stank of sweat and mildew. I put my head on the pillow and collapsed into a tired sleep. Sometime after midnight, Mrs. Cunningham opened my door.

"Ronalda," she said with surprise. "Is that you? When did you get home?"

I rolled over and stared at the swaying room. "I don't know. A long time ago."

"Well, you missed dinner."

"I'm sorry," I said. "I had homework."

Mrs. Cunningham grumbled. "Next time show some manners and call me from the school. I don't make meals to have them rot away in the refrigerator."

I mumbled agreement and rolled back into my pillow.

By morning the news was all over town. Raven's had burned to the ground. All that wood and timber, those ancient beams blackened by time and kerosene soot, could not withstand the pressure. People had seen the flames from as far as away as Sealers, not to mention the National Park headquarters. At first they had thought it was the northern lights – crimson streaks, curtains of orange and yellow rising up into a sky flecked with snow – but eventually someone had realized Raven's was on fire. Still, there was little anyone could do. Snow blocked the access road and wind from a late-night storm had whipped the flames into something fierce. There was nowhere the fire could spread, no fire department nearby to pump water from the lake. Nobody knew if anyone was inside, but some suggested mice had nibbled on matches or a gasoline leak followed by a spark of lightning.

As the days wore on, word spread that the warden had discovered a Lincoln Continental parked in front of the access gate. The RCMP became involved and discovered the charred remains of a body. When the news got around that Louis had already missed a morning full of appointments, rumours began to fly. Louis was an upstanding citizen, a member of the Rotary club and the Oddfellows Hall, but his interests in the local mill had floundered in the wake of the water shortage. Some people inferred that he needed money, and that the insurance coverage was particularly good on a place like Raven's. Others denied all this. The deal with the National Park was almost sealed. Surely he wouldn't stoop to burning down a place he had already sold.

I stayed in our Shelter Bay house eating Mrs. Cunningham's soggy vegetables and shivering with chills and a headache. Nightmares of Raven's going up in flames plagued my thoughts, but I kept on watching the news in case there was any word about Lee. There wasn't. The whole town seemed preoccupied with Louis and the charred remains of my father's legacy, which broke my heart every time the camera flashed over its blackened hull. When I failed to track down Alex and Bo, I tried to formulate another plan. Hadn't Lee mentioned "crash pads"? There must be an underground network of safe houses that would know something about where he'd gone. I didn't know where to begin.

When the police showed up on Sunday morning, I was feeling desperate.

"Are you Alice Page?" One of them asked when Mrs. Cunningham opened the door.

Mrs. Cunningham shuddered. "Heavens no. I'm the housekeeper. Mrs. Page is not at home."

The policeman leaned in the doorway and looked at Marcia who sat on the living room couch reading a magazine. I was next to her, struggling with the lid on a jar of pickles. "Will she be back anytime soon?"

"I don't know. I'm waiting to see her. You see, she's in the hospital." Mrs. Cunningham said this in a hushed voice.

"Unwell, is she?"

"Yes. Something like that."

"Well," the policeman said, and I heard the shifting of feet on the cement walkway. "Do you mind if we come in? We'd like to ask the girls a few questions."

The police officers were congenial, understanding men of about forty and twenty-five years who stood on the living room rug in their heavy boots. A thin yellow stripe ran the length of their polyester pants, and in the pocket of the older one's vest, a walkie-talkie crackled on and off with a mix of scratchy voices.

"You girls knew Mr. Moss," the older one began. He had a pair of bushy eyebrows and a long and rounded nose.

"Yes," Marcia said. "Why? Do you know where

he is?"

"Well now, that's what we're trying to find out. I'm sorry to have to ask you these questions, but we won't take up much of your time. How did you know Mr. Moss?"

"He is a friend of our mother's," Marcia said. "He's been helping us out."

"How's that?" the younger one said.

"With money mostly. Just until we're back on our feet."

"You lost your father last year."

We both quietly nodded, and I saw Marcia stiffen.

"I'm sorry," the older one said again. "But did either of you girls know if Mr. Moss was having money troubles? You know the sort. Short on cash?"

Marcia paused. There was really nothing I could say. I didn't know very much about Louis, nothing I wanted to tell. Eventually she looked up. "Louis is very generous. He gives us a lot of things and never once said anything about needing money. You can ask his secretary –"

The policeman nodded. "I'm sure we'll do that. Now, there's just one more thing we're trying to pin down. Did either of you see or talk to Louis on Friday night?"

I was about to shrug when Marcia spoke. "I did," she said. "I called him on the phone."

"About what time did you call him?"

"I'm not sure. It might have been six or seven o'clock. It was dark. I remember because I looked out the window."

"What did you talk about?"

Marcia stared hard at the floor. She twiddled with the strings on her lace-up skirt, and I thought that she should stop or else the policeman would think she was lying. As far as I knew, she wasn't. "I was upset about my mother being in the hospital. I talk to Louis a lot because he knows how to make a person feel better. We always turn to him for help. He hired Mrs. Cunningham to take care of us until my mother comes home."

"Did you talk about anything else on Friday night?"

Marcia went quiet, and for a long moment I thought she might have misheard the question. Then she spoke. She looked ghostly pale. "No," she said. "That's all."

The policeman returned his hat to his head. "Thank you, girls. That's all for now. You take care of yourselves." He turned to leave. "And I hope your mother gets better real soon."

The rest of the day was a blur: Mrs. Cunningham fussing in the kitchen, Marcia collapsing periodically into her magazines. Outside rain pounded the windowpanes, splashing across the lawns and garden beds and making pools in the driveway. I sat on the couch and tried to avoid thinking about what had happened. The only thing I knew for certain was that I didn't want to be alone.

"Why do you hate him?" Marcia said at last.

"What?"

"Louis? You've always hated him, and he knows it. It isn't easy for him, you know."

I stared, flabbergasted at my sister. "Why do you

like him so much? That's the question I should be asking you."

"What do you mean? He helps us. He takes care of us. He's the only one who does."

I stared at the carpet. "You spend time with him when you could be here with me. We're a family, remember? He broke that up. He wrecked everything we ever had. Mom, Dad, whenever they fought it was about him." I was crying now and I hated letting her watch. "If he was gone, things would be better. You know they would."

"He didn't wreck the family, Ronnie. That was unavoidable, or it was beyond his control. Things just happen. You can't always blame them on someone."

"Let's just forget it," I said.

"If only you knew how hard he tries to help us. He's always wanted what's best."

"I don't think that's what he wanted," I said. "Not that it matters now."

She eyed me with suspicion and hurt before picking up her magazine. "One of these days you'll understand, Ronnie. And then you'll thank him. You'll see that he was the one who really pulled through."

"I don't think so," I said, throat clenching. "Louis Moss was never my friend."

"Stop talking about him like he's dead," she said.

# Part III

Part II

# Chapter 13

I returned to school on Monday, stepping into the dark hallways hushed by the solemnity of the first day of the week or the long and tired prospect of exams. A committee of grade eleven girls was getting things ready for the holidays, stringing up garlands and cardboard reindeer in the spaces between lockers. I watched them administer snow from a can onto the panes of glass in front of the guidance office. One of them stood on a chair, her long legs disappearing into the bell of a suede mini-skirt. Her inane giggling brought to mind the kind of life I used to have before my father died. I wanted that life back again.

At break I saw the squad car in the turnabout. The police were in the lobby, talking with Jim Brower who leaned back on his heels and folded his arms across his chest. His voice boomed, and I heard something about *absolute cooperation*. I turned around and headed to the library, my footsteps echoing with a foreboding click along the hallway tile.

At four o'clock, when I had exhausted my will to procrastinate, I headed down the hallway to the back door. Mr. Brower intercepted me in front of the automotive shop.

"I'm sorry to hear about your parents' lodge, Ronalda. It's a terrible tragedy, and it'll be a loss for the entire valley. I remember my father going there, years ago. He had the time of his life. Caught a big fish, if I remember correctly."

I shifted uncomfortably. Mr. Brower prided himself on knowing each one of his students by name, but it was common knowledge that he didn't always get the details of their lives right. "They didn't own it anymore," I said. "My mother had sold everything. Someone else was going to sell it to the National Park."

"I see," Brower said. "Still. If you ever need to talk to someone, I want you to know I'm always here for you. I want you to feel welcome. The door, as they say, is open." He hesitated awkwardly, and I took a step toward the cafeteria. I didn't know what he wanted from me, except perhaps a display of gratitude, no matter how slipshod; but I was tired of waiting for this show of concern. I had needed it months earlier, and now I had nothing left to offer.

"Thank you," I said, and headed toward the door.

On the way home the wind picked up, blowing leaves across the sidewalk. I huddled deep within my raincoat, feeling the events of the past few days come at me with astonishing force. I couldn't think about Louis's face, his mouth twisted into a confused grin. Where had I left him? What, exactly, had happened? When I was two blocks from home, the noise of a motor idling up behind me broke my reverie. I whirled around to see the squad car pulling up to a stop.

"Ronalda?" the man said when he got out of the car.

I stood for a moment before nodding. This man was different from the one who had questioned us yesterday, and yet oddly familiar. He wore a pale coat and a dark yellow hat that reminded me of wild mustard. He held out his badge.

"Inspector Alex Lamb. We've met before. In the principal's office at Shelter Bay High? I recall you were in trouble for starting fires. We had a little chat." He waited until I had registered this fact. "We just want to ask you a few questions."

I noticed the same young officer from the other day lurking behind the inspector. "About Louis Moss. We understand that you might have been having some trouble with him at home? That you and he didn't exactly get along? Could you tell us why that might be?"

I shivered in my coat. "Who said that?"

"It doesn't matter at this point," said the inspector.

"We're just interested in his state of mind."

"Did you find him?" I asked tentatively.

The officer ignored my question. "I understand you served your suspension following our little run-in during the summer."

I stared into his yellow hat. I said quickly, "Some of the other kids asked me to show them how to –"

"And that you used to be a very good student, but you have slipped over the past few months."

I felt the tears welling up. "No," I said.

The officers exchanged glances, and then the inspector withdrew a notepad from his pocket and started scribbling. "What time did you get home on Friday night?"

"I don't know. I was home on Friday afternoon. And then I went out again to the library. After that I went for a walk."

"What time did you get home?"

"I don't know. Eight o'clock. Maybe later. "

"Well after dark then?"

"Yes."

"And did you see anyone?"

"Mrs. Cunningham, our housekeeper, was sitting on the couch watching television."

He scribbled for a moment, before closing his notepad and flashing me a smile. "Thank you very much for your help. We'll be getting back to you if we have any more questions."

I stared after them as they rode away, the squeal of their engine following them down the street. In their wake, the pavement shuddered, or maybe my legs shook from the knee down. I couldn't tell the difference.

I went home and found my mother on the couch watching a television commercial. Her eyes were puffy and rimmed with shadows. She turned to me and smiled. "Ronnie, I'm home."

She lifted her arms in a weak arc, as if time had melted away and she was my mother again, sad-eyed and innocent, deserving of a hug. I sat down beside her and leaned half-heartedly into her jersey. She smelled of hospital bleach and mint toothpaste, of castile soap and resignation. Her usually pale face was scrubbed to an uncooked pink.

"Louis is dead," she said. A tear spilled down her cheek. She reminded me of the actresses in soap operas. In the background, the television rhapsodized the joys of effective laundry detergent. *Clean and white, clean and white, such an absolute delight …*

"Oh," I said, feeling suddenly ill.

When the five o'clock news came on the television, Mrs. Cunningham and Marcia joined us in the living room. Marcia's face was stained with tears. She sat down and hugged a pillow.

The news anchorman flashed a tight smile before rattling off a list of tragedies. Within seconds he was focused on Louis's story. "And now back to Shelter Bay," he said. "The fire that consumed Raven's Lodge is now believed to have taken the life of nearby resident, Louis Moss. Moss was a businessman and the current owner of Raven's Lodge, an internationally acclaimed resort located in the heart of the Coast Mountains. He had entered into negotiations with Parks Canada to transfer the title of the building and leasehold by donation, and went missing some time early Saturday morning –"

"Did he say 'by donation'?" Marcia asked.

"*Ssh*," Mrs. Cunningham hissed. "I can't hear."

The anchor continued. "Ellie McMurtry is standing by with this report."

The camera flashed to a small woman cinched into a raincoat. Her hair whipped back and forth in the wind. "Thank you, Travis. I'm here in front of the Shelter Bay detachment of the RCMP where details of the case are coming to light following an autopsy. Pathologist Erwin Stent made the report earlier today after positively identifying Mr. Moss at the scene of the fire."

The camera swung again, this time to a tall thin man hunched over a clutch of microphones. His eyebrows were knitted together in a look of concentration. "Yes," he was saying. "We can determine a lot by examining the remains. Investigators look for fingerprints and dental patterns, but in the absence of those, two other things can be useful. Male bones are heavier than female bones and arranged in a different composition. There are also notable differences in the skulls. Hardening of the arteries may also play a role. This occurs with age and helps narrow the possibilities. In male victims, the size of the prostate gland can be of some assistance. In this case, given the car parked at the entryway, we had something to corroborate our findings. We were able to determine quite quickly that the body was that of Louis Moss."

The lights were back on Ellie. "Stent went on to explain that his findings supported the investigator's report, made earlier this week, that the cause of the fire was indeed kerosene. As of yet there has been no word on what Moss might have been doing at the scene, though foul play is suspected. This is Ellie McMurtry reporting for *TV Six*. Back to you, Travis."

The TV flashed and then went black. I saw Marcia's fingers on the knob, her hair falling across her shoulders. She stared into the empty screen.

"How could she say that? How could she talk about foul play in the same breath as reporting Louis's death? How could she stand there and lie like that, when she knows, when everyone knows –" her voice quivered.

Mrs. Cunningham piped in. "If they had asked me, I would have set them straight. All the things he's done for the people of this town, including everyone right here in this house." She scanned the living room with a frown.

"They didn't ask you," I said.

"No," Mrs. Cunningham turned. "They didn't. They listen to shameless numbskulls. Gossips, all of them, with nothing better to do than stand on a street corner wrecking a poor man's legacy. It makes me sick. I have half a mind to call the police."

"Why don't you?" Marcia said.

Mrs. Cunningham let out a grunt of indignation and rustled out.

In her absence, my mother stirred, turning her eyes on Marcia. "Don't worry about that reporter. No one listens to people like her. Everyone here knows Louis's true character." Her voice drifted off. I watched as she settled back into the sofa, and my sister gazed out the window. I had a thought that things couldn't get any worse now that Louis was really dead, but like most conclusions I came to, I was wrong.

"Ronnie?" my sister said after dinner. "Can I talk to you alone?" She stepped into my bedroom and closed the door. Her eyes darted nervously from the window to the bedspread like a trapped mouse.

"What?"

"I didn't tell the truth to the police about calling Louis Friday night."

"What do you mean?"

"I told them I called Louis, but what really happened was that he called me."

"So?"

She huddled down on the bedclothes. "He called me looking for you. He was worried about something he'd seen in the papers, some article or other that had to do with you. He didn't tell me very much about anything, but he thought you might be running away."

"What?"

"He said something about you having a boyfriend, and I thought at first he was just worried the way a dad would be worried. But the fact that you weren't at home bothered him. I told him that's just the way you were – independent – and that you were probably at the library. He said he'd already checked and that you weren't there at all."

I digested this bit of news.

"He'd driven around to both the school and public libraries. He'd checked at the Watermark. He had something he wanted to talk to you about that he wouldn't tell me." Here she stopped and looked at me with pleading eyes. "I might have mentioned something about seeing you go off with your pack. I know it's not really strange, but he seized on the idea and got it in his head that you had run away. I still couldn't figure out why, but I remember saying, 'Well, if she went anywhere, she probably went to Raven's.'" She turned her head and stared. "Ronnie," she said. "You didn't go to Raven's on Friday night, did you? Because if you did –"

I looked at my sister. Her eyes were red and her face resembled a piece of Silly Putty that someone had imprinted with a caricature from the funny papers: bug eyes, nose swollen and red from too much honking. She was asking me for the truth, and I wasn't sure that things were as simple as truth and lies.

"No," I said. "I didn't."

\* \* \*

The day of Louis's funeral I put on a black dress smelling of somebody else's laundry detergent and stared into the mirror: dark eyes, a tense and quizzical mouth that I tried – without success – to relax into a smile. I felt a wave of paranoia developing at the base of my ribs, a hard knot like a lump of undigested potato, as well as a mouthful of stomach acid boiling its way up my throat. I washed my face with lavender soap. Then I pulled back my hair and fastened a bauble around the ponytail. Before leaving, I rubbed deodorant into my palms to take away the sweat.

At the funeral parlour, a long line of parked cars and sodden pedestrians gathered around the entrance. There was a sea of black suits and worsted jackets, of tall black boots and overcoats. Umbrellas bloomed along the sidewalk, enveloping bodies crouching to miss the rain; some of them were black to match their holders, but others were oddly festive, plaids and solids and floral pastels shining from gloved hands. The crowd inched toward the entrance.

Almost immediately we were ushered into a small room off the main gathering area, a rectangular chamber ripe with the smell of refrigerated flowers. Blonde wood panelled the walls and from a number of small tables, clusters of pale carnations sprouted from porcelain vases.

As my eyes adjusted to the dimness, I saw a lone

man seated in the far corner, toying with the skin on his bottom lip. When he realized we were watching him, he fell from his trance. "Hullo," he said, springing to his feet and offering my mother a timid hand. "I'm Alfred, Louis's brother. But you can call me Alf. The man – " he motioned beyond the closed door to who must have been the funeral home director, "– he said you'd be coming along. This is the private room. For close friends and family."

My mother registered a sign of recognition. "So you're the elusive Alfred. I remember Louis mentioning you years ago, but you seem to have disappeared since then."

Alf smiled and gave a little tug on the hat he was holding between his hands. "I went off to Montana soon as I could. Haven't been back much since, now that I have a family down there and my business – ranching actually – something you can't do much of around here. Guess I always did have farming in my blood. Some sort of genetic disorder." He laughed nervously. "You're Alice?"

My mother nodded.

"I gather you're Louis's –"

"Friend," my mother said. "I'm his friend, and I have been for a long time, though he's been like family to us this past year since my husband died. My girls were very fond of him."

I turned my head.

"Well," Alf went on. "It's been years since I saw ol' Lou. He was different, ya know, younger than me by a good eight years, and always getting into trouble." He paused and scratched his head. "When he was a kid, I mean."

My mother nodded sympathetically as the man rambled on about the good ol' days in the valley, paddling around with Louis in a dugout rowboat, jigging rockfish. She seemed remarkably composed when he started to sniff, standing on the edge of some distant abyss that filled her mind with pleasant thoughts. I wondered what kind of pills her doctor had her on now.

"Sure was an ideal upbringing," continued Alf. "But o'course, as soon as I became a man, I wanted broader horizons, so to speak. I didn't think I'd stay away, not this long, and if I'd known I'd never see him again, well, I'd certainly have come around." He turned to my mother and gulped. "He was the last one, you know, after my parents and Grandma Hazel –"

His voice broke, and I saw with horror that he was going to cry. Tears welled up in his eyes, and he let out a tremendous sob. My mother looked startled.

"Excuse me," he said, gathering himself and forcing a monogrammed hanky under his nose. "It's just not right that he's gone. I really don't know what to say."

I sat still as the organ music started up and voices joined together in mewling song. *On a hill far away stood an old rugged cross/The emblem of suffering and shame/And I love that old cross where the dearest and best/For a world of lost sinners was slain.* A number of speakers followed the opening hymn: the funeral home director, a colleague from the mill, and then a buddy from Louis's high school football team. Each one coughed a little and spoke at length about Louis's upstanding sense of justice, his love of life and his desire to help others. They motioned periodically to a glass-topped table where a marble urn held his remains. I wondered briefly if he had been cremated, or if this small casket contained all that was left after the fire.

When a member of the Rotary club stood up to speak, I felt my cheeks filling with saliva. I poked Marcia in the arm. "I'm going to be sick," I said. "Let me out."

She stepped aside as I pushed my way out of the crowded bench and down the aisle to the front door. When I was safely outside I emptied my stomach next to the concrete steps. For a moment I felt better. The rain had slowed and the air echoed with the faint music of birdsong; the grass was fragrant with moss. Then I lifted my head and saw two police officers looking in my direction.

"Ronalda?" one of them said. "Is that you?" I recognized Inspector Lamb.

I wiped my mouth with the back of my wrist. The two men had been smoking cigarettes under the yellow awnings when I startled them with my interruption. I straightened and watched as they approached.

"We were going to find you later on today, but now it seems as though you've saved us the trouble." The inspector took a final drag from his cigarette and butted it into the ground. "How'd you like to come along with us right now? I could give you something for your upset stomach. Funerals, you know. They're never easy."

I looked at them warily. "Where do you want me to go?"

"To the station," Lamb said. "We need you to sign that statement you gave us yesterday, when we talked to you on the sidewalk. It's a minor formality, but we have to have everything signed and sealed before we can get anywhere. We're asking everyone."

I looked back at the funeral parlour, at the sombre brick and wrought iron railings leading up to an empty foyer. The music from a second hymn was now pouring through the walls, bleak and melancholic like a medieval dirge. I didn't want to go back inside, but I didn't especially want to go anywhere with the police.

"I should tell my mother," I said. "She would worry."

Lamb shook his head. "This won't take a second. We'll have you back in a jiffy. The way I see it, your mother won't have a chance to notice that you're gone."

I looked at the funeral home again. I knew very little about police procedure or criminal rights, but what I did know suggested listening to police officers when they told you what to do. Somewhere in the back of my head, I believed in the power of authority to seek out justice; I believed they were telling the truth. "OK," I said.

They weren't telling the truth. Under the laws of the day, the right to go to the bathroom was not even clearly defined. I sat squirming in the squad car until we pulled up in front of the station. I clenched my toes inside my shoes.

"Here we are," said Inspector Lamb. He led me through the information area into a room with three chairs and a table. He told me to sit down.

"Well," he said. "We might as well get started."

"Can I go to the bathroom first?" I said.

He flashed me a grimace, a hard-boiled combination of raised eyebrows and furrowed skin. It was the sternest look I had ever seen on a grown man. "Not right now," he said. His voice had slipped from coaxing and cajoling into something with sharp edges. He flipped through a stack of pages on the table.

"What time did you say you got home on Friday night?"

"I don't know. Maybe eight o'clock."

"And you said you saw Mrs. Cunningham, on the couch?"

"Yes."

"But Mrs. Cunningham didn't see you. She told us so herself."

"She was asleep."

"Was the television still on?"

"Yes."

"What show was playing, when you walked in the door and saw Mrs. Cunningham asleep?"

"I don't remember."

"How do you know it was eight o'clock?"

"I don't know. I don't remember."

He scratched the hairs on his temples. "Mrs.

Cunningham says that you had been having trouble with Louis. Or rather, that he had been having trouble with you. Do you know what kind of trouble that might be?"

"No."

"Well, she indicated that Louis was concerned for your well-being, and that he took a keen interest in keeping up with both you and your sister. Can you tell us why you didn't like him when he was giving you so much assistance?"

"I never said I didn't like him."

"Mrs. Cunningham said this."

"I don't know what Mrs. Cunningham said. I never said I didn't like him."

The inspector drew back. "We have reason to believe Louis was looking for you on Friday night. Two separate witnesses have verified that Louis turned up – first at the high school library, and then at the public library – looking for someone of your description. When he didn't find you, he left."

I said nothing.

"Do you know why he might have been looking for you?"

"No."

"Do you know why he was so concerned that he had the librarian go around the study area five times?"

"No."

"Perhaps you were angry with him for spending so much time with your sister. Perhaps you had threatened to tell someone about their relationship."

"They didn't have a relationship."

He shuffled through some papers. "I have a statement from a Stephen Logier who says otherwise." He levelled his voice into a higher, more callow version of his own. "'Marcia and Louis were an item, if you know what I mean. Everyone saw them around town. Everyone knew what they were doing.'" He looked back at me.

"Stephen who?"

"Stephen Logier. He works with your sister at the Watermark Theatre. I believe he is your age, or a few years older? Louis turned up at the theatre on Friday night, apparently looking for you. Mr. Logier was on duty."

I sat back in my chair.

"He also stated that you, and I quote, 'led him to the bush one day on the pretence of a walk, and there you proceeded to take off your clothes.' Is that true?"

"No," I said, my face flushing.

"He said that you were 'known for taking guys behind the warehouse' and that you were 'really hot for it.' Is it possible that you were trying to lure Louis somewhere on Friday night? That you set up a rendezvous for –"

"No!" I shouted, springing up and planting my hands on the table. The inspector looked at me for a long moment, and then asked me to sit down.

"I think we'll take a short break, Miss Page. Please wait here." He stood up and went out the blue door. After less than five minutes, Constable Ronning stepped inside.

"Well, Ronalda," he said. "Shall we pick up where you and the inspector left off?"

They kept me squirming in the room for almost five hours. The blue door looked at first like a rectangle and then like a large and menacing gorilla. I tried to keep my eye on the window, which leaked a small amount of light in from the corridor, but my eyelids drooped; the light swam, and then faded away. Overhead a single row of bulbs cast an incandescent glow onto my inquisitors, first Lamb and then Ronning. Both of them were sallow, with stubble protruding from knobbly chins. When they opened their mouths I saw rows of green teeth, and a tongue like a serpent that lay coiled beyond their gum lines in a cool nest of saliva. Throughout the evening they took turns asking me questions, stepping from the room to let the other have his way, and then returning like the member of a relay team. Their single-minded intent seemed to be my destruction.

As the evening went on, I knew that I was getting the details mixed up, that nervousness and fatigue were taking their toll. I tried to speak in sentences, but exhaustion rattled my brain. Sometimes I was at the library, but other times, I was walking down the street, heading in the direction of the cut-off before I realized what I was saying; I detoured myself into the dark woods before Lamb could have his confession. At the end of the interviews, they had only a single sheet of notes between them.

Around eleven o'clock, Inspector Lamb informed me he had just contacted my mother.

"I called after you first got here," he said with a snide little grin. "I called again at eight and at nine, but I didn't have any luck. Why do you suppose that is?"

I shrugged wearily. "She was at the funeral the first time."

He paced the perimeter of the room, growling from the bottom of his throat. Outside, I imagined, the sun had gone down. A cheerless gloom had settled over the landscape.

"Ronalda," he said. "You have been here over six hours. It is now ten o'clock. That's pretty late for a young girl like you. Don't you agree?"

"I don't know."

"It most certainly is. It is very late. Is it not strange then, that no one has come here looking for you? That no one has called to report you missing?"

I didn't know what he was getting at.

"Let me explain. In my books, if a fourteen-year-old girl doesn't come home for dinner, if she disappears after a very important funeral like thin air, chances are her parents would be worried sick. I know I would be worried sick if my daughter did something like that. Why do you suppose we didn't hear from your mother?"

"I don't know."

"You don't know. You don't know very much. Let me venture a guess. Your mother did not come looking for you, and she did not report you missing, because she was used to you not coming home. You so rarely come home, or rather, your mother so rarely sees you there at this time of night, that she probably didn't even notice."

I cringed at the thought. "I stay late at school a lot. She might have been thinking –"

"Your mother," he interrupted, "has some trouble with the bottle, is that not right? It's not a pretty thing in a lady, I'll admit, and I'm quite sure you don't like talking about it, but this is a small town. People know these things." He sidestepped the vacant chairs.

"People talk, they tell one another all sorts of things and eventually word gets around. Your mother has a lot of old friends. There has been a lot of worry over you and your sister – Louis himself expressed that. There was worry for you when you lived at the lodge. A place like that is not safe in winter."

"My father said –"

"Your father," the inspector continued, "may have been a good man. He may have been a clever man, but he was not a smart man. There were his debts, you see, he had a lot of those, and the fact that he didn't go out of his way to make friends with local people did not do him any favours."

I thought for a moment about my father's opinions of the people of Shelter Bay. Most were not complimentary.

"Your father was different, you see, and people who are different are perceived as outsiders. The way he did things, the way he lived –"

"How?" I asked defensively.

"Louis, on the other hand, was an outstanding citizen. A businessman and member of the Royal Canadian Legion. He donated to charity. He made pancakes on Shrove Tuesday in front of the Oddfellows Hall." He paused to take a breath. "Louis had a lot of friends, people who want to help him in death the way he helped them in life. These people are going to come forward. They are already coming forward. They're telling us he was looking for you on Friday night. Some of them even saw you walking along the highway with a large packsack." He leaned across the table and looked down into my face. I could smell onions, the dregs of rancid coffee. "Things are not weighed in your favour."

I considered the knob on the end of his nose.

"But," he swivelled and raised his arms. "Let's not get carried away. There's one way to bring things back. If, let's say, Louis was hurting you or your sister, if he was abusing his power as a father figure in your life the way Stephen Logier suggests," his voice moved back to its earlier softness, "people would understand your rage. They would understand why you might try to stop him from causing more damage. Even go to serious lengths to get him out of the way." He leaned in closer. "Everyone knows how hard it is for you at home. Everyone knows life is not easy. No one would blame you for doing something drastic. No one would expect any less."

Now I could see the hairs inside his nostrils. They quivered as he breathed out like sedges in a marsh.

"We all know your father died. We know how hard that can be. And your dislike for Louis, well, that's only natural in light of your recent ordeals. The loss of your home, your mother's health. It all makes sense." He breathed deeply, lowly, gazing into my eyes as if examining them for clues. He continued. "And what if Louis knew something about you that you didn't want him to know? What if he knew you were in contact with a wanted criminal, maybe even protecting him as girlfriends are apt to do? What if he was planning to turn that criminal in and it made you very angry?" He leaned back as if he'd just delivered the *coup de grace*. "Tell the truth, Ronalda. Make everyone happy."

I shuddered, careening now on the edge of restraint. My tongue would not move and I did not know what he wanted from me. To admit that I hated Louis would do very little, save get me into trouble; to admit that I was at the lodge was even worse. I had to protect myself. I could not come clean without revealing everything, and by the sounds of the inspector's breathing, he wanted a confession of murder.

I sat in silence for a weighty moment, until I thought the inspector might be ready to let me go. I had done nothing; I had said nothing, and in theory, I was innocent until proven guilty. But Alex Lamb was not finished with me yet. He stuck his head out the door to beckon to the night guard. "Constable," he said. "Get D'Angelo in here."

＊　＊　＊

Dr. D'Angelo was a tall man with grey hair and a sagging chin. He wore dentures – I could tell by their rigid perfection – and a three-piece suit with a pinstriped waistcoat. When he stepped through the door, he flashed me a shrewd grin. Inspector Lamb stepped in behind him.

"Ronalda, this is Dr. D'Angelo. He'll be performing the medical exam, and I ask that you do exactly as he says. The sooner we can get through all this, the sooner we can all go home to bed. Wouldn't that be nice?"

"Why do I need a medical exam?"

The inspector turned. "Because we say that you do. Your mother has already given her consent, or didn't I tell you? A team of officers visited her just after midnight. Constable Ronning did the honours and she signed the necessary forms. You have nothing to worry about. Your mother knows what's going on."

The doctor gave a discretionary nod and Inspector Lamb disappeared. I looked back at the blue door, at the cool and gleaming surface that shone like a layer of ice on a warming lake. I could almost see my reflection.

"Mrs. Page?" I imagined that Constable Ronning saying. "Mrs. Page, we have a warrant to search your home. Would you mind getting out of bed?"

Even in the heat of questioning, the constable had always been a polite man, with a smile like a scolded dog and the habit of removing his hat as if going into church. By the time he had tapped my mother on the shoulder to read her the warrant issued by the magistrate, I imagined he would have been fidgeting, rapping his fingers against his pant leg or kicking his boots into the rug. Marcia would have been standing in the hallway in her Orlon nightgown. I imagined her hair braided into rope, a look of sleepy confusion and then anger as she resisted the urge to tidy my room. Mrs. Cunningham would have been long gone, sliding into a peaceful slumber at her daughter-in-law's down the street.

My picture of that terrible night, then, is cobbled together from anecdotes I heard from my lawyer, and from a blow-by-blow my mother gave me later through a glass partition. The search lasted a half an hour, with a team of officers poking into crevices and cracks in the kitchen, bathroom, and my room. Items of clothing were held aloft; a number of treasures were sniffed and then stolen away in plastic bags. Later, when my case came to trial, the prosecution waved these items around the courtroom as evidence of my guilt.

Back in the station, Dr. D'Angelo opened his satchel. He withdrew an ear-viewing tool, a small flashlight, and a magnifying glass with a Bakelite handle. "Well, would you mind removing your clothes?"

The medical exam was cold and humiliating. I stood

shivering in my underwear while the doctor went over my body with the precision of a watchmaker. When he came to my elbows and knees, he flattened the creases of puckered skin and examined me with the magnifying glass. I didn't know what he was looking for. I was so tired that I could have fallen asleep standing up; and indeed I might have, because the lights went out and the blue door winked on and off like a planet in the night sky. Now you see it, now you don't. I stood still as a stork, lifting one leg and then the other, my thoughts drifting across the coffee cups on the table. It seemed natural that things would end like this: strained silence, hands working over my body like small and prying suctions.

"Do you know how you came by this?" the doctor said eventually.

"What?" I asked, but my voice was not my own. Instead it belonged to someone far off, an unfortunate girl with a rattle in her throat.

"There is a scratch mark, about three inches in length, running across the side of your neck and just above your shoulder. Beneath it is a coin-sized red mark."

I thought for a moment. "Maybe walking through the bush."

He raised an eyebrow. "Indeed?"

"The bush around the estuary. There are brambles there. I might have run into them on one of my walks." I thought of the tangle of blackberries, of the dark and wooded thickets sprouting buckthorn and wild roses. Birds lived in these thickets, taking shelter in a storm by huddling between the branches and puffing out their feathers.

"Very tall brambles," he eyed me suspiciously. "You like to take walks then, as a rule?"

"Sometimes," I said.

He made a note on his pad. "And what about the red mark? Could that be caused by brambles too?"

I didn't know what to say. I had no idea what red mark he was referring to, but I distantly remembered wearing a muffler on my long walk to Raven's, a woollen tartan that gave me a rash. "Maybe," I said. "It might have – I might have fallen down and scratched myself, or stepped over a log to get where I was going." I was rambling now, ready to fall over. The effort of keeping myself upright seemed harder than giving in. My legs shook; my hands were filled with lead.

"And where might that have been, Ronalda?" the doctor said. "During a walk to the lodge? To your parents' old lodge in the mountains?"

A soft and pleasurable liquid seemed to be filling my ears, coming in through the top of my head like a rush of warm water. My eyes closed; the lights were barely on. Far off I could see Raven's, the warm glow of the cook stove and fireplace, the kerosene lanterns left like beacons in the windows. "Maybe," I said, my voice a ghost. "It might have been."

"And was Louis there? Was Louis waiting for you?" His voice was insistent now, a mosquito working at my ear. I had the idea that if he would just stop talking, everything would make sense. I would be back at Raven's, back to the way things used to be. My father would be there too. If I just told the doctor a few details, everything would return to normal.

"No," I said. "I was waiting for him."

They booked me sometime after three in the morning. Their evidence consisted of my garbled confession, a pair of footprints at the scene similar in size to my own, and a lone strand of red fibre extracted from a spruce tree not very far down the access road. During the search of our Shelter Bay house, they had also gleaned a box of Red Bird matches, the emergency magnesium fire starter my father had given me for my thirteenth birthday, wet running shoes caked with mud, and my winter clothes rolled into a garbage bag and stuffed into the bottom of my closet. The fibre from the goose down jacket appeared to be the same colour as the one from the access road.

☆　☆　☆

"Oh, Ronnie," my mother said, when she saw me the next day in the visitor's cubicle, just before my bail hearing. She looked rougher than usual, with a tangle of hair tucked into her winter cap and a lack of sleep imprinted around her eyes like an ink stamp. "Oh Ronnie, what are we going to do? The policeman told me what they think you did, and I just can't understand it. Why are they treating you this way? You're just a little girl." She took a breath, and pressed her nose into her kidskin glove. When she showed her face again I saw tears pooling in her eyes, the glaze of sedation burning off into fatigue. "If only," she said with a little sniff. "If only Louis were here."

I was remanded into custody following the bail hearing, a five-minute waltz before the magistrate where I attempted not to fall asleep. It would take one more week and three more hearings before the same magistrate moved me up to adult court for a trial by judge and jury.

"It is certainly clear that the offence is indictable under Canadian law, and that under the provisions of the Juvenile Delinquents Act, the accused is fourteen years of age or older. I am also convinced," the man went on, "that the interests of this community demand that the accused be proceeded against by indictment in an ordinary court and so I order."

I turned to the duty counsel, a grizzled man who had been designated to represent me until my family could secure a lawyer. He looked morose and disinterested. He extracted a cigarette from his foil pouch. "What did he just say?" I wanted to know.

The counsel shrugged and flicked a hair from his eye. He rifled in his pockets for a package of matches. "Just that you'll be tried in adult court, and there you may be subject to adult penalties. Not a good sign, but your lawyer will take care of everything. They don't hang 'em any more, unless they kill a cop or a prison guard." He inserted the cigarette into his mouth and slipped from the courtroom. I watched him fade amidst the stream of rustling bodies, one of the many people free to eat his lunch in peace.

*   *   *

In the days following my arraignment, eleven students from Shelter Bay High came forward with information concerning my potential guilt. Stephen Logier I already knew about, but Regina Fitzgerald, Nathan Caplan, and Donny Orr: who were these people and what did they have against me?

"Nothing in particular," said my lawyer, Lars Johansson, on the day that we first met. My mother sat beside him in a tailored dress. In her hands she clenched one of my father's handkerchiefs, pressed and smelling of bleach water. "In all likelihood, they want to be famous, get in on the gruesome act. I will disallow their testimony as hearsay and hogwash, the same way I'll disallow anything those conniving police officers managed to get out of you in that fiasco of a questioning."

I looked puzzled.

"What do you mean, 'fiasco'?" my mother said.

"Under the law, the police may question Ronalda the way they did. It is technically not illegal." He paused and picked a spot of lint from his sleeve. "Having said that, no judge in the land will permit such behaviour. There are guidelines that explicitly suggest minors should be allowed to have a parent present. They should be given a warning and told their rights. In my opinion they should be allowed counsel, at the very least. And they certainly picked her up under false pretenses, nabbing her in front of the funeral parlour with the story of bringing her back in a jiffy." He shook his head. "It's absurd. They were setting a trap. They had no intention of letting her go."

My mother looked into her handkerchief. "I just can't understand."

"Of course," Lars went on, "the police will say that they wanted her to sign a statement, and that it was only after they got her into the station and she started talking that they realized they had a suspect on their hands. It's unconscionable, but they do it all the time. Intimidation, capitulation. When they have a juvenile on their hands, they think they can go to town." He looked at his watch. "These are the very things being addressed by the new legislation – reforms the present government is trying to bring in even as we speak. Unfortunately for Ronalda, reforms take time, and when discussing anything as controversial as juvenile law, the opposition is liable to stretch things out from here to eternity. 'A bill of rights for social wrongs,' I believe the New Democratic Party spokesman called the bill. 'A half-pint criminal code for children.' I wouldn't be surprised if it takes them ten years to get this bill through the house." He looked at me and sighed. Then he turned to my mother. "Unfortunately, Mrs. Page, you should not have consented to a medical exam, but at this point, that may be neither here nor there. A doctor never has the right to question a witness, certainly without the presence of an investigating officer, and anything he uncovered will be inadmissible, I'm sure. I'm speaking in terms of Ronalda's so-called confession, which if you ask me is nothing more than a hallucinatory rambling. The physical evidence may be another matter."

My mother coughed and flashed a guilty smile in my direction.

"You could not have known how they twist the logic of the law, and being half asleep the way you were, well, it just adds to their discredit." He looked into his briefcase and shuffled more papers. "Now, we are going to have to do something about these stories circulating around town and school, and go through these students one by one to ensure their stories are fabrications. That is, I'm assuming, what they are." He looked at me and I nodded hopefully. "Good. And to cover all the bases we will have to tackle any evidence gathered during the medical exam as well, in case I can't get the whole thing thrown out. We should start with the scratch marks. And what's this about a hickey?"

My mother turned and looked at me with swollen eyes. Lars rustled some more. "Dr. D'Angelo describes a small red mark on the side of Ronalda's neck, character-istic of suction being applied to the surface of the skin. Now I'm sure it's nothing more than a harmless kiss, but in light of the scratch marks, we need to find out exactly how it got there. There is the ridiculous assertion that Ronalda was associating with a wanted criminal, someone capable of leading her into trouble with the law. But given that there's absolutely no evidence of that connection, I believe that argument will be dropped. Still, it would be better if you could let us know in advance of any mysterious boyfriends, Ronalda."

They looked at me expectantly and I felt the urge to run. I hadn't noticed any red mark, and since the medical examination I hadn't been given a mirror. I felt rumpled and unkempt. If I had a hickey, it must have come from Lee. "I don't have any mysterious boyfriends," I said.

# Chapter 14

The Capital Jail sat perched on a hill looming over a gravel driveway, clusters of hardhack, and a bright, expansive view of the Olympic Peninsula. I saw the view the day I arrived and again on the day of the preliminary hearing; then I didn't see it again. The building itself was solid and imposing, engineered from English brick and a series of arched windows that reminded me of the Shelter Bay armoury. Vast lawns led to an oaken door. Inside polished surfaces reflected light and the sound of angry boot steps.

My cell was three walls and a bed, with a ceiling full of plaster cracks. Sliding doors and locked gates with two-inch metal bars sealed me in for the betterment of humankind. The first weeks were the hardest because I had to adjust to the weak light, the stale air smelling of floor cleaner and other people's sheets; to the lineups of women closer in age to my mother than myself. When the guards walked with a prisoner in an arm hold or a pair of handcuffs, I was reminded that I could not wander freely over the concrete floor.

Not long into my stay I developed a reputation for panic attacks. I learned from the prison library that the jail had been built in 1898 and had an "illustrious history of incarceration and disposal for persons afflicted by the criminal mind." At one time the gaol administered the following punishments for disobeying prison rules: solitary confinement in a dark cell, with or without bedding, not to exceed six days for any one offence; bread and water diet, full or half rations, combined or not with solitary confinement; cold water treatment with the approval of the visiting physician. I could sense the loud voices and clenched throats, the whispered prayers and half-choked confessions meted out over a final meal of bread and stew in the presence of a chaplain. Other prisoners joked about it, but there was one woman with a cell down the hallway who was convinced she shared her bed with a ghost. Mary, as the ghost was known, was a Cowichan woman who had been executed for killing her white husband; now she haunted the jail. Nobody knew her last name, and when I asked the guard, she told me in a short-tempered voice, "She didn't have one. She was just Mary. They didn't record Indians or Chinese before 1904."

The months inched by: long mornings and yawning afternoons; nights filled with sweaty, convulsive dreams about Louis and Lee and too much heat. My claustrophobia, for that's what the doctors called it, improved with the weather, settling down into a mild discomfit, a shortness of breath and the uneasy chill of too much darkness. Sometime after the preliminary hearing, I began to appreciate my cell – its blank walls and iron gate – and the solidity and safety of regular meals, routine walks, the firm voices that told me when to wash and how long to do it. I spent a lot of time looking out my small window, a transparent glass block painted yellow that muddled reflections and shapes into amorphous blobs.

At the end of January, I took to napping in the afternoons, hiding away from the common area where other inmates paced with strict regimentation. All of us were on remand, awaiting trial or sentencing. Christmas had passed with a meal of cold turkey and tinned cranberry sauce and a half-mocked round of *O Holy Night*. My mother came by in the early morning, when I should have been opening presents like other teenagers, to look at me through the glass partition.

"Where's Marcia?" I said, fiddling with the strings on my prisoners' uniform.

"She's not feeling well."

I knew Marcia was angry with me, but there was nothing I could do to fix things from inside my concrete box. I wrote her a careful letter asking how things were going. I spent a lot of time asleep. Between the preliminary hearing and the start of the trial, I met with Lars Johansson twice to discuss my defence. He brought me papers and magazines.

"See that?" he said. "The national paper has moved on to other things. You are no longer on the front page. You are no longer in the front section." He fingered through the contents, flashing images of Pierre Trudeau with his infant son, pictures of the FLQ members who received safe passage to Cuba in exchange for the release of the British Trade Commissioner. "There is the merest mention of my request to have a publication ban in place, a request which was unfortunately denied. I don't know what to say about that – the judge obviously has his bones to pick – but the good 'news is that the judge who did the *voir dire* determined what you said to D'Angelo was inadmissible."

"What does that mean?"

"It means he won't allow them to bring up what you said in court. He didn't feel the same about the medical exam, however, mainly because your mother gave her consent." Here he stopped and furrowed his caterpillar eyebrows. "Not that the exam gave them much to go on in the first place," he scoffed. "I don't think any of that will be a problem. A small hickey, if that's what it was, and a few teenaged war wounds. The point is that we're home free. That pseudo confession given to D'Angelo was the prosecution's main link. Their case was built around it. Now they have nothing to go on but hearsay and lies."

I scanned the article; the words "girl-child" and "accused slayer" popped out. I moved my fingers over the text.

"Well?" said Lars. "You want to ask a question, I can tell. Out with it, because we have to get things moving if we want to work together."

I felt for my tongue and formed the words. "But Mr. Johansson, if some of what I said is disallowed and the jury finds out, won't I look guilty? I mean, is there any way they can find out? The police called it a confession, but that's not really what it was."

"My dear Ronalda," Lars said, putting his fingertips together the way he had done when we first met. "Just because you are pleading *not guilty* does not technically mean you are innocent. If the charge cannot be proved to the court's satisfaction beyond a reasonable doubt, whether you are guilty or not is unimportant. You are entitled to be acquitted."

I looked into the spaces formed by his fingers, which seemed very much like praying hands. I opened the pages of *The Gazette* and looked to the inside where the debate about my trial still raged. Lars talked on.

"The burden of proof is weak," he continued. "Moyers will propose a lesser charge, but that won't be enough. I may not be a star, but I know a frame-up when I see one. The police had you pegged before they gathered all the evidence –" His voice drifted and my eyes snagged on a letter.

*Dear Editor,*

*I am just sick about this whole thing. A girl killing a grown man is horrific and evil. And killing a man who helped her family is worse, by far. I agree with the judge's decision to send her to adult court. I say bring on the punishment, and since we seem to be too civilized for the death penalty like our smart American cousins, lock her up and throw away the key.*

*Yours truly,*
*A concerned citizen*

"– and that's the reason you will be free in a very short time." There was a pause, and I felt my lawyer's eyes upon my face. "Ronalda? Did you hear what I said? I am not making promises, but I have a very good feeling about this case."

I looked up into his motionless face, earnest and sun-spotted, the cheeks hanging low at the jowls. For a moment, he looked very much like my father when he tried to tell me that everything would be fine.

It is a lonely thing to have strangers wishing you death, and it may have been those words in the *Gazette*, however ill-conceived and full of small town boredom, that brought my fainting spells back the week before the trial. Whatever the reason, the walls of my cell began to once again press in around me, closing me up like an object inside a trash compactor. I lay on my mattress trying to summon the hills surrounding Raven's, the deep valley and whispering trees; trying to smell sweet balsam and the pungent odour of skunk cabbage and prevent the room from swirling. Instead I blacked out, feeling the pressure of time and space around my head. When I came to, a guard was bending over me, slapping me firmly in the face.

"Come now, luv, I thought you'd stopped this nonsense long ago. You know you're all right, that nothing's going to get you. Wake up or I'll have to report you to the warden. Here we are."

I looked into the face of an English woman who I knew from the day shift. She was kind but relentless, with a collection of warts on her chin and a nose that prompted some of the inmates to call her "old toad."

"Some bee in your bonnet –" she went on.

"What happened?"

"That's for you to tell me. Your neighbours heard you screamin' and a shoutin'. Seems as though you thought you were on fire or something like tha'. Smelling smoke and all, running around telling everyone to get out. You tried to get ou' yourself, and then you keeled over. Hit the floor like a bag o' sand. You'd better be careful, luv, or you're going to be black and blue."

I looked into her eyes. On the air I could smell her eau de cologne and close-range armpit sweat. Beyond that, the smell of smoke faded away, curling out of my cell and down the hall like a vague and distant campfire.

The trial started in early March. I sat with my mother and Lars Johansson in a locked room, going over the last-minute developments they had neglected to tell me while I lay waiting in a cell.

"There's only Janice and Stephen left," Lars was saying from across the table in his impervious woollen suit. A set of wing-like lapels stirred on either side of his purple neck. Over his right lung the head of a pen peeked from a leather pocket. "The others have recanted, or chickened out. Apparently the prosecution couldn't bring them round to their original stories, which had grown somehow confused with the passage of time. They started adding lurid details, and eventually they couldn't remember what they had said in the first place." He chuckled softly to himself, and then forced his attention back to the matter at hand. "Now Janice and Stephen are another story, because they actually knew you once upon a time. But I feel I have a solid background on their behaviour, not to mention their desire for revenge."

"I just don't understand," my mother said. "Why would these children want revenge against Ronnie? She was a friend. It seems so cruel."

"It is cruel," agreed Lars. "But give a teenager the opportunity to belittle a former friend, and I tell you they'll take it every time. There's no reasoning with the jealous mind, Mrs. Page, particularly the adolescent one. Look at it from their perspective: Ronalda is famous. From what authorities are telling them, she may even be dangerous. Wouldn't you want to get in on the action and add excitement to your boring life if you could do it from a safe distance? It elevates you among the ranks, so to speak."

My mother smiled tepidly.

"Whatever the case," Lars said, "they do not know what they're up against. Edgar Moyers may be an excellent attorney, but he doesn't have the burden of proof to link Ronalda to the scene." He coughed and eyed me stoically. "Even if she had been there in the first place, which no one on this jury will ever know."

The inside of the courtroom was large and crowded. Hanging limp from copper brackets at intervals over the bench, flags protruded displaying the types of things you could see for real on the outside: a maple leaf; our own provincial sun rising or setting on the British Empire. The whole effect was of an indoor mall, with ferns and feathers and imported stone. The kind of environment people visit when they are too far away from the real thing, I thought. People like me.

I followed the bailiff to a box near the centre of the courtroom, a small wooden crate made up of three half-walls and a swinging gate, and sat down on a hard wooden chair. From there I could see the judge's bench and a portrait of the Queen. I thought I should feel nerves or the cold sweat of emotions boiling up inside me. Instead I felt soothed by the formality of it all. This had nothing to do with me, I pretended.

The whole procedure was like a play, with much pomp and circumstance, the sitting and standing of spectators, the gruff and heavily eyebrowed Judge Fitzpatrick peering out from metal spectacles as the jury filed in. I could hear their collective rustling and sighing as they settled their tailored suits, and their housedresses and blouses purchased on sale from a rare trip to Woodward's, into their assigned seats. Slowly I felt their eyes roll over me. I felt white and naked, goose pimpled by fear and a waft of cold air that followed them in the door.

I had chosen to wear a blue turtleneck and a corduroy skirt, and had pulled my hair back into a ponytail to reveal the little fat left in my cheeks. My mother had thought a reminder of my age would be a good idea, though Lars had waved her off. "She's a sweet young thing," he had said. "Anyone can see that. She can wear what she likes. As long as it's not too short." Behind me reporters jostled and sparred. When their lowing finally ceased, the judge called the court to order.

"Upon this indictment, how do you plead?" he said.

"Not guilty," I whispered.

The opening statements were brief and to the point: I was a vengeful girl with murder in her heart, I was a model citizen who loved nature, I was a troubled teen, I was an excellent student, I was the product of a broken family, I was well loved and carefully monitored, I was a bad girl with no concept of morality, I was a good girl who loved my family, I was a conniving plotting seductress, I was a normal fourteen-year-old teenager. I sat quietly sweating, wondering how the jury could choose one of the two sides when some element of truth existed in all of them.

The prosecution's case rested squarely on four pillars: the autopsy placed the time of death between seven and nine o'clock. During this time, Moyers said, I was on the prowl in the dark of night without one witness to back up my story. Several witnesses saw me heading up the cut-off to the highway, despite the fact that I denied being there in the first place. Secondly, his evidence would prove I was a disturbed and vengeful girl, who lured Louis to the lodge with the premise of running away. As evidenced by the testimony of my former friends, who saw the light in time to do the right thing, Louis came to find me at Raven's, and when he did, I had a surprise waiting for him. "A very big surprise," Moyers enunciated.

The third pillar was more concrete. I was an arsonist and had been warned by the police about the seriousness of my crime when I set fires at school. Lars objected to the word "crime" and to the pluralization of the word "fire." What I had done was not illegal, he pointed out, and I had only done it once. After the judge struck the insinuations from the record, Edgar Moyers went on to summarize evidence discovered in my bedroom. All of this would prove, he proselytized, that I was like a pyromaniac at a campfire.

Lastly, the prosecution deemed that evidence would prove me to be a liar. I had told the police that I was home by eight, but no one saw me there and Mrs. Cunningham had been keeping a watchful eye on the kitchen clock in her worry for my return. There was no other reason for me to lie about my whereabouts, save the fact that I was hiding something; and he had further evidence to add to my guilt. "You will be shown pictures of the fire, of footprints that match the size of the accused. You will hear testimony that supports a conviction. Today and over the course of this trial, you will be the judge. I urge you to make a just and moral decision." He sat down with a satisfied grunt, and I saw the jury stir.

Listening to the prosecution's case was painful, because up until that point I had avoided the details. Now they flashed before me in all their shock and horror: Louis's remains, the single withered shoe he left floating in the lake. Constable Ronning described the scene as he encountered it, carefully recalling the long slog down the access road to the smoking heap of Raven's. There were footprints going in and out, he said, from several points along the road. There were some fibres in the bush. Moyers stood up and entered photographs and a bag of threads as evidence.

When Lars began his cross-examination, he nodded professionally to the witness. "Constable," he said, "isn't it true that there were other footprints discovered at the scene? Footprints other than those you have mentioned."

"Yes, sir."

"Can you tell us how many?"

"If you mean how many sets of footprints, sir, I would say that there were anywhere between two or three others."

"Two or three? You can't be more specific?"

"I'm afraid not, sir."

"Why is that?"

"Because the tracks on the deck were somewhat obscured. There were a number of prints over top of one another. There was some drifting of snow from the previous night. With the rise in temperature, some of the tracks had blended together. I would like to be more specific, but I can't." Constable Ronning gave his sheepish smile.

"I see," said Lars. "You can't distinguish how many sets of prints there were in total, but you can say with certainty that there were others on the scene. Is it possible that some of these other tracks were made after the smaller prints?"

"It is possible, sir, though unlikely," Ronning said.

"And why do you say that?"

"Because we followed the tracks from the deck into the woods heading north. Unlike the smaller set coming in from the access road, these tracks disappeared completely under the cover of snow. That led us to believe they were at least six hours older."

"Couldn't they have simply been located in a windy corner, an exposed tunnel, a place where snow gathered more deeply than on the access road? I understand the road itself is partially under cover of trees. That in itself would preserve the smaller tracks for a longer period."

"Yes," the Constable said. "It might. Though on the lake it wouldn't."

Lars ignored his last point. "So why did you not investigate the other set? Why, when you have a dead man and the possibility of arson, did you not follow up on the possibility of some other parties being involved?"

"I don't know, sir. I suppose we did investigate them, as far as they went, and then concentrated on what looked like the recent ones."

"And who did you determine the tracks belonged to, the two or three other sets that seemed to be all over the deck?"

"Squatters, sir."

"Squatters?"

"Yes, sir. Those hippie types who take over abandoned buildings."

Lars nodded. "All right, Constable. For now let's just say those two or three other sets of prints belonged to squatters. Where do you suppose these squatters were when Louis Moss arrived and shortly thereafter Raven's Lodge went up in flames?"

"Objection, my Lord. We do not have any proof as to the schedule of events on the night in question. The defense is linking Moss to the fire when we do not have any evidence securing that fact."

Lars rephrased his question. "Where do you suppose they went?"

"I don't know," said Ronning. "I imagine they left."

"Do you imagine why they left?"

"No sir. I don't."

"Don't you think it odd that a group of squatters, possibly living in a place like Raven's Lodge, would suddenly get up and leave on the same day that the owner arrives and the lodge burns down?"

"Maybe someone had warned them, sir."

Lars drew back and made display of his distaste. "I see," he said. After a moment's pause he continued to grill the constable, asking him to verify once more the details of the scene. The lone shoe – how did he suppose it came to be in the lake? – and the fibres: could they not have come from a million different sources? A scarf? A pair of overalls? My own jacket had been ordered from the Sears catalogue over two years ago, and in the province of British Columbia alone there were hundreds covering the backs of girls like me, innocents zippered into their coats by parents who likened their pink cheeks and red fabric to the dimpled Red Riding Hood. The Constable nodded and commented politely. He circled back to the lost shoe. The way he recounted his discovery, I pictured Louis's Oxford slipping from his sinking foot. I saw his cold skin, the pale expanse of his ankles as he withdrew his leg and started the march to the lodge. A sick feeling crept into my stomach.

"What do you think the shoe was doing in the lake?"

"Well, I suppose he fell in or lost his footing temporarily. When he brought his foot out of the water, his shoe was gone."

"And do you suppose," Lars continued, "that after losing his shoe on a cold and stormy night, Mr. Moss might have been cold?"

"Yes, sir. I imagine that he was."

"So might it not also follow that Mr. Moss, chilled and frozen the way he was, raced up to the lodge to keep warm? There he lit himself a fire and lay down beside the blaze?"

"It could follow that way, sir, but it's not very likely."

"Why not?" Lars asked.

"Because, the fire was not in the fireplace."

Throughout the cross examination I snuck glimpses at the jurors. Some of them seemed to be twiddling their thumbs or gazing with vacancy at the portrait of Queen Elizabeth, including a man with puffy cheeks and a pout like a basset hound, and another in green coveralls with his hair slicked back against his forehead. One of the women in the front wore a hat like a toy poodle, while another was done up in a poplin jacket. She kept her hands folded in her lap and focused her eyes directly on Lars. I imagined a tentative smile playing with the edges of her mouth, which shows how much I was projecting. When the recess came she turned to me and scowled.

The second witness was Erwin Stent, the pathologist from the newscast who towered over the stand. When he got going, he furrowed his brow and repeated his earlier intonations about the art of pathological identification. I could see some of the jurors squirming at his intimacy with Louis's prostate gland.

"And what would you say was the pathological cause of death?" Moyers asked when Stent had completed his description.

"That's difficult to say given the extent of the burn. The corpse was badly decomposed, and at that stage even identification is a challenge. But given the investigators found him lying on the couch, supine in position, my opinion would have to be smoke inhalation," said Stent.

There was a satisfied nod from Moyers. From somewhere behind me I heard my mother let out a little moan, a weak sound like the mewing of a kitten. I felt the eyes of the jury, unanimously squinting, peering out at me from behind half-moon glasses and cataracts. Their offence was absolute.

At lunchtime I ate two pieces of white bread and a package of saltines. I looked out the windows of the courthouse and saw people in the streets. Nearby a clutch of pigeons was doing a pompous dance. My mother and Lars Johansson were talking at the end of the table. Lars was telling my mother how well everything was going even though I could hear the strain in his voice, a deep warble that had developed since we had first met. He made ticks with his pencil against a list of the prosecution's pillars; my mother nodded with a faint smile. I tried to block them out, to imagine myself in a normal life with routine sleep patterns and allotted hours in front of the television set. But it was no use: I couldn't imagine away the guard at the entrance to the lunchroom, nor the acid in my stomach that had vivified to a nasty fizzle with the addition of the saltines. My life was unfolding like the fake and improbable dramas chronicled on *Days of Our Lives*.

I thought about Erwin Stent's proclamation: *Death by smoke inhalation.* Up until his testimony, I had not consciously thought about Louis's demise. I had imagined him dead, but I had not pictured how he got there, lying prone on the burned couch. Instead I had skimmed over the words *dead in fire* and *charred remains* with the ease of a speed-reader. For the first time since that night at the lodge, I pictured Louis back at Raven's, his bare foot planted in a puddle of blankets while the flames lapped at his clothes. Smoke would be rising around him, filling up the air like a nebulous curtain. For a moment he would see the door, and then it would be gone. Was that when he decided to lie down? Was he simply tired? I shook off the image, feeling as desperate as he had been.

Edgar Moyers started off the afternoon by calling on

Inspector Lamb. I watched Lamb saunter up to the witness box, bursting out of his jacket from one too many trips to the donut shop. Strands of grey had sprouted from his eyebrows and a long series of whiskers protruded from his ear canal. With his face washed and his hair combed over a partial tonsure, he lacked the former enmity I had noticed the night of my arrest. The stand had reduced him, aged him; he seemed tired.

Within forty minutes Moyers had him summing up the investigation that led him to my door: his interviews, his tireless search for truth and justice through a maze of blind deceit.

"But you saw through all that," Lars said at the beginning of his cross-examination. "You brought the defendant in, just thirty-six hours after Louis's death."

"We work fast."

"I see," said Lars. "So if you work so quickly, why did you not warn Ronalda that she was a suspect when you picked her up at the funeral parlour?"

"She wasn't a suspect," Lamb said. "Not in the true sense of the word. We brought her in to corroborate her testimony and to have her sign a statement. It wasn't until we had her down there that she became the subject of our investigation."

Lars paused. "Inspector Lamb, you had the defendant in your custody for how many hours of questioning before you decided to warn her that she was a suspect?"

"I wasn't questioning her at first. I was simply talking."

"And is there a difference, Mr. Lamb?"

"In my mind, there is."

"I see. How many hours, then, did you have her in your custody? In total?"

"Five-and-a-half hours."

"Five-and-a half hours. And during all that time, you and Constable Ronning took only one page of notes."

"That's correct."

"So what," Lars asked impatiently, "changed during all that time, to transform Ronalda from a witness into a suspect in your eyes? What changed, Mr. Lamb? I do not see anything on your one page of notes that indicates this change."

Lars expected Inspector Lamb to cave in and admit to wrongdoing. Without his interview from Doctor D'Angelo, and with the stern warning he had received at work and again at the beginning of the proceedings for his lack of standard questioning procedure, he was supposed to appear a brute. Even better: I was supposed to appear a victim. But somehow Lamb didn't falter, and things didn't go the way Lars had hoped.

"Mrs. Cunningham's testimony, which came in sometime during the time I spent with Ronalda, changed my mind. Constable Ronning contacted me with this testimony and gave me a full run-down on the telephone. I decided it warranted a full cross-examination of the witness, and later, a search warrant."

Lars looked ruffled. "And can you tell us exactly what time that testimony came in? And how long afterwards you changed your mind?"

"I don't know the exact timing of the phone call," said the inspector ruminatively. "But I changed my mind immediately."

⁜  ⁜  ⁜

More police testimony and a handful of expert witnesses took up the third and fourth days of the trial. On the fifth day, the fire chief, followed by an arson investigator, gave hard evidence that a deliberate act burned down Raven's. I tried to concentrate, to catch glimpses as Moyers entered photographs into evidence. From where I sat I made out a collapsed roof, and the remains of the river rock fireplace my grandfather had built settling into the blackened living room. I felt my heart break.

The chief was a mumbler, with two front teeth that protruded from his lips like a beaver's. The arson investigator was more articulate, with an uncontrollable moustache that threatened to seal his mouth. Unfortunately he kept on talking, and I could understand everything he said.

"That's right," he went on as Moyers questioned him. "We noticed a number of key things that usually lead us to believe that arson is involved. First off, there were burn holes in the floors. Then there were other low burn patterns, which usually means a flammable liquid was used in that area. Gasoline, kerosene, and paint thinners are the most common."

"And did you determine that any of those were used in this case?" Moyers said.

"We did," said the investigator. "In this case, we determined that both gasoline and kerosene were used."

"And were there any other signs? Of flammable liquids I mean?"

"There was some spalling of concrete, a bit of crazed glass, and of course, the collapsed bed springs, all of which happen in an intense fire. Typically deformed or melted metals show the same results. All of those were present at the scene."

"I see," Moyers said. "Thank you, Mr. Keavy. No further questions."

Lars rose and proceeded to question the investigator for over an hour. He drilled him on his credentials and on his experience with arson investigations, which seemed considerable in light of the average annual precipitation thrown in from the Pacific. He asked him to explain the minute procedures of taking samples at a fire investigation.

"Isn't it true, Mr. Keavy, that recent developments in fire investigation state that low burn patterns simply mean an intense fire is burning in the area?" Lars said.

"Could be," the investigator said. "Low burn patterns can mean a lot of things, but usually intense fire means a flammable liquid –"

"And isn't it also true," Lars continued, "that spalling concrete, annealed springs, blistered wood, and any of the other signs you testified as indicating the presence of flammable liquid at the scene are no longer considered sure signs of a liquid accelerant? That low burn patterns can be misleading?"

"If you mean they don't indicate the presence of a possible accelerant, I'd have to disagree."

"Disagree that they are not sure signs?" said Lars.

"That they are not signs at all."

"Let me put the question another way. Do you think that the evidence that you gave this court irrefutably leads to the presence of an accelerant? That there is no other cause for low burn patterns, blistered wood, annealed bedsprings –"

The investigator paused and considered. "There could be other causes. Fire investigation is not rocket science. You have to use your head at the scene."

"Not rocket science?" Lars raised an eyebrow.

"I mean, the nature of a fire means that it consumes some of the evidence. You have to go on science, but you also have to go by experience and instinct."

"And did you go on instinct in this case?"

"Some."

"How much?"

"I'm not sure. That's not a question I can answer very easily."

"All right, Mr. Keavy. Maybe you can tell me whether or not your instinct helps you with these samples." He extracted a number of photographs from his briefcase and placed them before the jury. Then he brought them to Mr. Keavy. "I'd like to enter an exhibit of sample burn patterns for the investigator's examination. These are photographs similar in size and quality to the ones entered by the prosecution. I think you will agree, Mr. Keavy, that these are examples of low burn patterns? Do any of them stand out to you as being obviously caused by flammable liquids?"

"Objection, my Lord. The witness has been qualified. I don't see what this exercise has to do with the matter at hand."

"A great deal," Lars persisted. "I'd like to make a demonstration to the jury regarding the validity of the photographs submitted by the prosecution. I believe I can shed some light onto what appears to be a very technical subject."

"Very well," said the judge after a moment. "Continue, Mr. Johansson."

"Mr. Keavy?" Lars said.

Mr. Keavy shrugged. "Without seeing them first hand, I can't really say. They all look more or less the same."

"They do?" said Lars.

"More or less."

Edgar Moyers wrung his hands.

"But isn't it true, Mr. Keavy, that you made an initial

assessment of the fire at Raven's Lodge based on the photographs of the burn patterns taken by the fire chief? That you, in fact, did not go to the scene until you had seen the photographs and determined arson to be a factor?"

"That's true," Keavy said. "But I don't make a final judgement on photographs. I just make a preliminary one."

"Well then," said Lars. "You must be able to tell something from photographs, if only a preliminary judgement?"

"Yes. Usually."

"Well, can you tell me something about these?" he held up the photographs.

"Objection, my Lord. I strongly object to this line of questioning. The witness is not on trial."

"I'm being hypothetical," said Lars. "I believe that is allowed."

The judge paused. "I'm going to allow it. But get to the point, please, Mr. Johansson."

"I will, my Lord. Now, Mr. Keavy, please tell me, in your expert opinion, the cause of these burn patterns."

Keavy looked them over. He shook his head. "Well," he said vaguely. "There could be some evidence of flammable liquids, here and possibly here. But as I said, I can't really make –"

"Thank you, Mr. Keavy. Will the jury please note that Mr. Keavy identified the possibility of flammable liquids in the photographs? Photographs which actually contain samples from newspaper on carpet. In other words, no flammable accelerants."

Mr. Keavy shifted.

"Now, Mr. Keavy, I won't keep you here much longer. I'd just like to clarify a few things. You told the court that out of the samples taken at the scene, kerosene and gasoline were noted as possible accelerants."

"I did not say 'out of the samples taken.' I said that the accelerants were noted at the scene."

"How were they noted?"

"We could smell them."

"I see. Your nose is a scientific tool." He paused for a chuckle. "You also stated that the so-called 'pour' patterns observed at the scene indicated that approximately one quart of accelerant would have been needed to start the fire. Isn't that true?"

"That's what I said."

"Did you make a note of the chainsaw stored on the first floor?"

"I saw it."

"But did you make a note of it."

"No, I did not."

"Isn't it true that a chainsaw stored on a porous carpet may leave residual signs of gasoline?"

"It's possible."

"And isn't it also possible that the traces of kerosene you duly noted could have been caused by the variety of kerosene lamps evident at the scene?"

"Not unless they were knocked over."

"And were they all upright?"

"Excuse me?"

"Were the kerosene lamps at the scene all remaining upright?"

"I couldn't say. I didn't see any kerosene lamps at the scene."

"And why didn't you see any, Mr. Keavy? We know from the past history of Raven's and from a variety of police statements that kerosene lamps were the main source of light used at the lodge. Did you not think it odd that no lamps were present when you investigated the possibility of arson leading to a charge of first degree murder?"

Mr. Keavy shifted again and said acidly: "You've seen the pictures, Mr. Johansson. If there were any lamps, they were nothing but shards of glass by the time we got there. The weight of the debris and the pressure of the fire would have destroyed them."

"So there was little left to go on?"

"You could say that."

"Mr. Keavy, is it possible that Louis Moss set this fire, if indeed it was set?"

"It is possible," Keavy said.

⋇  ⋇  ⋇

During the recess, I sat in my locked room while Johansson spouted off about the idiocy of a small town police force. "That was no investigation," he said. "That was a frame-up. It's as if they arrested a suspect and then set out to build a case around her. I've seen some pretty dull cops, but this lot –"

I couldn't listen to him anymore. My mother had come up behind me; she had taken my hair in her hands and had whispered into my ear, "Your braid's undone." Now she was running her fingers through the mass. I thought about all the people who had touched my head, gently and with great intimacy: my mother, who used to wind my hair into baubles and barrettes; my father, who grazed my head with his thumb as I curled up into his lap for another story about frostbite; Lee, and possibly Moose, who clamped down onto my scalp with a mix of panic and tenderness; and the hairdresser from when I was six, who sat me in a chair that went up and down like a seesaw. I still remember her tall bouffant, teased and fitted with a bulging hairpiece, and the way she combed and clipped around my ears, marvelling at my ability to keep still. "You're just like an angel," she had said, handing me a lollipop on a compressed paper stick. I had eaten the lollipop and let the paper dissolve in my mouth. When I had returned home I looked in the mirror and saw my brown neck, the sharp ledge of hair that had receded like a crust of ice. For the first time, I realized how easy it might be to become someone new, simply with a change of style. Is that what I would have to do, I wondered now, if I made it through the trial?

At the end of the day, I followed my mother to the

edge of the waiting room and watched as she adjusted her purse. "Where's Marcia?" I asked. "I haven't seen her in months."

My mother bent down and put her hand on my shoulder. I could feel her shallow breath, the rush of lilacs and toilet water. "Marcia will be coming soon. She's still adjusting, Ronnie."

"Adjusting to what?"

"She had a different sort of relationship with Louis. You have to understand that. She's upset and you need to give her some time. She'll come around."

⋇   ⋇   ⋇

After the weekend I sat on my chair and watched as the jurors settled into a bland and familiar catatonia. The reporters at the back of the room had dwindled in number. There were a few stories in the local paper, ones that Lars had scoffed at over breakfast. "Girl Seems So Normal, But Is She Savage Murderer?" one of them read. Perhaps I was less of an interest now that I had refused to testify.

In the afternoon, Moyers called on the witnesses from Shelter Bay High. It was a strange thing to sit in that wooden box and listen to Janice Polanka give evidence against me. I could expect that from Stephen, though even he had exceeded my expectations when he told the jury I lured him into the bush with the promise of showing him some frogs. "Imagine my surprise," he had said with his leering mouth, "when she started to take off her clothes. She was like that with everyone."

"Every lawyer has a lying witness," Lars had said after Stephen's testimony. "You always hope it won't be the case, that what they're saying is as good as true, but you can never really know for sure. Stephen is the prosecution's lying witness. I thank God he is the only one."

"Who's ours?" my mother said.

Now I listened with feigned detachment as Janice told the courtroom of my faults: that I was suspicious and no one liked me, that I was a crazed sort of person who spent all her time in the bush, that I thought myself better than everyone else, and that I had told her – on two or three separate occasions – that I hated Louis and I wanted to get rid of him. Her account was cruel and damaging, though some of it might have been true.

Listening to her that day in the courtroom, droning on about my wicked ways, I imagined the hurt she must have suffered, a huge and unyielding ache that I had never understood. My mother had something like that ache inside of her; so did Marcia.

"But wasn't she your friend?" Lars asked her, when the time came for his cross-examination.

"No," Janice said. "She was never my friend. I just knew her, that's all."

Lars looked perplexed. "But Janice, teachers tell us that she was your friend. They say you were inseparable, at least for a while, and that you did almost everything together during the early days of summer school."

Janice looked chastened.

"Think hard. I know it's difficult to remember, but it's important that you do your best."

She bit her bottom lip, and then made a show of thinking back. "Well," she said. "Maybe for a short time, but then she got mean." .

"How did she get mean?"

"She stopped talking to me, and when I saw her in the school yard she walked by me like I didn't even exist."

"Isn't it true," Lars said, "that Ronalda started helping teachers during break and recess and that's why she was no longer available?"

Janice bit her lip again. "Yes, but –"

"And isn't it also true that you had Ronnie start the fire in the schoolyard because you thought it would make you more popular?"

"Objection, my Lord."

Lars rephrased his question. Janice's birthmark burned a bright red under the wave of her curled bangs. She looked sad and vulnerable, and for a moment I wanted him to stop.

"Miss Polanka. Have you ever been in trouble for lying? At school, I mean. I'll remind you that you are under oath, and that you stated very clearly that you understood the implications of swearing before the court at the beginning of your testimony."

Janice trembled and pulled her lip all the way into

her mouth. She thought for a moment before saying quietly, "Yes, but only once or twice. And I didn't mean anything by it."

"Thank you, Miss Polanka. Those are all my questions."

By the time the librarian and Mrs. Cunningham took the stand, one of the jurors, an elderly man, had fallen asleep in his seat. The judge urged the prosecution to continue so we could all go home for dinner.

"He's pushing for a marathon," said Lars. "That may be in our favour."

The testimony of both women seemed an exercise in confusion. The librarian could not say one way or the other whether or not I had been at her branch on the night in question. She did recognize that Louis had been agitated, and that when he asked for me, she did a search through the stacks and carousels and discovered I was not there. Mrs. Cunningham said that my entire family was deranged. She based her denunciation on the liquor bottles in the toilet tank, on the mould growing in the refrigerator, and on the quantity of dirt lingering under the beds. *Would any God-fearing family live in a place like that?* she asked the courtroom, her bosom jiggling inside her elasticized girdle. She went on to explain that she had never seen a house in a sadder state of affairs, and that Louis had taken us on out of the goodness of his character. I must have been lying when I talked about coming home at eight, Mrs. Cunningham affirmed, because she had been sitting on the couch the entire evening and hadn't heard a peep.

Lars dug almost at once into the timing of the evening. Mrs. Cunningham said she had been sitting on the couch for over three hours. What were the programs she had been watching that evening and what exactly had happened? Had she ever gotten bored or dozed off during the commercials when nothing exciting was going on? No? Never? Could she honestly say, in all God's truth, that she had never fallen asleep on the couch, not even once?

The last witnesses for the prosecution were people who had claimed to see me walking down the street on the way to the cut-off. Some of them were familiar in an over-the-counter sort of way: I associated them with grocery stores, bank lineups, and long and tedious outings to the hardware store. Others were strangers – a garage mechanic and a floral designer – who thought they had seen me but couldn't really be sure. I was like so many other girls, Lars had them admit, with my Barbie-issue hairdo, my small nose and plain features etched into my face beneath a white and gleaming forehead. Add a pair of long pants, a puffy jacket, and a toque with earflaps, and could they really be sure?

"I'm quite sure," said the floral designer, nodding in my direction.

"Quite sure, but not absolute," Lars emphasized.

I didn't know what had happened to the truck

driver or the German couple on their way to Alaska. Perhaps they were hidden away somewhere, out of reach of the newspaper and television reports. Perhaps they still thought I was a good girl.

At the end of the day, after Lars had finished his rebuttals, the guard led me to a room where I sat with a younger version of Queen Elizabeth. This time, she was apple-cheeked and stylishly poised, smiling out at the bright uniformity of her future which would no doubt be chock full of royal balls, jewelled tiaras, high teas, and games of croquet. She didn't yet know about the Second World War, or the way it would blow her country to smithereens.

# Chapter 15

Lars opened the defense's case by calling on a fire investigator, a man by the name of Eldon MacIntyre who worked for a private insurance company carrying out arson research all over the province. He was a specialist with a bow tie, and a little tuft of hair that sat on his head like a topknot. I thought he looked like a circus performer or a travelling encyclopaedia salesman.

"Mr. MacIntyre, you have read over the fire report concerning the destruction of Raven's Lodge. Evidence of holes in the floor, low burn patterns, blistered wood, among other things. In your opinion, what do these signs represent?"

"Not very much," MacIntyre said. "We used to think that signs like that meant an artificial accelerant was used to ignite the fire, but fire investigation has come a long way in the past few years. Some of our previous assumptions have been ruled out as 'old wives' tales.'"

"Old wives' tales?" Lars said. "Can you give me an example?"

"Yes," MacIntyre said. "Holes in the floors. These can be caused by an artificial accelerant poured directly on the floor. They can also be caused by radiant heat from furniture that is burning above an area or where the ceiling had been breached. Floors can also be charred when a fire reaches the point of flashover."

"Please define 'flashover' for the court."

"Flashover is a transitional stage of a fire from growth to its fully developed stage. After flashover, a fire spreads rapidly through doors and windows, consuming furniture and everything in the area. When a fire reaches flashover, the floor and carpet will be exposed to high levels of radiant heat. These levels may leave burn patterns on the floor."

"I see," said Lars. "Anything else?"

"We used to think that a very rapid burning fire meant that someone gave the fire a helping hand. Now it's not that obvious. Fires can burn rapidly when there are quick-burning items in the room. Things like curtains, upholstered furniture, shag rugs."

"And to your knowledge, were any of those items in the lodge?"

"I can't say."

"Why can't you say?"

"Because in the report, the report submitted by the fire investigator, there was no mention of furniture configuration. No mention of what was on the ground. No samples taken of any kind."

"Is this unusual?"

"I would say it is. Some officers go on smell for an initial test, but they usually use the lab to back them up. It's extremely important that investigators document specific items – couches, bedsteads, hanging drapes – to make it possible for others to duplicate their research."

"And did Mr. Keavy document such items?"

"No, he did not."

"So we have no way of confirming his findings."

"Not on the information that I've seen."

Lars smiled. "Now, Mr. MacIntyre. Mr. Keavy also made note of 'pour patterns' that he believed called for a quart of accelerant. Do you agree?"

"I've seen the patterns he's referring to. First of all, I'd like to make it clear that I do not agree that these are so-called 'pour patterns.' As I said before, the nature of the investigation and the lack of samples cannot determine that beyond a reasonable doubt. Secondly, to cause the extent of the pour patterns Mr. Keavy claims to see, you would need at least ten quarts of flammable liquids. But I'm not seeing that here."

"What are you seeing?"

"Well, ten quarts poured on the floor would leave a

considerable amount of evidence."

"What kind of evidence?"

"Evidence on the ground. Evidence on the defendant. It's very difficult to douse a place in flammable substances and not have any splash marks on your shoes and pant legs."

"And in this case the defendant did not?"

"Not to my knowledge."

"Thank you, Mr. MacIntyre. I just want to pursue one more line of questioning. A number of people we have heard from over the past week have indicated that the fire was 'suspicious.' How do you respond?"

"I don't know how to respond. It is my belief, and the belief of the International Fire Investigators Association, that people are suspicious. Fires are not. Either a fire is incendiary – that is, helped along by a person – or it is electrical, chemical, or natural."

"In your opinion, what caused this fire?"

"I don't know. I don't have enough information to make that judgement. People hate to declare a fire's cause unknown, but sometimes that's just what it is. There's no dishonour in that."

"But if you had to make a guess as to probable causes –"

"I would name any number of things: mice nibbling on matches; spontaneous combustion of a stored gasoline tank; the ignition of those newfangled plastics in the CB radio, provided the radio had first been turned on; and possibly a liquid accelerant like kerosene or gasoline poured or spilled on the floor and furniture by an intruder."

"Someone like Mr. Moss?"

"That is a possibility."

After taking a few pot shots at MacIntyre's credentials, Moyers began his cross-examination. His nostrils flared, and on the back of his neck a flush developed like a crimson collar. Wasn't it true, he said, that the fire could not have been electrical, seeing as how there were no electrical appliances or wiring of any kind? Yes, MacIntyre nodded. That was most certainly true. Wasn't it also true, Moyers said, that a chemical or natural fire was very unlikely under these circumstances? No, said MacIntyre. In the presence of so many combustibles, so many accelerants and aging components, lab samples would need to be taken; without them, his guess was a shot in the dark.

"Is it possible that in some cases, burn patterns from liquid accelerant remain after flashover?"

"That is possible," MacIntyre said. "But you are asking me to make decisive statements, beyond a reasonable doubt. With burn patterns, I'm afraid things are just not that conclusive. Maybe one day they will be, but not yet."

Moyers slouched and looked at the clock. He tried a number of other tactics, most of which produced little more than grumbling acquiescence or a cagey nod from Mr. MacIntyre. Lars chuckled, fidgeting in his seat like the child I was supposed to be. Eventually Moyers gave in. "Thank you, Mr. MacIntyre. I have no further questions."

The day Marcia testified the jury perked up; the woman with the scowl even smiled. Here was someone almost as lurid as I was, only she was vastly prettier with straw-blonde hair and a tragic mouth. Her floral-print dress billowed out around her, and as she walked to the stand her hair rippled across her face, flowing over her cheeks like a river of honey. I was so glad to see her.

"Tell us," Lars began, "what you told me the night that we first talked."

There was a hush over the courtroom, and then the timid rustling of a trapped bird. When my sister spoke she was unlike the experts and specialists who had gone before, frowning and postulating about the depth of burn marks, the quality of fibres, the thoughts and motives and processes of the common man. She was real and heated, sitting before us in the flesh. She was the meat of the story, and I could tell the jury found her refreshing. The man with the skullcap put in his hearing aid.

She talked at first about our life at Raven's, about the family values and summertime glories that encapsulated us like a wave of blessings: the lake, the animals, the wild birds. She moved on to the grief of losing our father, a man who exemplified honesty and perseverance, followed by our life in Shelter Bay. There were struggles and setbacks, a dwindling sense of structure. When she came to our relationship with Louis, she slowed down to a steady gait, pointing out his generosity, his feelings for both of us, which were doled out in heaping portions after the life and death of my father.

"He was a giving man," said Marcia. "A generous man."

"And what about the night of his death?" said Lars. "Tell us about that."

Marcia drew back and closed her eyes. When she opened them again they were glassy, covered by a film of tears. "It was around six o'clock. I ran into Ronnie on the street on her way home from school. I was going for a walk. I had just talked to Louis and I was upset about something. When Ronnie saw me she wanted to know what was wrong."

"And did you tell her?"

"Yes."

"What happened after that?"

"She got angry with me, or at least, very upset. She said that I was lying, that I was making things up because I wanted to make her mad. I tried to explain, but I was feeling pretty terrible and I didn't have the patience. She ran off towards the estuary and I turned around and went home."

"Your sister went off towards the estuary?"

"Yes. She walked there all the time. It was a place we used to go when we were children. Ronnie had been walking there a lot, always by herself. I think it helped her to work things out. I didn't see her again for two hours. By that time I had already eaten dinner with Mrs. Cunningham and was doing my homework in the kitchen."

"Two hours? You are sure it was two hours?"

"Yes."

"And is that enough time to get to the lodge and back, let's say, in a high-speed vehicle?"

"No."

Lars smiled. "And you saw Ronalda?"

"Yes, she came in the door at five minutes to eight."

"How can you be so sure about the time?"

"Mrs. Cunningham was watching the tail end of *Front Page Challenge*. I heard the theme song start up, and the little news flash that always happens between television shows. I also looked up at the clock, which was right over the sink."

"Why didn't Mrs. Cunningham hear Ronalda?"

"Because she was asleep. I often heard her snoring on the chesterfield, and that day was no different. She had dropped off. I could hear her snoring through the walls."

"So Ronalda came into the kitchen?"

"No, she headed down the hallway. I stood up and confronted her when she passed."

"What did you say?"

"I said, 'It's not your fault.'"

"And did Ronalda say anything?"

"She turned around and went off to bed."

"Did this make you mad?"

"Yes."

"Why?"

Marcia stopped and looked at her lap. Then she raised her head. "When you have lived in a family as close as mine and everything gets blown apart, you start to get mad at everyone, including yourself. We had been mad at each other for a long time. I didn't know how else to be."

Lars nodded sympathetically. "Marcia, what did you tell your sister when you ran into her on the street, the information that made her upset enough to run off toward the estuary, the same information that had upset you in the first place?"

"That Louis was my father."

Lars let the full weight of my sister's testimony sink in. There was a shift in the jurors' box, the hiss of rising whispers. "I see. And why didn't you tell the police what you just told us, or bring it up at the preliminary hearing? You must understand the seriousness of your silence."

"I was mad at my sister. I was mad at everyone. But mostly I was mad at Ronnie for being my father's only daughter. I knew what people were saying about Louis and me. They didn't know the truth. Louis didn't want to tell them because he was afraid it would ruin my mother's reputation. He did everything he could to help us, but he couldn't take us in because he was afraid of how that would look. Afterwards I was confused, and didn't want to believe that he was dead. When things finally began to sink in, it was too late. The trial had already begun."

"Why are you telling us now?"

"Because it's not my sister's fault. And I'm tired of being mad."

Lars paused again and the court focused on Marcia. "Marcia, do you know why Louis might have been looking for Ronalda the night he died in the fire?"

"I told him that she was upset. I phoned him between the time that I saw her on the street and the time that she came home. He was already very upset about not being able to send me to college – his business wasn't doing very well and he didn't have the money to pay for my tuition. He knew my mother couldn't afford it either, and he felt that it was his responsibility. When I told him that Ronalda knew his secret, he wanted to find her and explain things for himself. He was very upset that she was feeling badly about the situation. He had it in his head that she was going to run away, and said that he was going out looking for her."

"Did Louis tell you where?"

"No. But I remember saying that if she was running away, she would probably go to the lodge. She had always wanted to go back to Raven's. It had never stopped being our home."

"Did you ever talk to Louis again?"

"No," my sister said. "I didn't."

The judge called for a recess and the collective weight of the courtroom struggled to its feet. I could feel the surge toward the door. There would be details to talk about, the gritty scandal of promiscuity to dissect over insipid tea and sticky buns. For a moment I sat blinking in the light – too tired to get up, but too wired to stay seated, my head buzzing with my sister's performance. When the guard beckoned, I looked at the sun on the wall, streaming in through the window and landing with a splash across the Queen. There was an instant when I knew I wasn't going to make it, but by then it was already too late: I stood up, the room shifted, and I fell to the ground.

# Chapter 16

They told me after the trial was over, after Marcia had completed her testimony and my mother had given her tearful confirmation concerning my sister's paternity, that my final panic attack was the simple result of low blood sugar and iron deficiency anaemia. My three months in the Capital Jail had not been enough to replenish my iron stores, following so closely on the heels of a year of malnutrition. Combine that with the jellied egg I had shunned at breakfast, and the half-round of grapefruit I had picked apart with my spoon on the morning of the fainting, and it was a wonder that I had been standing at all. Several of the papers put my behaviour down to a weak nature, a fragile constitution from too much romping and neglect. Others said this was evidence of my guilt. Whatever the case, the jury believed Marcia, and after three more days of witnesses and specialists, of people swearing on the Holy Word, her sad eyes were what people remembered.

In the aftermath of the trial, more than one newsman decried the result. Some were on my side, but most acknowledged the alleged confession, which was deemed inadmissible by the *voir dire* but talked about after my acquittal. The floral designer from the crown's case – who I came to see as my nemesis – swore up and down on national television that she saw me thumbing my way up the cut-off; but even if she were correct, as many champions of justice pointed out, my presence on the highway did not indicate culpability for murder. The premise of Canadian law, you see, is that it is better to have a thousand criminals walking free, than to have one innocent convicted and held in captivity. For my part, I'm inclined to agree.

✻ ✻ ✻

The battle over juvenile law reform that Lars had talked about taking place in the House of Commons continued to rage as he had predicted. When an opposition justice critic cited my case as evidence for much-needed change, he inflamed the papers all over again. It would be five more years before the proposed legislation, *Young Persons in Conflict With the Law*, called for the safeguards of adult criminal justice to be applied to juvenile cases.

Though time has allowed me to put the trial more or

less behind me, the details keep rearing up: the smell of Lee's lambs' wool vest, an earthy scent like a bog in spring; my days at the Watermark before everything fell apart. Then there is the feeling of shackles upon my wrists, the darkness and fear that clutched at my chest when I slept in the Capital Jail and Mary crept in through the bars. The most difficult souvenir of the whole affair seems to be my fear of wide-open spaces, which has lessened to some degree since I last visited the alpine: a dismal and sweaty dread; a slow choking like a bone in the throat. I never did find out when Marcia came to Lars with her story about the night in question, but I do know that she was our lying witness. Louis may have been her father, but the rest of her story was a fabrication. As far as I can tell she was the only one.

Since that day many things have changed. My mother entered Alcoholics Anonymous. She climbed on the wagon and fell off again; then she climbed back on and made a valiant attempt for the finish line. By my senior year of high school, she was studying to be a real estate agent, sucking back pills only when she couldn't get through the night without them. I wrung my hands a number of times, but I finally came back to one realization: she was no longer the mother I remembered, but at least she was not the one I had tried to forget. For now, for this life, she was my mother.

I also had to admit that I was not the perfect daughter. Following the trial I failed my year at high school. I took the summer off and failed some more. By this time, Jim Brower had moved on to other things – ousted by the school board for his hippie ways – and it took me two years to get used to the old system. When I graduated, I was the same age as everyone else in my class.

In memory of Lee, I've had a number of boyfriends who eventually broke up with me when I accused them of plotting to leave forever. I'm not a jealous person, but in my mind's eye, I can see them moving away from me, slowly retreating against a backdrop of glaring white. Eventually, my prophecies become self-fulfilling.

I haven't heard from Lee since our last morning on *The Minstrel*. Sometimes I imagine him free, living incognito in some Mexican state. He is happy and probably part of a commune. In the months following my arrest, my access to the news was limited. For this reason I heard about his case only sporadically. The police had leads, but never anything concrete. They never caught him, and eventually I stopped paying attention, because with time, even he began to fade: first to a watery image, a hazy outline with features dissolving; and then to nothing.

When I graduated from high school, we moved to the city, where rain falls hard in the winter, but in early spring, flowers litter the landscape. They aren't as amazing as alpine flora, but they do push through cracks in the sidewalk, astonishing me with their persistence. There is a park close to our apartment. Last month I stumbled upon a theatre with a crying room, the same vintage as the Watermark with offers of discount popcorn. I sat for a moment in the stiff-backed seats, letting the noises of burping and suckling babies drown out the roar in my head.

Recently I have been seeing another therapist, different from the quacks at the Capital Jail and the high school guidance counsellors who told me to imagine myself filling up with pure white light. This is a woman I can talk to, though I do not tell her everything about my life. Our latest conversations have been about death; she thinks I have an unhealthy preoccupation. *Liken it to the state of existence before you were born*, she told me, not very long ago. *There is nothing to fear in that.* I try and tell her it's not fear exactly, but a morbid fascination. I understand life on a cellular level. I do not have that luxury with death.

Mostly she has been trying to help me overcome my nightmares, those sweat-filled visions that have been recurring with startling frequency. I no longer see them as panic attacks but as a sort of mental calisthenics. Recently I asked her to explain the old medical adage: *Though shalt not kill; but need'st not strive Officiously to keep alive.* She looked at me and said, "You think too much."

I started to explain that this was important for my nightmares, but at the last minute I thought I'd better not. There is one nightmare I would like to exorcise, though. It has something to do with what I told Dr. D'Angelo.

It goes like this:

I am struggling through the snow, waddling like a penguin in my layers of wool and rayon. All around me flakes are falling, and the sky above is darkening with impending dusk. At some point I realize I am snagged on a branch, and I pull with enough force to free myself from its clutches but leave part of my jacket behind. The impulse to pick up the remnant is heady, but not strong enough to make me act. I go on because I have to.

I'm moving now with greater speed. Ahead of me Raven's lurks on the hillside, adjacent to the lake like a haven in the stillness. I expect to feel better when I get there, but all I feel is despair.

I know I have been sitting on the floor for a long time when Louis enters the room. He is pale and shivering. The sound of his foot on the floor is a hideous squelching. My face is hot and wet, singed from crying or too much frost.

*What are you doing here?* I say. *Where did you come from?* I shiver in my layers, but Louis is the one who is cold. He shakes like a dog out of water and clambers over to the hearth.

When he strikes the matches, he holds them like a child, out and away from his body before tossing them onto the floor. I think he is deranged, or that I am deranged; then I don't even care.

I am sitting on the floor; I am standing. I am looking at Louis and shouting *you, you, you.*

Suddenly dread overtakes me. I want him to stop

lighting the matches, because there is something we are both forgetting. If I could remember what it was, everything would turn out fine. It is moments before I see him stepping onto the blankets, his pant legs wagging beneath him. He is clumsy and nonsensical. I think we are going to die.

*Louis*, I say. *What are you doing? You're going to get us both into trouble if you keep that up. Come here. Come away from there.*

He looks at me for a moment, and then he shakes his head. He says: *Alice?*

He hasn't heard me right. He wants me to speak up. He wants me to tell him all over again, but I can't move my lips. Instead I see Lee running away from me; I see my father snowshoeing out and over the lake. I see my sister stepping from the blue Lincoln, her thin ankle gleaming in the night.

He waits for my reply, but I cannot form the words. Instead I take a step toward the door. I say, "Never mind."

Outside the sky opens up before me like a tunnel into the future; there are infinite possibilities. One of them is that we will all live happily ever after; another is that we will both die; still another is that I will walk out and never look behind me, and that Louis will stay inside.

I do not go back into the lodge and tell Louis what I'm seeing. Instead I step down into the snow, feeling the chill of ice against my boots, the wind blowing snow down my neck. I smell the burn of cloth and cedar timbers, and something that smells like meat. I stand there for a long time looking at the stars, at the way the universe has become suddenly smaller because of one small step.

# Afterword

Although *Tin Angel* is a work of fiction, the story is based on the realities of Canadian law and history between 1969-71. Under the Juvenile Delinquents Act (JDA) – an act that tried to rehabilitate, rather than punish – an accused child was not treated as a criminal, but as someone "in a condition of delinquency and therefore requiring help and guidance and proper supervision." [1]As a result, the juvenile court could not convict an accused child of a crime, but could declare that the accused had committed "a delinquency." If the charges were serious enough, moving an accused child up to adult court enabled prosecutors to aim for the conviction of an indictable, or criminal, offence, which in Ronnie's case equalled arson and murder.

Throughout the early sixties and seventies, federal authorities struggled to create new laws that dealt with the criminal behaviour of children to replace the JDA. Although the law's focus on helping children was good for many people, the nature of the sentence depended largely on the judge. Children in different provinces might receive detention time or be required to pay a fine for similar crimes. The Act gave so much authority to judges and others in positions of authority, that there was great potential for abuse. The 1960 Canadian Bill of Rights (and later, the 1982 Charter of Rights and Freedoms) also raised concerns that the Juvenile Delinquents Act did not take into account the legal rights of children. Like Ronnie's treatment by police in the story, youth were not necessarily entitled to have their parents present during questioning. Police and others were also at liberty to act in what they saw as the child's best interest, but this didn't always mean that they followed the laws of evidence. For instance, a judge might convict a youth he or she knew was innocent, if the judge felt the sentence would help the youth in the long run.

In 1970, the Solicitor General, who was responsible for administering the prison system and other matters of justice in Canada, first introduced the Young Offenders Act (YOA). The YOA was both hailed and criticized for its attempts to protect the rights of young people while holding them more accountable for their behaviour. Among other things, the act allowed children the right to a lawyer and the presence of a parent during questioning by police. The YOA was not made law until 1984.

While I took the liberty of moving ahead protests

against the underground nuclear blasts on the Alaskan peninsula by approximately three months, Canadians were aware of the controversial plans to explode a five-megaton bomb near Cannikin. Since the mid 1960s, the United States government had been testing nuclear bombs in the Aleutian Islands. A previous explosion detonated 4,000 feet below the surface of Amchitka Island had created a shockwave registering 6.9 on the Richter scale. In addition to being concerned about nuclear testing out of principal, many people worried further tests would set off an earthquake. On March 15, 1971, the *Vancouver Sun* published the objectives of a group of Canadians planning to pilot a boat into the test site. The passengers on this boat went on to found the international organization Greenpeace.

Lastly, the manifesto of the Front de Libération du Quebec (FLQ) was read on CBC radio on October 8, 1970, while kidnap victim Pierre Laporte was being held hostage. The FLQ and its actions marked a willingness by Canadian citizens to get involved in terrorist activities in order to advance their political goals. Like Lee, who uses ultimately violent means to make a statement, many of the historical figures of the time were willing to take their actions to new heights to gain recognition. The 1970s were a period of ideological, political, and legal shifting in Canada, and all these things combine to affect Ronnie's story.

[1] Section 3(2) of the Juvenile Delinquents Act, 1975.

# Historical Timeline

| | |
|---|---|
| 1969 | Joni Mitchell releases her second album, *Clouds*. The album contains the single "Tin Angel." |
| August 1969 | The United States announces a one-megaton nuclear bomb test scheduled for October on Amchitka Island in the Aleutian Islands. |
| September 1969 | The *Vancouver Sun* reports the risk of an earthquake and the threat of a tidal wave as a result of the nuclear tests. |
| November 1969 | The U.S. Department of Defence announces a 5-megaton thermonuclear test scheduled for Amchitka in the fall of 1971. |
| February 1970 | Vancouver activists decide to send a boat to Amchitka to protest the nuclear tests. The *Vancouver Sun* runs a story about the intended voyage, calling the boat the *Greenpeace*. |
| October 5, 1970 | Joni Mitchell, James Taylor, Phil Ochs, and B.C. band Chilliwack stage a benefit concert in Vancouver for the protest efforts. |
| October 5, 1970 | British Trade Commissioner James Richard Cross is kidnapped from his home in Montreal by members of the Front de Libération du Quebec (FLQ). A separatist organization seeking to gain independence for Quebec, the FLQ demands the release of 23 political prisoners, $500,000 in gold, publication of the FLQ manifesto, and passage for the kidnappers to Cuba or Algeria. |
| October 8, 1970 | The FLQ manifesto is read on CBC Radio and Television. As well as calling on the working class people of Quebec to unite against Canadian federalism, it condemns governments that sell their souls to woo American investors and businesses at the expense of their own people. It reads: "We are Quebec workers and we are prepared to go all the way. With the help of the entire population, we want to replace this society of slaves by a free |

society, operating by itself and for itself, a society open on the world. Our struggle can only be victorious. A people that has awakened cannot long be kept in misery and contempt."

| | |
|---|---|
| October 10, 1970 | FLQ members kidnap Quebec's Minister of Labour, Pierre Laporte. |
| October 16, 1970 | Prime Minister Trudeau invokes the War Measures Act, the only time the Act has ever been used during peacetime, and only the third time the Act has been used in Canadian history. The emergency legislation gives the federal government sweeping powers, allowing them to govern by decree. Within 48 hours, more than 250 people are arrested. |
| October 17, 1970 | Pierre Laporte's strangled body is found in the trunk of a car in Montreal. |
| November 1970 | Canada's Solicitor General introduces the first Young Offenders Act (Bill C-192). The bill does not make it past the second reading in the House of Commons. |
| December 3, 1970 | James Cross is released when FLQ members holding him gain passage to Cuba. |
| December, 1970 | The four members of the FLQ responsible for kidnapping Pierre Laporte are now charged with kidnapping and murder. |
| September 30, 1971 | The U.S. Coast Guard arrests the *Greenpeace* and charges the crew with a customs infraction. Although the boat never reaches Amchitka Island, the publicity caused by its voyage stops the nuclear tests. |
| April 1984 | Following an extensive review process, Parliament replaces the Juvenile Delinquents Act with the Young Offenders Act (YOA). |
| February 4, 2002 | The YOA is replaced by the Youth Criminal Justice Act (YCJA), in force as of April 1, 2003. |

# Also Available from Lobster Press:

written by
Kimberly Joy Peters

*Painting Caitlyn*

## Painting Caitlyn
### by Kimberly Joy Peters
ISBN: 978-1-897073-40-7

"... an excellent book for any girl who falls prey to a boyfriend's abusive behavior." – *School Library Journal*

"... a provocative story with an important message."
– *CM: Canadian Review of Materials*

Caitlyn's artistic talent seems to be failing, her best friend is ditching her for a new boyfriend, and her mother and stepfather have gone to extraordinary lengths to get pregnant – leaving Caitlyn wondering where she'll fit in when *baby* arrives. Enter Tyler – older, gorgeous, and totally into Caitlyn. When she's with him, all of her problems seem to disappear. But just as things get serious, Caitlyn discovers Tyler's jealous side. Once she realizes her "perfect" boyfriend is as controlling as he is caring, she is faced with a choice: she can either let this relationship define her, or find the courage to break away.

# Death at Deacon Pond
## by E. M. Alexander

ISBN: 978-1-897073-42-1

"Those who want books about the supernatural will flock to this one ..." – *School Library Journal*

"With an intriguing and suspenseful plot, readers will be drawn into Alexander's story of murder, greed, and ultimate betrayal as experienced by an extraordinary young woman ..."
– *Connecticut Muse*

"... enough twists and turns to keep readers on their toes."
– teensreadtoo.com

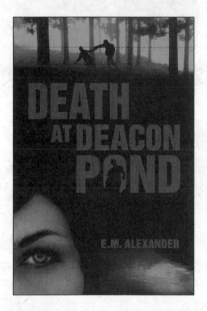

Ever since her father's suicide, Kerri Langston has been tortured by visions of his violent death, which make her believe that he was murdered. With no way to prove her theory, her psychic visions only serve to upset her mother and give her the reputation of being a "freak." When Kerri stumbles upon a body in the woods near Deacon Pond, she realizes her strange connection with the dead might help solve a crime – if she can convince the police to trust what she sees. What Kerri doesn't know is that there is someone close to her who will stop at nothing to ensure that her visions remain hidden.

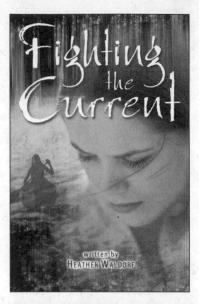

# Fighting the Current
## by Heather Waldorf
### ISBN: 978-1-894222-93-8

"... teenage love, divorce, disability, and death are tackled
without overwhelming or bombarding the reader ..."
*— Montreal Review of Books*

Shortlisted, Stellar Book Award — BC Teen Readers' Choice

Selected, International Reading Association
"Young Adults' Choices" Reading List

Theresa "Tee" Stanford figures her life is smooth sailing. But
everything changes when a drunk driver hits her father, leaving him
mentally disabled. With her last year of high school looming large, Tee
finds she can no longer rely on her old dreams for the future.

**www.lobsterpress.com**